Dreamtime

by

Paula Blais Gorgas

Dragonfly Publishing, Inc.

EAN 978-0-9817049-6-8 / ISBN 0-9817049-6-4
Paperback Edition

Text Copyright © 2000 Paula Blais Gorgas
Cover Art © 2003 Terri L. Branson
Dragonfly Publishing, Inc. logo © 2001

Published in the United States of America
Dragonfly Publishing, Inc.
Website: www.dragonflypubs.com

Dedication

For Chet:

Best husband, best father, best friend.
Thank you for sharing my dream.

Prologue

BY nine o'clock in the evening, westbound traffic on the Broken Arrow Expressway had cleared and was moving along at a fairly steady clip. The sun had long since set, but a full moon had risen in the eastern sky, and a field of bright dancing stars spread a blanket of light over Tulsa.

Alone in his small blue car, Dr. Loren Price was happily oblivious of sky, moon, or stars. Unaware that the speedometer had moved up steadily--five, ten, fifteen miles over the speed limit, he puffed on his favorite pipe and tapped his foot on the accelerator in time to the offbeat tune he hummed.

Up ahead and off to the right, Loren caught a flash of green. "Damn," he muttered. All in one motion, he clamped down on his pipe, glanced over his shoulder and shot across the right lane onto the exit ramp. His left foot hit the brake and his breath came out in a soft whoosh as the car squealed up to the stoplight. By the time he turned left onto Shannon Boulevard, he was humming again. A few more minutes and he'd be home. Barb would be waiting, and Buddy probably had the cribbage board out, ready for a quick game.

Later, Loren was never sure exactly when or why, he began to feel uneasy. Maybe it was the sudden absence of cars. Shannon wasn't one of Tulsa's main arteries, but as he drove through the familiar residential neighborhood, he didn't see another vehicle anywhere. And it was quiet, too quiet. His windows were rolled down, yet the only noise he heard was the steady hiss of his own tires eating up the asphalt paving. Frowning, he closed the windows and locked his door, then reached across the seat and locked the passenger side. Normally, he paid no attention to such things, but at that moment it felt like the right thing to do.

He was counting now. Ten more blocks and he'd be home. Nine…eight….

He approached Crossland Park, a pretty little bit of country on the southeast edge of town that he and Barb often visited with Buddy. A thick stand of pines marked the park entrance. They were beautiful, stately trees that Loren had often admired. Tonight he saw nothing but giant black sentinels silhouetted in the moonlight.

Moonlight? For the first time, he noticed an unnatural brightness in the sky. True, the moon was full, but this was different.

Then he saw it, a white glowing light below and slightly left of the moon. Even as he watched, the light steadily grew bigger and brighter.

Loren blinked and rubbed his eyes, but when he opened them, the light was even closer. It appeared to be coming straight toward him.

A surge of panic, unlike anything he'd ever known, washed over him. It must be a plane out of control and about to crash on top of him!

The park entrance loomed ahead, its gates wide open. It wasn't till later that he wondered why. The park always closed at dark. But right now, all he could think about was getting away from that light. Slamming on his brakes, he jerked hard on the wheel. His car careened wildly around the corner into the park.

Don't stop! Don't stop!

He tore down the two-lane road at forty, fifty. If he

could get far enough away, maybe it wouldn't catch him.

Narrowing to a dirt path with trees and shrubs on both sides, the road ended.

Loren stopped the car. Slowly, he looked up. Somehow, he wasn't surprised that the light still hovered in front of him, bigger and brighter than ever. He knew now that he couldn't fight it. Nor could he escape. With a calm acceptance of the inevitable, he sat and waited.

1

SIX o'clock on Halloween night. A pale yellow moon slithered behind dark clouds, casting an eerie glow over the hillside. The only thing missing was a silhouette of a witch slipping silently across the sky.

Chuckling to himself, Denis Earley downshifted his red sports car and started up the steep incline of Bentonville Road. Denis seldom indulged in such flights of fancy, but the night was perfect for ghosts and goblins, especially here on the eastern slope of Buckeye Mountain where his friends, Loren and Barb Price, had built their home in the middle of five virgin acres. They insisted they had the best of two worlds, real country living but only a ten-minute drive to Benton, a town of five thousand, the perfect place to raise their family, ten-year-old Buddy and in a few months, his new little brother or sister. Perfect as it was, however, Denis wondered how Buddy was spending Halloween. He sure wouldn't do much trick or treating out here in the middle of the woods. Denis had passed only one house since turning on this road.

Up ahead, his headlights caught the amber reflector that marked the beginning of Loren's long winding driveway, and Denis' thoughts shifted from Halloween to food. He'd spent the morning at City Hospital meeting the staff and touring the facilities, then the rest of the day unpacking, and he still couldn't walk around his house without stumbling over brown boxes. He hadn't even thought about lunch till an hour ago when he suddenly remembered Loren's spontaneous invitation to have dinner with them tonight. He had accepted, of course, but now he wondered if he should have called before he came. Loren was the original absent-minded professor, history professor, that is, and he'd been even more preoccupied than usual when Denis ran into him yesterday at a downtown restaurant. Suppose he'd forgotten to tell Barb there would be one extra for supper?

Well, too late now. Anyway, after living with Loren for more than ten years, Barb would probably just laugh and set another place.

Denis braked to a stop at the top of the drive and turned the key. The neat redwood and rock house sat in darkness except for the sentry light in the back yard, but he'd already caught a faint whiff of charcoal and beef. His stomach growled in anticipation. Grabbing the cold six-pack he'd picked up in town, he strolled up the path to the front door and rang the bell. He was really looking forward to the next few hours. Good times with old friends, a luxury he hadn't enjoyed for too long, one he'd finally realized he needed in his life, and one of the big reasons he'd moved back to Tulsa.

"What the--"

A vampire had opened the door. A green-faced, white-lipped, long-haired vampire! Bright blue eyes stared at him, eyes that should have clashed with that green face but somehow didn't.

"Oh my!" The voice, soft, silky, and just a bit unsteady, dissolved the thread of fear that had grabbed him.

"I'm Denis," he said, offering his hand. "Which Munster are you?"

"I'm not. That is, I guess I am, sort of, just for tonight."

Still staring, she wrapped her fingers around his.

Cool...damp...slimy....

"Damn." He jerked back.

"Don't do that!" She grabbed his hand again before he wiped it on his jeans.

"On second thought, maybe I won't." Fascinated, he studied her small green fingers with their impossibly long red nails.

"You must be a lady vampire," he said, letting himself absorb every inch of her small body, clad in a form-fitting black leotard that clung to her like a second skin. "The hair gives you away."

Even under all that makeup, Denis knew she was blushing. He could almost feel her embarrassment as she shrank back. Amazing. The lady was shy, a rare quality among his female acquaintances back in Washington.

Before he could pursue that thought, Barb swept into the living room. Tall, slim, poised, wearing a casual beige jumpsuit, she looked more like the model she had been than a thirty-year-old mother-to-be. "Denis!" She wrapped her arms around him in a genuine bear hug. "I'm so glad to see you! What are you doing here?"

He returned the hug, then quirked one eyebrow as he looked around the dimly lit room. Ghosts and witches bobbed from the ceiling, and a huge inflated skeleton lounged on the couch. There were several clear glass bowls filled with candy and chips, and for the first time he noticed ghostly cackling and high-pitched shrieks coming through hidden speakers. From the back of the house came a burst of childish voices, squealing and shouting. "Looks like you're having a party."

Barb laughed. "How did you ever guess? This is the price we pay every year for having a son born on Halloween." Again, she looked at Denis curiously. "What brings you here tonight, of all nights?"

If she'd been anyone else, Denis would have felt like an

intruder. When Loren met Barb twelve years ago, Denis had already left Oklahoma for graduate school in Washington. He hadn't been home since, although he and Loren had kept in touch over the years, and his friend had insisted on meeting him at the airport last week when Denis finally moved back to Tulsa. That was the only time he'd met Loren's family till Barb walked into this room a few minutes ago, but he had decided then that she was the perfect mate for his old friend. With that in mind, Denis didn't apologize for tonight's unexpected arrival. Instead, he picked up one of the bright orange paper napkins lying on a nearby table, calmly wiped green makeup off his hand, and sprawled out on the couch beside the skeleton. "Pleased to meet you, too," he said, shaking a long bony hand.

The plastic bundle of bones bounced around several times and ended up in his lap. Barb and the lady vampire burst out laughing. Denis grinned.

"Did Loren invite you to dinner tonight?" Barb asked.

Denis nodded. "He didn't say anything about a party though."

"Of course not. He didn't remember. I had to call him at work at five-thirty and remind him to come home. And he still forgot the cake. Jeannie ran out and picked it up. Oh, did you two introduce yourselves? Denis Earley, this is my sister, Jeannie MacLeod. In real life, she's a reporter for the *Benton News and Sun*, but once a year she does her vampire thing. As you might guess, Buddy and his friends love it."

Denis tried to catch Jeannie's eye again, but she seemed to be looking everywhere else. "I don't blame them," he said. "She's a most bewitching vampire."

Jeannie rolled her eyes. Barb just laughed and changed the subject. "Anyway, you're in luck. Loren's been cooking the hamburgers, and we have plenty. If you don't mind sharing with a bunch of little boys, come on out back."

"Thanks, I'd like that. Are you coming, Jeannie?"

She shook her head. "You two go ahead. I'll be there in a minute."

Strangely disappointed, Denis watched the slim black figure fade into the hallway shadows. He turned and followed Barb through the family room onto the back patio.

"Look who's here!" Barb called to her husband, who stood over a smoking grill, flipping hamburger patties. Half a dozen boys in costumes ran around the yard playing a game, but Loren paid them no attention. Hearing Barb's voice, he nodded absently and kept on cooking.

"Now that's concentration!" Denis declared.

"It's something," Barb muttered. "He's been like that all week. I'm beginning to think I'm married to a zombie."

"You mean, he's worse than usual?" Denis teased.

"He's impossible," she said, her voice tight. "See if he'll talk to you. I'm going to get the drinks."

Denis leaned against the doorjamb, arms folded in front of him. How long would it take Loren to realize someone was staring at him? He started counting seconds. It was a game he had played when they were roommates at OU. No wonder one of their frat brothers had named them the odd couple, but in spite of their differences, they'd been best friends. Loren was the brother he'd never had.

Denis frowned. He'd been staring for well over a minute. "Hey, Loren!" he called, walking toward the grill. "How's it going?"

Loren straightened up slowly. "Hi, Denis." A puzzled look crossed his face. "Are you sure this is where you want to be tonight? These kids are just getting warmed up."

"If I didn't know better, I'd say you don't want me to stay for dinner."

Denis grinned, but Loren didn't even crack a smile. "You know better than that. You're always welcome here. Better make up your mind though. If Buddy sees you, you won't get away."

Right on cue, a scar-faced, one-eyed pirate, chased by a

junior spaceman, tore around the corner of the house. The pirate stopped short, then with a bloodcurdling cry, he changed directions and ran at them full speed. "Denis! I didn't know you were coming to my party!"

Denis managed to catch the charging pirate before he was bowled over. "Can I stay even if I'm not wearing a costume?"

"Sure! Mom and Dad didn't wear 'em either. They never do, but Aunt Jeannie did. She's a great vampire. Did you see her?"

"Sure did." A vivid image of Buddy's svelte little aunt flashed through his mind.

"Is it time to eat, Dad?" Buddy asked, switching to a more important subject. "We're starved!"

The spaceman peered over his shoulder. "They look real good, Mr. Price."

Still flipping burgers, Loren didn't look up.

"C'mon, Todd," said Buddy. "Let's get the rest of the guys."

Denis watched them race off. "Temporary reprieve," he observed. "I hope those things are almost ready."

Still no answer. He tapped his friend on the shoulder.

Loren whirled around, his eyes wide. No, wild was a better word. The spatula he held came within an inch of Denis' nose, and several hamburgers went flying.

"Hey, calm down." Denis reached out a steadying hand.

"No!"

Denis pulled back, but even as he watched, Loren blinked and rubbed his hand across his forehead. When he looked up, his face was pale but calm. He shook his head. "Sorry about that."

Sorry? The man had freaked out and he was sorry? Denis started to protest but changed his mind as Loren abruptly stalked off toward the house.

* * *

UPSTAIRS in the master bathroom, Jeannie dipped into Barb's cold cream and removed her eye makeup so she could wear her contacts. Without them, she was practically blind at three feet, which didn't bother her when she was dealing with ten-year-olds, but Denis Earley was a different story, a disturbing one. She remembered every word he had spoken, every little inflection of his smooth deep voice. She especially remembered the way his gray-green eyes, flecked with tiny bits of gold, had looked at her. No man should have eyes like that. They saw too much. Without half trying, he would strip away a woman's defenses and leave her unnerved. Vulnerable.

Squinting into the mirror, Jeannie popped in her lenses. Her image flashed into focus, sharp and clear, just the way she wanted to see Denis Earley the next time she faced him.

The house was quiet when she walked downstairs and paused on the bottom landing, listening. Nothing. Nothing at all. She gripped the railing. Was everyone outside? They must have closed the patio doors. And turned off the stereo. She couldn't imagine why, not this early in the evening. Maybe she would check the kitchen before going outside. Barb might have left something behind.

Slowly, she walked through the foyer. She had never felt such quiet. The silence was heavy, oppressive, almost like an invisible fog. Jeannie felt a prickling at the back of her neck.

I don't like this. Something's wrong.

She walked up to the swinging kitchen doors and stopped as a long shiver ran through her. Her hand reached out to touch the smooth varnished wood. Then she quickly pulled back.

She didn't want to open those doors.

Don't be ridiculous. Don't even think about it.

She pushed the doors open.

Loren stood at the window across the room, watching something outside. His tall rangy body hunched forward as he leaned on the sink. Another inch or two and he'd poke his nose right through the screen.

As Jeannie stepped into the kitchen, one of the doors creaked on its hinges. Loren didn't move. The stifling stillness she'd felt in the other rooms settled around her as she walked across the floor and stood beside him. If he noticed her, he gave no indication. He seemed totally engrossed in whatever he saw outside the window.

What was it? The same reluctance she'd felt about going into the kitchen filled her now. She didn't want to look outside, yet she seemed to have no choice.

The window faced a wide grassy area adjoining the nearby woods to the east. Off to the left was the attached, two-car garage, and beside that a small corral where Barb and Buddy kept their prized quarter horses. The window was open, and Jeannie heard Golden Girl and Prince whinnying restlessly. In the shadowed light from the yard, she saw them pacing the length of the fence. Whatever held Loren's attention was bothering the horses, too. Jeannie saw nothing, but something wasn't right.

"What is it, Loren?"

This time he heard her. Pointing a shaking finger toward the woods, he whispered, "Over there."

She peered into the blackness beyond the clearing. As her night vision improved, she could distinguish vague shadows. Tall skinny tree trunks, mostly oaks, and the thicker bushy cedars and pines. Here and there, tiny twinkling lights darted about. Fireflies, no doubt.

"I don't see--"

"The lights," Loren said hoarsely. "Look at the lights!"

He wanted her to watch a bunch of bugs flying around? Jeannie suddenly remembered Barb telling her how strange Loren had been acting this week. Watching him stare out the window, she decided her sister might be right. So what should she do? Stand here and humor him?

He grabbed her arm. "Look at that!" His eyes were

riveted on the northeast corner of the woods.

Jeannie looked. The tiny lights she had assumed were fireflies appeared larger than they had a minute ago. They darted here and there, but they seemed to be coming closer to the rail fence at the edge of the woods.

"What is it?" she whispered.

His only answer was to tighten his grip on her arm.

She hardly even noticed. She was too busy watching the lights. There were six of them now, about the size and brightness of car headlights at fifty yards. And they were definitely headed toward the fence. An inexplicable sense of danger gripped her. "What are they?" she demanded again.

No answer, but something sharp digging into her arm brought her back to the reality of the kitchen and the man standing beside her.

"Loren?"

His body was rigid, his face a ghastly shade of gray. A thin film of perspiration had broken out on his upper lip, and his eyes bulged as he stared unblinking at the lights. He looked deathly ill.

Afraid he might be having a seizure of some kind, Jeannie managed to pry his fingers loose. His arm dropped to his side, but otherwise he didn't move. Thoroughly alarmed now, she backed up slowly. When her fingers finally touched a door, she turned and ran.

Barb. Get Barb!

She had just slid the patio doors open, when a scream pierced the night air.

2

"WHAT was that?"

Denis jumped up and moved toward the patio. The lawn chair he'd been sitting in hit the ground at the same moment he burst into the family room.

"What's going on?" he demanded, noticing Jeannie for the first time. "Was that you?"

Eyes wide, she had time only to shake her head before Barb ran in and grabbed her. Eight little boys, some of them still munching hamburgers, trailed along behind.

"It was Loren!" Barb cried, shaking her sister. "What happened? Where is he?"

Recognizing the beginning of a genuine panic situation, Denis quickly crossed the room and put his arm around the distraught woman. "Easy, Barb," he said, carefully loosening her death grip on Jeannie's arm. "We don't know what happened but you're scaring the kids. Why don't you take them back outside? Jeannie and I will get Loren and find out what's going on. We'll be back in a minute."

Mentioning the children was the right thing. Barb took a deep breath and backed away from Jeannie. "Don't be long." With one hand on Buddy's shoulder, she herded the boys through the door. "Come on, guys. Let's finish up those hamburgers."

Denis shut the door behind them. "Was it Loren?" he demanded, turning to Jeannie. "Where is he?"

She didn't answer. She was already running toward the kitchen with Denis right behind her.

Loren stood at the window, still staring into the yard.

"Thank God! I was afraid--" *Of what? Lights that grow bigger as you watch them?* She pushed away the thought and headed toward Loren.

"No." Denis' voice, soft but sharp, stopped her. "Let me."

She did, although she couldn't have said why. Jeannie was used to taking charge. After the past few years, she did it automatically, yet here she was standing back, watching.

Denis moved slowly toward his friend. Loren didn't turn around, but Jeannie was sure he was aware of the man standing beside him. His shoulders slumped, and his whole body relaxed. When he finally spoke, it was as though Denis had been there all along.

"That was really something," he said, shaking his head.

"What do you mean?"

"Those lights. Did you see the way they got bigger and bigger the closer they came?"

"I didn't see them," Denis replied carefully. "What about you, Jeannie?"

"They were different," she admitted, walking up to the two men. She glanced out the window. Just as she suspected, the lights were gone.

"What do you mean, different?" Denis asked.

How could she explain the heavy stillness that had settled over the house, or the sense of danger she had felt? She couldn't, nor did she want to, not to a stranger.

"Just different," she said, shrugging. "Why don't you ask Loren? He was here the whole time. He's the one who screamed."

Denis shook his head and she knew she'd made a mistake, but it was too late. Loren's eyes had widened and he gripped the edge of the counter for support. "What else did I do?"

"Probably nothing," Denis said quickly. "Do you remember what happened?"

"I saw some weird dancing lights moving toward the fence, getting bigger and bigger." He ran a shaking hand through his hair. "Head hurts," he mumbled.

When he finally looked up, his eyes were haunted. "What's the matter with me, Denis? Am I going crazy?"

Jeannie flinched. It was the exact thought that had crossed her mind.

Denis looped an arm around Loren's broad shoulders and led him toward the table. "That'll be the day!" He grinned. "Not 'Old Reliable' Price!"

Loren eased himself into a chair. "That should make me feel better since you're the shrink, but I'm not sure it does. I'm not sure about anything any more."

Jeannie stared at Denis. "You're a psychiatrist?"

"Psychologist."

Before she could digest that surprising bit of information, the kitchen door swung open.

Barb burst into the room and ran to Loren. "Are you all right?" she demanded.

He reached for his wife's hand. "Denis says I am. I haven't decided yet whether to believe him."

Barb glanced at Denis, then back at Loren. "What was that god-awful scream we heard? Was that you?"

He shrugged. "I guess. I don't remember."

Still gripping his hand, Barb sank into the nearest chair. "Oh no," she whispered.

Loren scowled. "Don't worry about it, Barb. It's probably nothing."

"Just like last Friday was nothing, I suppose. People don't forget a scream like that one, Loren, and they don't lose a whole hour out of their lives."

"I told you, it's just a matter of time till I figure out what happened that night. I've always been a little absent-minded."

"Absent-minded? I don't buy that, not this time."

"Then what do you call it? Crazy? You think I'm crazy, is that it?"

Denis couldn't believe this. His good friend, who also happened to be very much in love with his wife, was practically nose to nose with her, glaring and shouting. What was going on here?

Jeannie must have wondered the same thing. "Just a minute, you two," she said, pulling up a chair between them. "Do you suppose you can calm down long enough to discuss this like two adults?"

A sheepish grin spread across Barb's face. "Sorry, honey." She squeezed Loren's hand. "Guess I got carried away."

He groaned and shook his head. "I don't blame you. This whole business is tearing me up."

"What business?" Jeannie demanded. "Will somebody please tell me what is going on?"

Denis glanced at the troubled faces around the table. Jeannie was obviously bewildered. Loren and Barb were deeply troubled and scared. He wanted to help if he could, but they had to ask first. Laying a hand on Loren's shoulder, he said, "Maybe I should check on the kids."

"No!" Loren gripped his arm. "The kids are fine." He looked at Barb and she nodded. "I want to talk. I need to."

Denis eased his arm away. "Why not start at the beginning," he suggested. "When was that, last Friday?"

Loren nodded. "Up till then, I considered myself a pretty normal person. Within limits, of course."

Not much of a joke, but typically Loren. At least he hadn't lost his sense of humor. "What happened Friday?" Denis asked.

Loren reached in his shirt pocket and pulled out an old corncob pipe. Tapping it on the edge of the table, he fumbled in the pocket again, hunting for a match. With shaking hands, he finally managed to light the pipe. Barb didn't say a word, although he seldom smoked any more and never in the house, now that she was pregnant again.

Denis waited, more patiently than Jeannie, he noted, watching her out of the corner of his eye. She fidgeted in her chair, trying to find a comfortable spot. She had washed off the shiny green makeup, but she still wore the luscious black outfit that revealed all those tempting curves. All in all, a most bewitching woman.

He turned his attention back to Loren, who was now puffing on his pipe and staring into space. "About last Friday...."

Loren's shoulders jerked, then he seemed to collect himself.

"I was on my way home from the college, a little after nine. I'm teaching an evening seminar this semester." He stopped and Denis nodded encouragingly. "I had just turned off the expressway onto Shannon when I noticed that something was different."

Jeannie leaned forward. "Different? How?"

Frowning, Loren reached into his pocket again and pulled out his tobacco pouch. "It's hard to explain. I felt different, like I was waiting for something to happen."

"Had you seen something?" Denis asked.

"Not then, but soon, about the time I crossed over Fifty-First Street. You know how it is out there, with Crossland Park on the right and those old homes set way off the road on the left. It's the middle of Tulsa, but you feel like you're out in the country, especially when there's a full moon and not much traffic. That night the moon was bright and the street was practically deserted. I wondered why there were no other cars."

Loren laid down his pipe and pouch. "Out of nowhere, I saw a light coming toward me. A big, bright white light. I remember thinking, 'It's a plane and it's going to crash right on top of me!' That's when I noticed the turnoff into the park, and I headed for it. I don't know how long I drove down that road. A minute, maybe two. I just kept driving, expecting to hear a crash any second, but it never came. Then I looked up, and that light was still in front of me."

By now, Jeannie was sitting on the edge of her seat. "You mean it followed you?"

"So it seems."

"What did you do?" asked Denis.

With a shrug of his broad shoulders, Loren slumped in his chair. "That's the crazy part," he said, avoiding Denis' eyes. "I don't know."

"You don't remember?"

"I just don't know. I remember sitting in my car, looking at that light. It was almost directly overhead and I couldn't figure out what it was. And I remember feeling funny, kind of lightheaded. The next thing I knew, I was turning the car around and driving out of the park. Ten minutes later, I got home."

The room was quiet for a moment. Then Jeannie stood and began to pace the floor. "That's an interesting story, but nothing to get all bothered about. I'm sure there's a logical explanation."

"I haven't finished."

Denis frowned. Barb reached for her husband's hand again.

Jeannie walked slowly back to the table. "Something else happened?"

"Not exactly. When I walked into the house, Barb was sitting up waiting for me. She was watching the ten o'clock news."

"Wait a minute." Denis shook his head. "I thought you went straight home."

"I did." Loren leaned across the table, his face unreadable. "Denis, it takes nine and a half minutes to drive from Crossland Park in Tulsa to this house here in Benton. What happened to me between nine and ten o'clock last Friday night?"

The room was quiet, only the steady humming of the refrigerator breaking the stillness. Denis wanted to say something reassuring, but what? Loren's story had really thrown him. He had already considered several theories and discarded them. They just weren't possible. Maybe Denis didn't know his friend as well as he once had, but he would bet his life that Loren was solid, stable, and altogether sane. So how did he explain sixty minutes just gone?

"What about tonight?" he asked abruptly. "What happened out here?"

Loren pushed back his chair and stretched out his long legs. "A good question. Maybe we should compare stories. I seem to be missing something again."

"You were here," Denis said to Jeannie. "What happened?"

"Go ahead," Loren said. "I want to hear this, too."

Just thinking about those few minutes gave her the shivers. She took a deep breath, as though trying again to breathe the heavy cloying air that had filled this room.

Or had it?

"Jeannie?"

No! She wouldn't think that way. She had seen something and felt something. Quickly, before she could talk herself out of it, she told them about the stillness in the house.

"The tape!" she said suddenly. "Somebody turned off the 'Sounds of Halloween' tape!"

Barb glanced at Denis. "I don't think so, Jeannie. I can hear it all the way in here."

Incredibly, so could Jeannie, and yet she knew the house had been quiet. But no one would believe that. "Okay, maybe not." This wasn't the time to argue. She'd think about it later.

She continued her tale of the twinkling lights outside and

how strange Loren had looked and acted. "I was really afraid you were sick," she told him. "And then, when I heard that scream...."

Denis stood up and walked to the window. "What did you see out here, Loren?"

"Lights," he replied promptly. "Tiny, twinkling lights that moved toward the corral."

"And got bigger the closer they came," Jeannie added.

"Not so unusual," Denis mused, staring into the yard.

"Very unusual," Jeannie corrected him. "The last time I saw them, they were as big as car lights, all headed toward the fence. They bothered the horses, too."

"Maybe we should check outside," Denis suggested.

Jeannie nodded. "Good idea."

Loren looked less than thrilled, but he agreed.

"I'm going back to the kids." Barb stood. She reached into a drawer and pulled out a large flashlight. "Better take this. And I hope you figure it out."

"What are we looking for?" Jeannie asked Denis, as they walked through the yard toward the corral. The horses had calmed down, but she noticed they had moved as far away from the woods as possible and stood close together, head to tail, as though seeking comfort from each other.

Denis matched his long strides to hers. "I have no idea, but I figured anything was better than sitting in the house doing nothing."

Jeannie agreed. She needed a little time and space to mull over an idea, that had crossed her mind as she listened to Loren tell his story a few minutes ago. True, it was a wild and improbable idea, but she wanted to check it out. And the place to start was out here where they had seen the lights.

"Has anyone seen Dicey?" Loren asked suddenly, looking around the yard. He whistled, but no little black and white dog appeared.

"I saw her in the back yard with the boys," Jeannie

offered. "She's probably still there."

Loren shook his head. "She always comes when I whistle, no matter what she's doing. She should have been out here investigating those lights, too, but I didn't see or hear her."

Much as she liked Dicey, Jeannie couldn't get excited about her right now. She was much more interested in watching Denis sweep the area with the flashlight.

In a minute or two, Loren joined them.

"I guess she'll show up when she's good and ready." Denis didn't sound convinced.

They covered the cleared acreage quickly, ending up at the wooden fence that enclosed the horses. Denis ran the powerful beam over the rails, then along the ground beneath. Nothing.

Leaning against a sturdy post, he turned the light toward the nearby woods and watched it plunge between oaks and pines, then sweep the thick carpet of leaves that covered the ground. The night air was cool and dry. The last rain had been over a week ago, which left the fallen leaves brittle. They would hear as well as see anything that moved.

Again, nothing. Not even the hoot of an owl or the rustling of small creatures settling in for the night. Only the occasional childish shout or peal of laughter from the back yard broke the silence.

"Sure is quiet out here tonight," Loren remarked, running his hand along the top rail of the fence.

Jeannie agreed. Too quiet. And too still. Not the heavy oppressive stillness she had felt inside, yet something...

"Shine that light over there at the shed," Loren said suddenly, pointing toward the small, three-sided building at the far side of the corral, a crude shelter for the horses when they weren't in the barn.

Denis obliged. Almost immediately he saw what had caught Loren's attention, the small dark lump huddled into the farthest corner. Dicey.

When they reached her, she hadn't moved, nor could she be coaxed outside. She cowered in the corner, shivering and whimpering soft, pitiful little sounds.

Loren picked her up and checked her carefully. "She doesn't seem to be hurt. Just scared." He shook his head. "This is a first. I didn't think old Dicey was afraid of anything."

"Poor little thing!" Jeannie ran her hand over the quivering dog. "What do you suppose happened?"

Denis shrugged. "Could have been most anything. A noise, an animal."

Loren disagreed. "She would have barked. I've seen her back up an armadillo twice her size."

"Maybe the lights scared her," Jeannie offered.

The two men stared at her, Denis skeptical, Loren thoughtful.

As they started back to the house, Loren said, "There was something weird about those lights. Something different."

This time Denis asked the question. "Different how?"

"I'm not sure. I just know something wasn't right. Damn! I wish this headache would go away. I wish I could remember!"

Denis could feel the man's frustration. What was it he couldn't remember? More important, why couldn't he remember? Had he experienced another memory lapse? Denis hoped not. He probably could find a fairly simple explanation for the first one, stress or fatigue perhaps, but stress wouldn't explain repeated incidents or Loren's other erratic behavior.

Denis took a long hard look at his friend, who still held Dicey. Even in the pale, half-light of the moon, he could see the dark shadows under Loren's eyes and the pulse beating rapidly in his temple.

For some reason, this normally calm, pragmatic man was strung tight. No wonder he complained of a headache.

He appeared close to the breaking point. The question was why.

* * *

BY the time the last youngster left for home, the clock had struck eleven and Jeannie was ready to call it quits. Barb was still upstairs, getting Buddy settled down. Loren had turned off the gas grill and cleaned up the yard, while Jeannie, with Denis' help, put away the food and washed the few dishes that weren't disposable.

She didn't want his help, had tried to tell him that but he paid no attention. He cleaned and straightened right along with her, and she had to admit she appreciated it, even though he made her nervous. It wasn't actually anything he did. It was just him.

Finally, she laid down her dish towel and leaned back against the sink. "That's it! Enough for tonight." She had closed her eyes, but she felt Denis right there beside her.

"It has been eventful."

Jeannie's eyes opened wide. What did Denis think about those *events*? Did he have any idea what had happened to Loren tonight and a week ago? Was something wrong with her brother-in-law? And what about Dicey? Something had spooked the little dog. If not the mysterious lights, then what?

"I'm almost afraid to ask what's going on inside that head of yours," Denis said, grinning. "From the way you're scowling and the steam that's rising, it must be pretty serious."

Jeannie flushed and moved out of his reach. She wasn't used to being teased. "I was thinking about Loren."

The smile disappeared. "Me, too," Denis admitted. "Do you have any idea what the lights could have been?"

One wild idea.

She almost voiced the thought, but she heard herself saying, "Nothing you'd want to hear."

"Try me."

He stood close again, so close she could feel the soft whisper of his breath on her cheek. His sleeve brushed hers as he leaned back against the counter, arms folded in front of him. She caught a faint whiff of spicy aftershave, a clean masculine smell that set her nerves jangling. Unconsciously, she inched away.

The swinging doors opened and Loren walked into the kitchen, his arms laden with popcorn bowls and two sacks of trash. "This should be the last of it." He set the bowls down and stacked the trash in a corner. "What a night! I'm ready for one of those cold beers I saw in the refrigerator. Denis?"

"Sure. How about you, Jeannie?"

She almost said no. It was on the tip of her tongue to tell him she hated beer, but she surprised herself. "Sounds good."

A few minutes later, Barb joined them. When she saw the silver cans, she patted her still flat stomach. "That looks great, but I'd better not."

Denis groaned. "Darn! I forgot about the baby. Sorry, Barb."

She laughed and reached in the refrigerator for the orange juice. "I'll take that as a compliment, but next April you can bring a six-pack to the hospital and we'll all celebrate."

"I'll drink to that," Denis said, raising his can.

Barb sat next to her husband. "Did you find anything outside?"

Silence. An uncomfortable silence. Denis stared intently at Loren who cleared his throat and tried not to look at anyone. Jeannie started to say something, then decided no one wanted to hear it. Her fingers strummed and fidgeted on the table as she looked around the room.

"Don't everyone talk at once!" Barb declared. "Did you find something or didn't you?"

Loren shook his head. "I wish we had. Anything."

"Something scared Dicey," Jeannie offered. "She was really spooked."

Denis leaned forward, his arms resting on the table. "I'm not so sure there's a connection."

"Neither am I, but surely it's worth investigating." Jeannie knew she sounded sarcastic, but she didn't care. She hated it when people made up their minds and refused to see another side of a story. In her business, she couldn't afford to do that. A good reporter had to be open-minded, and Jeannie was good. The *Benton News and Sun* might not be big, but for six years she had given it her best. Quite often, that was very good indeed.

"We already checked the yard pretty carefully," Denis reminded her.

"Walking around in the dark with a flashlight doesn't prove much. We could have missed lots of things."

"Like what?"

Two simple words and a challenge in his green eyes that made her careless.

"Like tracks. Or footprints," she blurted.

Silence again, then three voices all talking at once.

"Tracks?"

"Footprints?"

"You think somebody was out there? Who?"

Now she'd done it! Jeannie pushed her chair back and stood up. Should she tell them what she was thinking, bizarre as it sounded? Barb and Loren would probably laugh it off, just another one of her wild ideas. She didn't mind that so much. She was used to it. But the idea of Denis Earley laughing at her didn't set well at all.

"Come on, Jeannie. Let's have it," Loren urged.

She walked over to the open window and stared outside. Except for the sentry light by the corner of the house, the yard was inky black. Golden Girl and Prince still stood side by side in the southeast corner of the corral. She felt the cool breeze drifting through the screen, heard the nearby cry of a night bird. Nothing disturbed the stillness now, but she was sure, absolutely sure, something had been out there.

What?

Did she want to find out?

Without turning around, she said softly, "Maybe it was a UFO."

3

"SURE it was!"

"Come off it, Jeannie! You've been reading too many of those science fiction novels."

She looked at Denis. He was staring at her, too. So far, he hadn't added any snide comments, but he probably would. She already wished she'd kept her idea to herself.

Barb was smiling. "You think a flying saucer landed in our yard?"

Jeannie winced at the popular term. No wonder so many people laughed when they heard it. The idea of a saucer flying was pretty funny. But Denis wasn't laughing. Not yet.

"I've been reading a lot about them lately," she said. "Lots of people believe they exist, intelligent people. Scientists, engineers, military pilots."

"And you." Loren grinned. "Do you really think little green men are buzzing around the world in spaceships, scaring people half to death?"

"Of course not!" Jeannie snapped. "I'm saying people see things they don't understand. Not everything that happens can be explained in logical terms, at least not logic as we know it."

"Whose logic are you talking about? The Martians?

Venusians?"

"No! You're being ridiculous, Loren. Forget I even mentioned it." She tipped up the beer can she'd been cradling in both hands and drank deeply, shuddering as the bitter liquid fizzed down her throat. Whatever had possessed her to open her big mouth? She knew what people thought of anyone who believed in such things.

"Why did you mention it, Jeannie?"

She turned toward that deep voice on her left.

Denis regarded her steadily, thoughtfully, as though he really cared what she might say.

"Like I said," she replied, her words edged with caution, "I've read a number of books lately, and the consensus of opinion, among those who bother to investigate, seems to be that something is out there. We just don't know what."

Denis nodded. "And who writes these books you've been reading? Scientists? Journalists?"

"People who are involved with UFO's," Jennie replied.

"Yes, of course. Otherwise, they would have no interest."

Loren slammed his fist on the table. "Don't tell me you go along with this nonsense, Denis!"

"I didn't say--"

"You didn't have to. And you know where that puts me. Right there with all the weirdoes who see things that don't exist. Pretty soon, I'll be hearing things, too. What does that make me? Schizophrenic? Isn't that the fancy word you shrinks call someone who hears imaginary voices?"

Shocked silence.

For the first time in her life, Jeannie understood the meaning of those words, and no wonder. She had never seen Loren in such a state. His longish brown hair, always reasonably neat, stuck up in several directions where he'd run his fingers through it. Behind thick rimless glasses, his pale blue eyes, usually so steady and thoughtful, darted here and there around the room.

Barb stood and edged toward her husband. "Nobody believes that, Loren, and neither do you. You're talking crazy."

Loren threw up his hands. "That's what I've been saying. Crazy, just like me!" He stomped across the kitchen, his long legs eating up the few feet to the doorway. In seconds, he had disappeared into the dark hall.

"Dear God!" Barb's words came out a whispered moan. She grasped the table with both hands, and then took off after Loren.

Shaken, Jeannie walked to the sink and emptied her can and Loren's.

Denis tipped his one last time, then crushed it with one hand and tossed it across the room into the trash can. "I take it you're not much of a beer drinker."

Her mind was a million miles away. "No, I never acquired a taste for it."

"I guess that's right. It's an acquired taste, although it seems to happen pretty naturally to most guys sometime between fourteen and eighteen. Loren and I became connoisseurs our freshman year at OU."

Jeannie knew what he was doing. Using calm soothing words to ease the tension in the room. Taking a deep breath, she went along with him. "Is that where you met, in college?"

"We were roommates and ended up best friends." Denis laughed. "I played baseball and golf and partied. Loren worked, although every so often, I'd get him out to the golf course or the lake. Not many people know it, but he's a great sailor and a pretty fair golfer. At least he was fifteen years ago."

Jeannie studied the tanned, smiling face across the room. Playboy looks, but she had a feeling there was a lot more to Denis Earley than just good looks. Yes, she could see him and Loren together. He'd be good for her quiet, serious brother-in-law.

Unable to keep her fears inside any longer, she blurted, "Have you ever seen him like this before?"

"Never," he replied immediately. "Loren's as steady as they come. I can't tell you the number of times he kept my head above water. We're the same age, but he always seemed older, more mature. I looked up to him. I still do," he added quietly.

"What do you think is wrong with him?"

"I honestly don't know."

Common sense told Jeannie not to say what she was thinking. She didn't want to be laughed at. She especially didn't want Denis Earley to laugh, yet she couldn't stop, not with her family hurting. Besides, if Denis made fun of her ideas, which she'd spent considerable time researching, she would know he was too narrow-minded to advise Loren or Barb. Better to know now.

She pulled out a chair and sat down, one foot tucked under her. "Do you think Post Traumatic Stress Syndrome is a possibility?"

Denis lifted his left eyebrow in surprise. Then he opened his mouth. Frowned and shut it again.

Jeannie plunged ahead. "It seems to me Loren shows some of the classic signs of the disorder. Insomnia, irritability, nightmares, paranoid responses to harmless cues, possible flashbacks, the feeling he may be going crazy--"

"Whoa there! Hold on just a minute." Denis leaned forward. "Did I misunderstand? I thought you were a reporter, not a psychologist."

"You're right, but I'm a reporter who does her home-work."

"And you've been hitting the psych texts pretty hard."

"Among other things. What do you think?"

"I think you've named several symptoms that might or might not apply to Loren."

"Do I hear a 'but' in your voice?"

"You do. Unless I missed something tonight, Loren

hasn't been traumatized. Without the trauma, your diagnosis doesn't fit."

Her heart pounding, Jeannie played her ace. "Some would consider contact with a UFO quite traumatic."

Denis leaned back, his blunt-tipped fingers steepled in front of him. His eyes were hooded, unreadable. "You're serious about that, aren't you?"

"Very serious."

"Why?"

It was the sixty-four-thousand-dollar question with no answer. How could she explain something she didn't understand herself?

Again, the steady hum of the refrigerator cut through the still night, and from the front of the house came the rhythmic tick-tock of Barb's antique Grandfather clock. Jeannie heard nothing upstairs, although she knew Barb and Loren must still be talking.

Restless, she paced the floor, peering out the window each time she passed it. Finally, the words came. "I've always liked puzzles. A question without an answer drives me crazy. My boss says I don't know when to leave well enough alone, but I like to think persistence makes a good reporter."

"And are you?"

"So I've been told, but that's not the issue here."

Denis smiled. "You're right. Go ahead. I'm listening."

He shouldn't smile like that. It was most distracting.

"Puzzles drive you crazy," he prompted.

"Mmm. Yes, they do." She managed to pull her wayward thoughts together. "So a few months ago, when I heard about a woman in Benton who had seen a 'funny' light in the sky, I decided to find out what it was."

"Did you?"

"Sure did. It turned out to be Venus, but by the time I figured that out, I had talked to two astronomers, an airline pilot, the Air Force and a meteorologist."

Denis whistled. "All that and you didn't even get a story."

"But I didn't go away empty-handed."

"How do you figure that?"

"I found a puzzle, a big one, probably the biggest of the century, or longer, and most people don't even give it a thought."

"UFO's?"

"That's right." She grabbed a chair and sat down again. Leaning on the table, she spoke quickly, urgently. "Denis, if you could talk to the people I've talked to, read the books I've read, you'd understand what I'm saying about Loren. What happened to him last week and tonight, the way he's been acting. Absentminded. Afraid of his own shadow. I've read these same things dozens of times."

"And the people you've read about have all seen a UFO?"

"They've all had close encounters, yes." She didn't dare explain that one any further. Not yet.

"So you're saying that seeing a strange light in the sky is enough to induce Post Traumatic Stress?"

Jeannie heard the skepticism in his voice and she really didn't blame him. She should have known he wouldn't accept a simple explanation. "Sometimes it's more than just seeing a light," she said carefully. "Sometimes they see the craft up close, and I'm talking about something alien, something totally out of the realm of human experience."

"Alien beings?"

"Sometimes."

At that, he shook his head. His look nearly screamed disbelief. Still, he hadn't laughed.

Encouraged, Jeannie said, "I'm not asking you to accept everything I'm saying. Just keep an open mind, okay? I'm giving you one possible explanation for Loren's problems."

No answer.

"You do agree he has a problem, don't you?"

"Something's bugging him. I'll go along with that."

"And you're going to help him, aren't you?"

"If he asks. So far, he doesn't seem to want any help."

"Whether he wants it or not, somebody has to do something. He's driving Barb crazy with worry, and that's the last thing she needs now."

"Because of the baby?"

Jeannie nodded. "This baby is a minor miracle. After what she went through ten years ago, they never expected to have another child."

"What happened?"

"I'm not really sure. Barb's always been a friendly, outgoing person, but all that changed when she got pregnant with Buddy. She hardly left the house any more, and when she did, she was always looking over her shoulder. She had convinced herself someone was going to hurt her and take the baby." Jeannie shuddered. "Those seven months were a nightmare for everyone in the family. Besides Barb's problems, my mom's M.S. had just been diagnosed, and we were trying to adjust to the fact that she would only live a few more years.

"At one point, Barb had to be hospitalized and sedated. When Buddy finally arrived a month and a half early, we almost lost her. He was two days old when she saw him for the first time. I'll never forget the look on her face when she realized she had a healthy baby. It was like--well, like she'd been born again, too. Her problems completely disappeared. She was her old self again. And I want to make sure she stays that way. She doesn't need to be worrying about Loren."

Denis nodded. "I understand your concern, Jeannie, and I'll be glad to help Loren and Barb, too, if they ask."

He had made his position clear, and Jeannie respected that--to a point. She just didn't think she could sit by and let her sister and Loren fall to pieces. She would figure out something, but not tonight. As though backing her decision, the grandfather clock slowly gonged twelve times.

"Sounds like the witching hour." Denis eased out of his chair and stretched his arms over his head. "Guess we get to let ourselves out tonight."

"That's no problem," Jeannie replied. "I have a key."

"Well then, I'll say good-night."

In the dim glow of the overhead light, his eyes burned a golden green as he studied her. Cat eyes, Jeannie thought, and fought back the sudden shiver that rippled through her. Too much Halloween, too much excitement, and much too much Denis Earley!

He brushed one finger lightly across her cheek. "Sweet dreams, Jeannie MacLeod," he whispered.

Mesmerized, she watched him curl his slightly green forefinger into his hand. "Oh no! I didn't get it all off! Wait a minute. I'll get you a towel."

Grinning, he shook his head. "Nope. I've always wanted my very own vampire on Halloween. At least now I have a little part of one."

Jeannie had to laugh. "You're impossible, Dr. Earley."

"Yeah, I know."

Without another word, he spun around and strode out of the kitchen and through the house to the front door, leaving a slightly bemused vampire staring at his broad back as he disappeared into the night.

* * *

JEANNIE dreamed wild dreams. She was standing in her back yard, gazing up at a star-studded sky. The dewy grass felt cool under her bare feet, and the damp autumn air whipped through her flannel granny gown, chilling her to the bone. Yet she stood perfectly still, frozen to a grassy mound six feet from her house on the northeast side of Benton. She tasted the wind on her tongue and heard it singing through the tall pines off to her right, but somehow, dreamlike, no other night sounds touched her ears. The stars twinkled like silver jewels catching the light, and as she gazed upward, several of the stars grew bigger and brighter, filling her with an awe both familiar and frightening.

I'm dreaming, she thought, and immediately relaxed.

The dream changed. Now she was in a colorless room. Large birds hovered all around. Her pulse quickened, her breathing became rapid. Long sharp claws stretched down, down...

"No!" Then louder, "No!"

The claws vanished.

Eyes. Large black eyes watched her. She should be scared, but they wouldn't hurt her. These were peaceful creatures, kind and loving. She sighed and slept deeply.

Deer. Three full-grown deer stood in a rest area just off the highway as Jeannie and Denis drove toward Benton. Without a word, Denis touched his turn signal and eased off the road. Such beautiful deer, smooth and sleek, with huge liquid eyes.

Denis stopped the car and opened his door.

"Where are you going?" Jeannie called, scrambling after him.

No answer. He didn't even look at her, just kept walking toward the three deer.

Fear swallowed her whole and left her trembling. What was wrong with the man? Had he lost his senses?

"Wait a minute, Denis. I'm coming, too!" Her words seemed to bounce around, like she was standing in a vacuum chamber. Then nothing. An eerie silence fell on the area, and her whole body tingled, as though each fine hair had been activated. Jeannie didn't like this, not one little bit. Denis could darn well quit staring at those deer and start talking to her!

She took a step forward and froze. *Denis*! Even the word froze in her mind.

Terror. Stark, raving terror gripped her. In her mind she

screamed and fought the power that held her till she feared she might explode with frustration.

Then, mercifully, she awoke, suddenly, completely. For a moment, she didn't move, didn't know if she could move. The dream had left her feeling lethargic. Her head, especially, felt weighted down.

"Mee-owr!"

"Kenworth!"

The weight lifted, and a soft furry body slid off her head to the pillow.

"Darn cat!" No wonder she'd had nightmares, sleeping with a sixteen-pound cat on her head! She reached for her pet and snuggled his warm body till he squealed and squirmed out of her arms. By then, she had almost stopped shaking.

Jeannie squinted at the digital clock. Five-seventeen. She'd only been in bed four hours.

"Mee-owr!" A damp raspy tongue touched her bare arm.

"Breakfast? At this hour?"

Another lick.

She sighed. "You're not going to leave me alone, and I can't sleep anyway." She unwrapped her legs from the tangled covers. "Come on, Ken. Let's raid the kitchen."

Jeannie managed to push her nightmare away into a deep corner of her mind, although she couldn't quite forget that she had dreamed about Denis Earley. Obviously, the handsome young doctor had made quite an impression on her. She couldn't remember ever being so very aware of a man she had just met and knew so little about. Was he a good psychologist? She hoped so, because she had a feeling Loren might need the best.

She jumped, as Kenworth's cold wet nose touched her bare foot. "Watch it, fella!" she muttered, measuring exactly three ounces of liver bits from a six-ounce can. A smile crossed her lips as she realized the absurdity of this little ritual. In an hour or two, Ken would be hungry again.

He'd pester and beg and she'd give him an *advance* on tonight's Kitty Chow. By mid-afternoon, he'd do the same thing all over again and he'd get another little bit. Truth was, he ate as much as he wanted.

"A con artist," Jeannie murmured, watching her pet attack his early breakfast. Denis Earley's smiling face popped into her mind at that very moment.

Coincidence?

* * *

BY eight o'clock, Jeannie felt almost human again.

She'd taken her usual brisk stroll around downtown Benton, spent an hour at Mack's Diner reading the Sunday paper over breakfast, then used up every bit of hot water for her morning shower. And managed not to think about her disturbing dreams till now, three hours later, as she restlessly ran her dust rag over the dining room furniture. She always cleaned house on Sunday, so what was wrong with her today?

Maybe that's the problem, she mused, carefully wiping a delicate, gold-rimmed demitasse cup, one of four that decorated the hutch, along with the other hand-painted china and glasses that had been passed down from her German grandparents to her mother and now to Jeannie. Grace MacLeod had succumbed to MS fourteen months ago, yet here was Jeannie, still living in the same house she and Barb had grown up in, still following the same routines her parents had laid down years ago.

Still alone.

Her hands began to shake. She set the fragile little cup back in its place and sank into one of the maple ladder-back chairs. Was she that predictable, that completely unimaginative? Was she on the verge of becoming an old maid?

The idea wouldn't let go, snowballing through her mind. She was twenty-six years old, living alone in her deceased parents' fifty-year-old home. She still worked at the same job she'd taken when she left college and probably would never advance any further because she didn't graduate. With good reason, but that didn't change the fact that here she was, dusting furniture in a big empty house on a beautiful Sunday morning.

Why? Mom didn't need her any more. Neither did Barb. So, why was she still here in Benton, Oklahoma? What had happened to her ambition to become a famous reporter? Once she had believed in herself. Whatever happened to her big hopes and plans?

With a strangled cry, she threw down the dust cloth. Those crazy dreams last night must have really knocked her off balance. Jeannie MacLeod didn't indulge in bouts of self-pity. Why should she? She liked her job, her life just fine.

Didn't she?

Again, jumbled images from last night flooded her mind, and again she pushed them away. She didn't want to think right now. She didn't want to know why she had dreamed those disturbing dreams, and she especially didn't want to know why she had conjured up Denis Earley.

Peering through a window she had planned to wash today, Jeannie deliberately turned her attention outside, to the blue sky and the bright sun sparkling on three dew-tipped pine trees that guarded the south side of the yard. It was a beautiful day, much too good to waste.

When it finally came, the solution was obvious. She would finish what she had started last night. Barb and Loren wouldn't mind her poking around outside their house. She would get away from here and maybe, just maybe, she'd come up with some answers, something that would help them. Okay, so it wasn't likely, but she wanted to go back. In fact, quite suddenly, she knew this was what she'd wanted all along.

* * *

HER sister and brother-in-law weren't even home when she showed up half an hour later. Dicey greeted her with happy yips, but after knocking on the door and getting no answer, Jeannie peered through the garage window and saw that Barb's little blue station wagon sat alone inside.

They must have taken off on a family outing, probably something Barb had talked Loren into last night. Maybe a day away from here was just what they needed, Jeannie mused, unlocking the back door with her own key and letting herself inside. Although she was pretty sure Loren needed a lot more than one day to get over--what? His ailment? Trauma?

She turned on the kitchen tap and filled a glass full of cold water. Sipping it slowly, she leaned over the sink and studied the yard through the window. How normal it all looked this morning with a bright November sun sparkling through the tall trees. No unexplained lights darted through the woods, no sinister shadows lurked around corners. She could even see the movement of wild birds from branch to branch, tree to tree in the thick woods. So peaceful.

So different from last night.

The perfect time to check every inch of her sister's property with a fine tooth comb, the way she'd wanted to do it last night. Setting down her glass, she hurried out the door.

As soon as she stepped outside, Dicey bounded around the corner of the house and practically jumped into Jeannie's arms. Laughing, she picked up the little dog, cuddling and petting her. "Looks like you're back to your old rambunctious self, little girl."

Dicey licked and yipped and finally jumped down, as Jeannie took off sprinting across the back yard. "Come on, Dice! Race you to the fence!"

She was no match for the hyper little terrier, but that didn't matter. They both ran just for the sake of running. Then, two-thirds of the way across the grass, twenty yards from the corral gate, Dicey stopped in mid-stride. Her floppy little tail slid down between her legs, and with one loud anguished yelp she turned and ran back, disappearing around the corner into the front yard.

Jeannie spent the next ten minutes trying to coax the little dog out of her house next to the garage with no success. Lying flat on her stomach, she talked, cajoled, even tried bribery with half a link sausage, but Dicey would have none of it. She lay as far back as possible in her little house. Her big brown eyes seemed to plead for understanding, but she adamantly refused to budge.

"You're something else, dog!" Jeannie muttered, and left the sausage on the ground, just inside the doghouse. She watched and waited, but Dicey didn't even try to snatch the tasty treat. Shaking her head, Jeannie finally conceded defeat. "Weird, dog, totally weird!"

Just like last night.

She stopped dead in her tracks as she realized the meaning of what had just happened. Something *had* spooked Dicey last night, and whatever it was must still be here! Why else would she refuse to go near the woods?

Jeannie swallowed hard. Did she really want to find out what it was? Suppose she met up with something really scary, even dangerous?

Suppose she turned around and left, avoiding the whole issue?

She knew she would never forgive herself if she ran away now from whatever lurked in those woods. That much settled, Jeannie left Dicey safe in her doghouse, and with grim determination, if not exactly courage, she marched back across the front yard toward the thick woods on the eastern edge of the acreage.

4

WITHIN seconds, a thick mantle of evergreens, hard-woods, and scrub oak enveloped her.

Standing perfectly still, she listened and watched as the world around her came alive. A strangely melodic bird call she had never heard before; the crunch of dry leaves under a small padded foot; the soft clicking of insects as they chattered back and forth; the swish of a light breeze passing through the branches. It was a new and different world, one she seldom entered, but Jeannie was quite sure this was a world at peace with itself. Whatever had intruded here last night was long gone, yet something urged her on.

Carefully, she stepped over fallen limbs and made her way through the thick brush.

After several minutes, the land eased into an upward slope, and gradually the trees thinned. Now she could see several feet around her. A few more steps and she stood in a natural clearing atop a small hill. High above, the cloud-less blue sky stretched forever.

A new sound intruded, the soft hum of running water. Puzzled, Jeannie's eyes skimmed the area till suddenly, straight ahead, she spied a miniature waterfall, probably the runoff from a nearby underground stream, spilling its waters over the upper edge of a dry creek bed. Delighted with her find, she ran through the soft grass and knelt down across from the mini fall.

And that's when she saw it.

At first, she didn't understand what was wrong with the grass on the other side of the gully. Not all the grass, she realized, as she slowly got to her feet, but a sizable section, a large circle.

Her heart gave one thump and began to pound loud and hard. It's probably nothing, she told herself, as she scrambled through the dry bed, her eyes fixed on that patch of grass. It's a fungus. A blight of some kind that has turned the grass brown.

She stood at the edge of the circle and cautiously pushed her shoe over the stiff brown blades. They crumbled into tiny flakes and sifted down to the ground.

Burned. This grass had been burned!

Hunching down, she tried to pick a few blades. As she expected, they fell apart in her fingers. She stood up and scanned the open area around her. The brown grass seemed to form a perfect circle, about ten feet across, with a long straight swath extending off one side, almost to the edge of the clearing, where it ended abruptly.

With her heart pumping overtime, Jeannie walked around the perimeter of the circle, searching for something, anything to confirm or deny the wild idea that kept bouncing around in her head.

She ignored the first hole until she saw another, a four-inch, shallow depression in the hard rocky ground. Then she found the third, this one with a deep crack running from end to end, as though it had been seared by intense heat. The three appeared equidistant from one another. Even her untrained eyes saw that these gashes could not possibly be natural. Something had put them there.

Hugging herself tightly, she continued to search the entire area for another ten or fifteen minutes, yet only one other thing struck her as strange. Here, unlike the area near the house, she heard no bird songs or twittering of small creatures. Was it coincidence that just a few feet away a ten-foot circle of grass had died?

When she finally jumped over the creek bed and started down the hill, Jeannie had a million questions.

And a burning desire to find the answers.

* * *

THE phone was ringing when she opened the door to Barb's house ten minutes later. Without thinking, she picked it up before the answering machine could cut in. "Price residence. Jeannie MacLeod speaking."

"Hello, Jeannie MacLeod. This must be my lucky day."

"Denis!"

"I'm flattered. You recognized my voice."

Even though he was miles away, Jeannie felt the heat creeping into her face. She could just imagine what he'd say if she told him she would never mistake his voice. She didn't say it, of course. Denis Earley didn't need anyone to bolster his confidence.

"If you're looking for Loren, he's not here," she said, switching to a safer topic. "He and Barb and Buddy were gone when I got here a while ago. I thought I'd look around. In the daylight," she added.

"What are you looking for?"

Nothing. I've already found it. The words danced on the tip of her tongue, but she didn't say them. "I'm not quite sure." At least that was true an hour ago. She hadn't known then what she was looking for or even what she had found. Not for sure.

"Jeannie? Are you there?"

"Mm-m. Right here."

"You sound different. Say, what did you find out there?"

"Uh, Denis, I've got to run. I'll leave Loren a note saying you called. Good to talk to you. Bye!"

Jeannie had already pushed the button to break the

connection when she set the receiver down and stood there staring at the phone.

"I don't believe I did that!" Pacing the floor, she muttered, "I might as well have told him everything. It won't take him long to figure it out. And he probably thinks I'm a complete idiot." Whatever had possessed her to hang up on the man?

Deep down she knew why. She was still afraid Denis would laugh at her. She'd been afraid last night, too, when she plunged ahead with her UFO theory, but she had just met him then. She hadn't dreamed about him. Somehow, the dream made Denis much more real to her. Dreams were so personal.

Well, whatever the reason for what she had done, the result was the same. Dr. Earley would dismiss her as a flaky twit, not worth the time of day.

Disappointed at this conclusion, she managed to scribble a note saying she had stopped by and Denis had called. Then she scooped up her keys and purse and left the house, her mind already racing with ideas on what to do with her startling discovery in the woods.

* * *

FROWNING, Denis hung up the phone.

That was the strangest conversation he'd ever had. At first, Jeannie had sounded okay. Surprised but normal, until he mentioned finding something at Loren's house. Then she practically hung up on him, without answering his question.

What did it mean? He didn't have to be a genius to figure out the answer. She must have found something she didn't want him to know about, although what, he had no idea. But he did know how to figure it out.

* * *

THE Sun Building sat on the corner of Wilkes and Main in downtown Benton, a two-story, yellow brick structure from one of the town's more prosperous periods in the late thirties when southeastern Oklahoma's abundant coal resources became an important national commodity. At present, Benton's economy was experiencing a pleasant lull, pleasant, at least, for many of its residents, who found the town's slow-paced lack of prosperity quite comfortable. Among them was Eddie Barnes, *News and Sun* editor-in-chief.

A few minutes after eight o'clock on Monday morning, Eddie strode through the Sun Building's front door and into his spacious office. Thanks to his late Uncle Jack, a major investor in the newspaper, young Eddie had been offered this position straight out of college in nearby Emmetville, and he made no secret of the fact that he considered it a lifelong appointment. Eddie was a simple man with simple needs and wants. He'd married his high school sweetheart, who kept him reasonably happy, had a growing family he was proud of and a job that gave him respect and a certain amount of clout in this small community. He couldn't imagine anyone wanting more out of life.

The lock in the front door thumped hard as it turned, and Eddie watched Jeannie MacLeod blow past the main desk headed straight toward his office. He sighed. Jeannie was one of the few thorns in his usually peaceful existence. Not that he didn't like her. He liked a lot of things about her, although she had quickly squelched any romantic notions he might have entertained when she came to work for him six years ago. Since then, their relationship had been strictly business and it, no *she*, drove him crazy. She was good, no doubt about it, but so damned intense about her work. Like now. One look at the determined jut of her small round chin and the fire in her blue eyes told him she had sniffed out a story and was hot on the trail. She'd get it, too, and do a great write-up. This was fine, as long as it didn't happen too often. With Uncle Jack gone these past couple of years, Eddie never felt quite as sure of his job as he used to, and he didn't need a hotshot reporter scooping him all the time. Why couldn't she stick to events at the local library or the Music Club's annual recital?

"'Morning, Eddie. What brings you in so early on a Monday morning?"

"I might ask you the same question, Ms. MacLeod. I believe your hours are nine to six."

"Come off it, chief. We both know this job doesn't work that way."

He ignored the hated nickname and changed the subject. "I assume you're working on something other than an assignment?"

Jeannie grinned. "Right on."

"And?"

"And what?" she asked, innocently.

Not for the first time, Eddie wished he had the nerve, or a reason, to get this woman out of his life. Since he didn't, he did the next best thing. Swinging around in his chair, he snapped, "Shut the door on your way out!"

* * *

JEANNIE walked down the narrow hall, swinging the oversized purse that doubled as her briefcase and grinning at the ridiculous charade Eddie insisted on even with no one else around.

They both knew she was his best reporter. They also knew that even without a journalism degree, she would make a better editor than he ever could. And they both knew that at this paper, in this town, she would never get the chance. There would always be a favorite son or nephew or friend--male, of course--from which to choose. These things should have pleased Eddie. Instead, he hated the fact that he depended on a woman, especially a younger woman, so he picked on her whenever he could get away with it. Recognizing the absurdity of the situation, Jeannie picked back, and life went on.

Still smiling at their latest encounter, she stopped at a small cubbyhole on the right. It wasn't much--a desk with her computer, two chairs and a single drawer file--but at least she had privacy. Well, sort of. A nine-by-nine space without a door wouldn't keep anyone out, but even a dead bolt wouldn't stop Eddie if he took a notion to come in. Anyway, privacy had never been an issue here, although that could change if anything came of the call she was about to make. Flipping through her card file, she found the right number and punched it into the phone. A few minutes later, she was talking to the Classifieds Department of the *Tulsa Star.*

"That's right, Linda. I want to run an announcement, a special notice. Ready? 'Anyone who noticed unusual activity, events, etc., in the Crossland Park area on Friday night, October 23rd, please reply to P.O. Box 832, Benton, Oklahoma. All responses will be kept confidential.'"

"Right. Run it for a week. And sign it, 'Investigative Reporter.' Thanks, Linda. Bye."

Taking a deep breath, Jeannie slowly hung up the phone. Done. She had committed herself to a project that could lead anywhere. Or nowhere. But that wouldn't happen. She knew it with a certainty that left no room for doubt. This was the big one, her chance to make a name for herself.

Excitement filled her and charged her like a shot of adrenaline. With hands not quite steady, she flipped on her computer and created a new file, which she labeled, "Tulsa Lights." When she finished entering her data, she copied the file onto a disk and tucked it into her purse. A quick glance at her watch told her she had twelve minutes to make her nine o'clock appointment.

* * *

WHEN the doorbell rang shortly before noon on Monday, Denis was sitting in the middle of the faded blue Aubusson rug in his study, surrounded by oversized cardboard boxes and hundreds of books.

He stood up slowly, stretching his cramped legs and surveying the clutter around him. He'd planned to finish setting up his office in here today, that is, until he got the bright idea yesterday to invite Loren for a round of golf. After the way his old friend had carried on the other night, Denis thought he'd have to talk him into the game, but Loren said he was free on Monday afternoon and he'd quickly agreed.

The doorbell clanged again, and Denis knew he'd better hurry. Loren might decide there was no one home and go back to work for the rest of the day. If that happened, it could be weeks before Denis pried him out of his history books again.

Sure enough, Loren was already walking down the front steps when Denis opened the door. "Going somewhere?" he drawled.

Loren whirled around, his eyes wide, his body tense. "You're home!"

Leaning against the door, Denis nodded toward his small red sports car sitting in the driveway. "I guess you didn't notice my car."

"No. No, I didn't." Loren's lanky body eased into its normal, loose-limbed posture as he ambled back toward the house. "But that probably doesn't surprise you."

Denis draped one arm around his friend's shoulders. "You quit surprising me our sophomore year in college."

"What about Saturday night?"

"What about it?"

"Your profession is showing, Doctor," Loren said, shaking his head.

Denis grinned. "You always were a quick study, Price. Tell you what, I'll lay off the questions if you'll relax and enjoy yourself. We have a lot of catching up to do today."

Loren straightened his shoulders and took a deep breath. "You're on, Doc."

* * *

DENIS sat sprawled on the sofa in his living room later that evening, a forgotten can of beer on the floor by his feet. He was thinking about Loren, his old friend who had once been like a brother to him. The friend who had urged him to come back to Oklahoma when Denis could no longer endure his life back East. Loren, a very troubled man.

And Denis couldn't even begin to imagine why.

As the city darkness stole into his front room, he closed his eyes and tried to remember. Had he noticed anything different about Loren ten days ago when he and Barb met his plane at the airport? Surely he would remember the unusual agitation, prolonged silences and memory lapses the man had exhibited today. Or would he? After all, they hadn't seen each other in twelve years.

But Denis still knew him. They had often talked on the phone, exchanged e-mail. He was Buddy's godfather, dammit! And Loren was still his best friend. A few years apart--okay, even a dozen years--couldn't break the bond between them. He sure felt closer to Loren than he ever did to his own family.

So what about Loren's problem? Try as he might, Denis couldn't think of a thing about his friend that had struck him as out of the ordinary, until two days ago.

This brought him back to the story Loren had told about the strange light in the sky. And his sister-in-law's absurd explanation for his behavior.

Ah yes, Jeannie MacLeod. A tantalizing package of contradictions with an astounding imagination. A far cry from Suzanne's cool sophistication.

His eyes flew open and his stomach actually churned at this unwelcome intrusion into his thoughts. He deliberately pushed his ex-wife's image back into a remote corner of his mind, hopefully for good. He'd spent the last five years trying to forget the most beautiful woman he'd ever met, and he'd be damned if he would let her ruin his new life here in Tulsa.

He stood, yawned, and walked over to the windows to close the blinds. All that fresh air and exercise walking around the golf course today had made him tired, but he'd enjoyed it more than anything he'd done in a long time. But then, he'd always enjoyed Loren's company. If only the guy didn't have this unknown cloud hanging over him, tearing him up inside.

Denis turned out the lights and climbed the stairs to his bedroom. He'd sleep on the problem and let his subconscious work on it. Maybe he'd wake up with some answers, or at least an idea of how to help his friend.

* * *

REPLIES to Jeannie's notice in the Tulsa paper trickled in during the week. One on Wednesday and two on Thursday. Not exactly an overwhelming response, but better than it could have been, and they all mentioned seeing lights.

The police told one man he had seen the planet Venus. Two people said the lights were explained as either a satellite or an airplane, again by the police. When Jeannie talked with the Tulsa Police Department, she was told politely but firmly she was wasting her time. People had always seen "funny" things in the sky and they always would. The officials checked because it was their job, but nothing ever came of it.

Maybe, maybe not. If she could just get one solid sighting by a reliable witness….

Friday morning, she was running late and almost didn't stop at the post office. A few hours more or less wouldn't make any difference. Then she remembered why she was hurrying. Eddie held a staff meeting at nine o'clock every Friday morning so he could play boss for an hour or more.

That settled it. She made a U-turn in the middle of Markct Street and shot down an alley to the back of the post office.

Standing on tiptoe, she peered into Box 832. Through the smoky glass, she saw one slim envelope. Darn! She'd been hoping for a handful. Good thing she only used this box for business mail. She could develop a serious inferiority complex depending on what had come this week. Still, one was better than none. She hoped.

At least this one had a return address. And neat typing.

She slid her finger under the flap and tore it open.

Dear Investigator:

In response to your request for information on 'unusual activity' in the Crossland Park area, this is what I observed:

At approximately 8:55 p.m. on October 23rd, while alone in my back yard, I noticed a bright white light in the sky northwest of my house, which is between Thirty-First Street and the Broken Arrow Expressway. The light was moving, so it wasn't a star. As it came closer, I saw that it had a reddish-orange glow that changed to silver-white as it went over my house in a southeasterly direction. It moved much faster than a satellite, which I have observed before. I watched till it finally blinked out at nine o'clock. At that time, I estimated its position as the general area of Cross-land Park.

I was curious as to what the light might be, so I asked some questions of a few colleagues. My wife and two sons had shared my observations and can corroborate what I've said. I learned that a number of people saw strange lights that night and several other nights during the past weeks. As you can imagine, I've heard all kinds of explanations,

*which I'd be happy to share with you if you're
interested. You can reach me at the phone
number on this letterhead.*

*Sincerely,
John Gregory
Engineer, City of Tulsa*

"Yes!" Jeannie's war whoop echoed through the small
post office, causing several heads to turn.

"Good news, Miss Jeannie?"

Waving the letter over her head, she smiled at a tall
elderly man who stood at one of the tables sorting his mail.

"Just what I've been waiting for, Mr. Cooper. How's
Mary doing? I haven't seen her column in a couple of
weeks."

"She's been a bit under the weather, but she's perking up
now. Say, you wouldn't be on your way to the newspaper
office, would you?" A gnarled hand reached around to his
hip pocket and pulled out a folded piece of paper. "She
asked me to drop this by. It's a dandy." His pale blue eyes
lit up as he opened the paper. "'Sammy Squirrel Stores His
Nuts,' by Mary Cooper. I told her this is one of her best
pieces," he said proudly, "and that's saying something. Did
you know she's been writing 'Backyard Friends' for over
twenty years? Why, I remember--"

"I'll be glad to deliver it, Mr. Cooper," said Jeannie
quickly, taking the paper. "There's a lot of folks in Benton
who count on Mary's advice. Got to run now. Bye!" She
squeezed his hand and hurried through the double doors
and down the front steps.

That was a close one. Once Mr. Cooper got wound up,
she usually didn't get away for twenty or thirty minutes.
Not that she really minded. He was an interesting man, a
retired schoolteacher who had traveled all over the country,
and she liked to hear his stories, but not today. Not when

she was on her way to talk to John Gregory.

She stopped short on the sidewalk beside her car and stared at the two pieces of paper in her hand. One went to the *News and Sun* office, where she was supposed to be-- she glanced at her watch--five minutes ago. The other would take her into Tulsa to an interview that could turn into her first real break in her investigation.

Without a second thought, she slid Mary's column into her bulging, brown leather purse and yanked open her car door. Okay, so Eddie would rant and rave and carry on like a madman when she finally showed up today, after the meeting. She'd chance it. Right now, she was going to find a phone and talk to John Gregory, even if it took her all morning to track him down.

Once she made her decision, Jeannie didn't waste time wondering what had possessed her to act so boldly, something totally unlike her. Sure, she sometimes teased Eddie, even deliberately baited him, but she had never defied him.

Until now.

With an impatient toss of her head, she backed her car out of its parking place and turned north on Jackson Street. First things first. She had places to go, things to do.

She had to find John Gregory.

* * *

TWO phone calls and thirty-five minutes later, she found herself on the third floor of a downtown Tulsa office building, talking to Gregory's secretary.

"I'm not sure Mr. Gregory is available," the gray-haired woman said doubtfully. "He has a meeting at ten. If you would like to make an appointment--"

Jeannie reached into her purse and pulled out the engineer's letter. "We've been corresponding," she said, stretching the truth just a little. "I'm sure he'll want to see me." She smiled and added one of her business cards. "Please show him these."

The woman didn't look convinced, but she took the card and the envelope and walked back to one of the two closed doors behind the reception area.

Jeannie tapped her foot and counted seconds. *Nine. Ten. Eleven.*

The door opened. "You can come in now," the secretary said.

"Thank you." Jeannie smiled and hurried past the woman, who nodded stiffly. Obviously, she didn't approve, but she had done her job.

John Gregory pushed back his chair and stood up when Jeannie entered the room. She took in his loosened shirt collar and rolled-up sleeves, along with the keen blue eyes that followed her as she crossed the room to the front of his desk. "Thank you for seeing me, Mr. Gregory. I know you're busy."

"Not that busy, Ms. MacLeod." He handed her back his letter. "I did invite you to contact me, after all."

She slipped the envelope into her bag. "Yes, you did. Do you mind telling me why?"

"Not at all." He sat down in his swivel chair. "Have a seat. And feel free to take notes, although I prefer to remain anonymous, if any of this conversation should make it into print."

"Understood. Although right now, all I have are questions, not a story."

A smile hovered at the corners of Gregory's broad mouth. "That's why I wrote the letter. I'm a practical man, Ms. MacLeod. Questions without answers bother me. When I saw your notice in the *Star*, I figured you were looking for answers, too. No need to duplicate efforts."

"I do the legwork. You get your answers."

He shrugged. "So do you. Sounds good to me."

A practical man. Jeannie decided she liked him. She rummaged through her purse and found a small notebook, then settled back in her chair. "Exactly who have you talked to and what kinds of explanations have you received for what you saw that night?"

Instead of answering, he swung his chair around and reached into the middle drawer of a filing cabinet behind him. Without comment, he laid a manila folder on his desk. "This is it, all the information I've come up with, including names and addresses. I'll make you copies, if you like."

Jeannie stared at the man, and then opened the folder, which was labeled simply: "Lights." It included statements from half a dozen people, as well as maps and precise scale drawings and diagrams, signed by Gregory.

"This is incredible!" she murmured. "But why?"

"Why give it to you?" He shrugged. "You plan to check it out, don't you?"

"Of course, but--"

"And you probably have contacts I don't. Is that correct?"

"Well, yes, but--"

"Ms. MacLeod, I'm a professional. So are you. I work with building codes. You track down stories. You wouldn't try to revise a building code for the city of Tulsa, would you?"

"Of course not!"

"But you do know who to talk to and which questions to ask to get a good story. I think there's a story here." He pointed to the folder. "I don't know what it is, but there are questions that need answers, the right answers. It's all yours, if you want it."

A cold shiver rippled through Jeannie. "I want it," she said quickly. "And thank you, Mr. Gregory."

"You're welcome."

They talked for several minutes more, but Jeannie soon decided he really had put everything on paper, and if she just studied his notes, she would have plenty to work with. Finally, she glanced at her watch. "If you don't mind making those copies, Mr. Gregory."

He picked up the folder and took it to the copier. "I get carried away when I talk about that night," he admitted. "It really has me baffled. You, uh, wouldn't care to tell me how you got involved, would you?"

The question sounded casual, but Jeannie detected a very real interest. "Sorry," she said and meant it. "But I promise to keep in touch."

"I figured as much. I'll hold you to that promise."

She walked across the room and held out her hand. "You have a deal, Mr. Gregory."

* * *

AFTER that very promising start, the day went downhill fast. Eddie did not believe any meeting could be more important than his, especially when Jeannie refused to tell him anything about it.

Her stubbornness undoubtedly influenced his decision to let Billy Whitecotton, his newest reporter, cover the drug trial at the courthouse while Jeannie interviewed newly elected class officers at the Middle School. She didn't really mind, she told herself. Billy needed the experience, and tomorrow Eddie would find something else to gripe about. Still, by the time she walked into her house shortly after six that evening, she knew she had done a day's work.

"But I'm not finished yet," she told Kenworth, who had greeted her at the door with a pitiful complaint about his empty food dish. Laying her purse on the kitchen table, she filled the dish. Then hurried into her bedroom to change into her favorite lavender sweats, her real work clothes.

Twenty minutes later, she sat curled up on the couch with a cup of mocha coffee and a lasagna entree in a cardboard box, straight from the microwave. Not a great dinner, but she liked anything with spicy tomato sauce.

"And so do you," she said, scratching Ken's chin, as she set the empty container on the floor for him to lick.

On her way through the kitchen, she grabbed an apple

from the refrigerator to balance her meal. Then settled at the table with John Gregory's file folder spread open in front of her. What a find! Someone intelligent and efficient, who had already done some of her legwork. That didn't happen very often. Sure, she would have to go back and confirm what his witnesses had seen and said, but still....

As she flipped through the dozen or more statements, her eyes caught a name in caps at the top of one sheet: "UFORA: UFO Research Association, a worldwide UFO organization."

All right! Now she was getting somewhere. She read the page carefully. It was a letter from an Allen Kendrick, the Oklahoma State Director of UFORA. He stated that in reference to his telephone conversation with Mr. Gregory on October 25th, he had checked into the matter of unexplained lights seen over Tulsa. He had only two trained investigators in that area, and neither was able to take on a new project at the moment. Therefore, he would look into the matter himself and call Gregory when he came to Tulsa. The engineer had made a note in the margin that as of November 5th, he had not heard from Kendrick.

Jeannie glanced at her watch. Friday, the sixth. Most likely, he still hadn't called. Gregory would probably have let her know, and there had been no messages on her answering machine today. She scanned the remaining pages, but this letter seemed to be the most promising lead. Making a quick decision, she picked up the receiver hanging on her wall phone and dialed Allen Kendrick's home in Oklahoma City.

"Hello?"

"Mr. Kendrick, this is Jeannie MacLeod with the *Benton News and Sun*. I'm calling in regard to a letter you wrote John Gregory on October 28th."

For a second or two, Jeannie thought the line had gone dead, then the voice spoke again, wary this time. "How do you know about that letter?"

She told him how she had met John Gregory and that he had handed his investigation over to her.

"I see."

Those two words spoke volumes, and Jeannie decided the man didn't "see" at all. "Mr. Kendrick, I understand your hesitation about speaking to a reporter, but believe me, my interest in UFO's is serious as well as professional. I am not a tabloid journalist, nor will I write any sensational copy about flying saucers and little green men. I'm looking for the truth."

"That's a pretty speech, Ms. MacLeod. Unfortunately, I've heard it before, believed it and regretted it."

Jeannie's mind raced with several possibilities. She just knew this man had access to all kinds of information, things she wanted to know. How could she convince him she was a serious investigator?

She tried a different tack. "Mr. Kendrick, I respect your position, but I really need help. I'd like a chance to talk to you in person. Would you at least be willing to meet with me? I'll give you a written statement, if you like, that our conversations are off the record until you tell me otherwise." She lowered her voice and considered her words carefully. She had to be very sure not to implicate Loren. "You may be interested to know that I have good reasons for my investigation. Perhaps we can help each other."

Another pause, then a soft chuckle. "You are a very persuasive young woman. My schedule has been pretty hectic lately, but since I come to Tulsa on Tuesdays and Thursdays, why don't we get together tomorrow, say five-thirty?"

Excited now, Jeannie scribbled a memo to herself. "Five-thirty is fine. Where shall I meet you?"

"Are you familiar with Northwest College?"

All Jeannie's systems went on full alert. "Northwest College?"

"Yes, it's off the Crosstown Expressway."

"I'm familiar with the college."

"Good. My office is in the Social Science Building, right behind Admin. You can't miss it. I'll see you then, Ms. MacLeod."

"Yes. And thank you, Mr. Kendrick."

She slipped the receiver back in its cradle. Yes, she knew Northwest College and the Social Science Building. She had walked through its double glass doors any number of times in the past ten years, since her sister had married Dr. Loren Price, head of Northwest's History Department.

5

JEANNIE parked her car in a visitors' slot directly across from the Social Science Building, and then leaned back in the seat and closed her eyes.

All her instincts told her she had made a right turn when she stumbled onto Allen Kendrick, and she'd been gearing up to this meeting all day. Long, deep, calming breaths.

Her eyes popped open. Time to get it on and meet the man. Grabbing her purse, she locked the car and hurried along the sidewalk to the main entrance, mentally rehearsing her approach to this interview.

If her mind hadn't drifted at that moment, if she'd been looking straight ahead rather than watching her own feet, she would have seen the man running down the steps. She would have stepped out of his way instead of walking straight into him, but at least he managed to twist aside at the last moment, avoiding a head-on collision.

She staggered, grabbed and ended up clutching a handful of bright green cotton lisle, the front of a very expensive polo shirt. "I--oh!"

"Are you hurt?"

The familiar deep voice slid over her like a stream of ice water. Refreshing, yet disturbing.

"Jeannie? Are you all right?"

She leaned into his solid chest. "Oh yes."

"Good! Uh, could you let go of my shirt? We're blocking traffic here."

Shirt? Oh, God! She jumped back, only to have Denis circle her waist with one arm and lead her toward a wooden bench several feet away. She went without protest only because their collision had already drawn some curious stares.

"You sure you're okay?"

"I'm fine. Really."

He didn't look convinced. Nor did he take his arm away. "Let's sit down for a minute. We didn't get much of a chance to talk--when was it? A week ago Sunday?"

Right. The day she had hung up on him. Without squirming too much, she managed to slip out of his grasp. "Denis, I don't mean to be rude, but I have an appointment in--" She checked her watch. "In two minutes. I really have to run."

"I hope Loren didn't forget you," he said, frowning. "A few minutes ago, he told me he had finished for the day."

"It's not Loren," she said, avoiding his eyes.

His scowl deepened. "Sorry. I just assumed--"

"I know, but this is business." Business not with Loren, but definitely concerning him.

His scowl deepened. "Well then, I won't keep you. Have a good meeting."

"Right. Take care, Denis." She walked away and quickly climbed the steps to the front door.

Much better, she assured herself. This time she had kept her cool and carried on a fairly intelligent conversation with the man. Not brilliant, but at least rational. She absolutely refused to think about how she had leaned in to him, how good and solid he had felt.

As the heavy glass door closed behind her, Jeannie caught a glimpse of Dr. Earley still staring at the building, his rugged face thoughtful. No, he looked puzzled, she decided, and wondered just what was going through his mind.

Fortunately, she didn't run into Loren as she hurried through the building's east wing, which housed a number of small offices. Telling him why she was here might be even harder than explaining it to Denis. At the far end of the hallway, she located the tiny room Allen Kendrick called his office. She knocked, and a soft voice with a distinctive Texas drawl bade her come in.

The professor surprised her. His voice over the phone and his involvement with a UFO organization had made her think young and slightly radical, long hair, probably bearded, maybe an earring. Instead, she found herself staring at somebody's grandfather from the suburbs. Short white hair neatly styled, clean shaven, and dark brown eyes that appraised her steadily from behind silver-rimmed glasses.

When she entered the room, he stood and walked around to the front of his desk. "Ms. MacLeod?"

Jeannie shook his hand. "Thank you for meeting with me, Mr. Kendrick. I guess I should say Dr. Kendrick," she corrected, remembering the sign on his door.

"No need to be formal," he said easily. "Have a seat."

She pulled up a comfortable-looking chair while he returned to his place behind the desk. "Before we begin, Ms. MacLeod, I'd like your assurance that anything we discuss today will remain confidential until I give you permission to print it."

"You have it," she assured him. "Do you want me to put that in writing?"

"No, I trust you."

"That's very flattering," she said slowly, wondering what came next.

Kendrick smiled. "Before you start thinking I'm a simple old man, I'll tell you that I did some checking. You are an excellent journalist, young lady, and your strong sense of ethics comes through quite clearly in a number of your stories. I'm satisfied with your word that our conversation will go no further than this room."

Pleased with his confidence, Jeannie said simply, "I appreciate that. Shall we get started?"

Without naming any names, she told him how she had become involved in this investigation and what she had uncovered so far, including the burned area in the woods. When she described the dead grass and the three distinct holes in the ground, Kendrick leaned forward, taking in every word. He had her repeat each detail several times while he jotted down notes.

"It certainly sounds like a classic landing trace," he said, tapping his pen on the paper. "Almost too good to be true. Together with what happened to the man living in this area and the data John Gregory gathered about Crossland Park, I'd say we may be on to something big."

Nodding, Jeannie said, "I've read the letters in Mr. Gregory's file. What do you think about them?"

"I think someone needs to do a thorough investigation," Kendrick said promptly. "Unfortunately, as I mentioned in my letter to Mr. Gregory, I haven't yet located a UFORA investigator who can take it on now. I've sent out a state-wide request, but so far, no takers. I'm hoping to have someone on it by the time we meet next week."

"UFORA," Jeannie said slowly. "Can you tell me something about it? How do you fit into the picture?"

Kendrick chuckled. "You mean, how did a college professor get involved with such a dubious group? Actually, it happened quite logically." He leaned back in his chair, his long legs in their tailored gray slacks stretched out under the desk, his hands folded behind his head. "By nature, I'm a curious man. I can't think of a subject I'm not interested in. Not that I know that much outside my own field, but I like learning new things. And I like logical answers.

"When I picked up a book on UFO's several years ago, I found many of the commonly held explanations just didn't make sense. They left more questions than they answered. One book led to another, until one day I ran across UFORA listed under 'UFO organizations.' I contacted them. Liked what I learned and joined. The rest, as they say, is history."

"What about this group convinced you to join?"

"First of all, it's a scientific organization, international in scope. Their Board of Consultants consists of almost two hundred members, mostly PhD's and MD's, from all over the world, representing over seventy-five areas of science. Membership is by invitation, and only those seriously interested in studying UFO's may join.

"It's a grass roots organization with most of its leadership at a local level. And it's effective. I'm convinced that the research we're doing will ultimately provide the answer to the greatest mystery the world has ever encountered."

"Wow!"

Kendrick shook his head and laughed ruefully. "Well, there you have it, a two-minute dissertation on my favorite subject. Next time you won't let me run on like that."

"No, no. I'm impressed," Jeannie assured him. "I had no idea such a group existed."

"Would you like to attend a meeting?"

Jeannie's eyes widened. "Really?"

"Sure. You have a legitimate interest." He glanced at his calendar. "Next Friday, seven p.m., at the Bainbridge East Library in Oklahoma City. Do you know where it is?"

She took down directions and promised to be there. She didn't look forward to the two-hour drive at night, but she had no intention of missing such a great opportunity. Maybe she could stay in the city for the weekend, take in a show. The idea began to have possibilities.

They talked for a few more minutes, until Jeannie glanced at her watch and realized she had taken almost an hour of the man's time. Slipping her notebook into her purse, she stood up. "Dr. Kendrick, I've enjoyed talking to you. You've given me several new ideas to work on. One of the first things I'll do is check out Crossland Park."

He nodded. "That's what I would do. I'm not sure I've been much help, but I can tell you that UFORA will be interested. They will definitely look into that trace you described, and our investigator will want to talk to the man who is involved. Can that be arranged?"

Jeannie hesitated. "I'm not sure. This whole business has really upset him. I'm hoping he'll agree to talk to a psychologist soon."

"That's a good idea. If you think he'd be interested, I can recommend a woman who works with UFORA. She's a psychiatrist who has taken a special interest in abduction victims. In fact, she will be our speaker at the next meeting."

"Abduction victims? You mean, people who have talked to aliens?"

"More than that. They are taken away against their wills. These people are victims in the truest sense of the word. Often their lives change forever."

"That's hard to believe."

"I know. Many people don't, although all the evidence supports the theory."

"And you think Lo--uh, this man could be one of these victims?"

"From what you've told me, it sounds likely," Kendrick said evenly.

Suddenly, she had to get out of this room. She needed time to think. Standing up, she said, "Do you have my number, Dr. Kendrick?"

He held up her small white business card. "It's been a pleasure, Ms. MacLeod. Good luck in your investigation, and I'll see you at the meeting next Friday?"

She nodded. "I'll be there. I wouldn't miss it for the world."

* * *

WITH a soft groan, Denis sank into his favorite armchair by the living room fireplace. God, what a day!

Two appointments at the hospital this morning, a fruitless hour of hunting through medical textbooks for a problem he hadn't identified yet, a trip to the college to visit with Loren, and the rest of the day unpacking, arranging and rearranging furniture. And his house still resembled a major disaster area. So far, the only room with any semblance of order was the study, which he had turned into his office, although he'd been in Tulsa almost a month. At least he'd had the foresight to hire a carpenter and painter to work in there before he moved in. Except for a few pieces, mostly nautical treasures collected by his shipbuilding ancestors and passed on through the family, that room was complete and ready for him to receive patients. Denis had packed the antiques himself, and he'd seen the boxes here somewhere. Oh well, they would turn up eventually.

Eyeing the clutter around him--boxes, books, extra pieces of furniture--he wondered again if he shouldn't have hired a decorator before he moved in. But he didn't want anyone else messing around with his belongings, trying to change things. He liked the comfortable furniture he'd accumulated since his divorce, and he liked the family heirlooms Suzanne had called monstrosities.

Shaking off the pall that immediately settled over him at the thought of his ex-wife, he reached for a newspaper lying on top of the stack by his chair. Last Monday's *Tulsa Star*. Maybe he'd read the comics before he went up to bed.

He probably would never have noticed the small ad in the middle of the classifieds, if the words "Crossland Park" hadn't jumped out at him. That was the place where Loren had seen the so-called mysterious lights. He kept reading.

"Anyone who noticed unusual activity, events, etc., in the Crossland Park area on Friday night, October 23rd, please reply to P.O. Box 832, Benton, Oklahoma. All responses will be kept confidential. Investigative Reporter."

Darn that woman! So that was what she'd been up to, chasing lights in the sky so she could convince Loren he really had seen something strange. Just what the man didn't need.

Anger and disappointment vied for Denis' attention. How could she lead Loren on like that? Supposedly, she cared about the guy. At least Denis had thought so after listening to her on Halloween night. Okay, so he began to have his doubts when he talked to her the next day and found out she'd been snooping around Loren's house. That sounded more like a reporter after a story than a concerned friend, but then he'd spoken to Loren several times this past week and spent Monday afternoon with him at the golf course, and he assured Denis that Jeannie hadn't even talked to him since the night of Buddy's party.

Denis had almost convinced himself that Jeannie MacLeod really had nothing more than her brother-in-law's best interests at heart when he ran into her this afternoon outside the college. Just business, she'd said. Nothing to do with Loren. Denis had given her the benefit of the doubt because he wanted to believe her, and now this!

Disgusted, he threw down the paper. He should have known he couldn't trust a reporter, even one so soft-spoken and shy, with a tantalizing innocence. Hadn't he learned anything at all six years ago when a pack of reporters had made his life a living hell?

Gritting his teeth, he slumped back in the chair. She wouldn't get away with it. Two could play her game. Whatever she thought she might find nosing around here and there, he'd just have to find it first and be sure she didn't use it to harm Loren. Unfortunately, Denis had no idea what to look for. He'd already checked the corral and the yard all around Loren's house and found nothing unusual. Well, now he had one more place Jeannie would

be poking through, if she hadn't already. His eyes settled
once more on the ad in the paper. Tomorrow morning he
would get up at the crack of dawn and make a thorough
search of Crossland Park.

                                        * * *

RON Siegel was curious.

He had arrived in Tulsa on Monday, expecting a routine
investigation. So far, it had turned out to be anything but
routine, but it was too early to get excited. He wouldn't
allow that, not yet. He hated being disappointed, and
ninety-nine percent of the time, that's what happened. No,
he wasn't excited, but he was definitely intrigued.

Crossland Park was quiet at seven-thirty on a Tuesday
morning, quiet and empty. That suited Ron perfectly. He
came here to look around, and he didn't want anyone
watching over his shoulder. He shouldn't have to worry.
The gates didn't open till nine, and he doubted that anyone
else would bother to crawl through the shrubbery.

His biggest problem was not knowing where to look.
The park covered more than a square mile of grassy acreage, tree-lined walkways, several ponds, and some fairly
thick woods, even in November. He decided to start with
the open areas, the easiest to comb with the most possibilities.

As he tramped through the grass, springy and wet with
morning dew, Siegel was only dimly aware of the soft
squishing of his rubber-soled moccasins and the faint
rustling in nearby bushes. As long as he was the only two-
legged creature around, he didn't care. He hadn't come out
here to enjoy the scenery. Sure, the sunshine felt great, a lot
better than the cold drizzle he'd left back in Washington,
but he would have kept on walking no matter what the
weather. He needed a good case, something to make
Biggers sit up and notice him, and this might be the one. He
had a feeling about it.

An hour and a half later, he wasn't so sure. He had covered the whole western section of the park and found nothing. That sun had turned downright hot and he was getting uncomfortable. Every time he took a step, the brand new camera he'd slung over his shoulder bumped his hip, and his briefcase felt more like a suitcase. Pulling off his sweater, he tied it around his ample waist, but he could still feel the dampness around his stiff collar and under his arms.

His legs felt stiff, too, and he was breathing too hard. All those hours behind a desk had taken their toll. He'd have to do something about that when he got back home, maybe join one of those health clubs or a gym. He'd heard that a new one had just opened over in Silver Spring. Probably expensive, but class doesn't come cheap.

He almost stepped on it. The brown grass stretched out straight in front of him for about fifty feet, ending in a perfect circle, maybe eight feet across. Ron stared at it for several seconds before the possibility of what he had found dawned on him. Then he dropped to the ground and ran his hands over the grass, the dead grass. He watched in awe as the brown blades broke off and crumbled through his fingers.

He'd need samples and tests. And pictures. Those jocks back in DC needed proof, lots of it. Well, he'd get it. He'd get them everything they wanted. This was the one he'd been waiting for. He knew it for sure.

His hands shook slightly as he slid the camera out of its case. He couldn't do it all today, but he'd take some pictures and a few samples, and tomorrow he'd be back. When he got through, he'd have enough to make Biggers jump right out of his three-piece-suit.

* * *

ON Wednesday morning, the sun had just risen when Jeannie squeezed through a hole in the shrubs on the eastern edge of Crossland Park.

Standing in the thick grass, she looked around uncertainly. The thought occurred to her that she was spending a lot of time in the woods lately, an ironic twist for a girl who had liked everything about Scouting except the camping trips. Determined to get this early morning excursion over with as soon as possible, she walked fifteen or twenty feet into a clearing then headed north, intending to make a sweep around the entire park, then cross the ball fields and playground searching for any sort of clue to the mysterious lights that had plagued this area.

When she first heard the engine, a distinctive low rumble through the trees, Jeannie stopped in her tracks. The duck pond had just poked into view up ahead, which meant the Shannon Boulevard entrance was still a good quarter mile away, too far for the sound of a car engine to carry. Yet, she definitely heard an engine and not very far off. What was a car or truck doing in the park at 6:10 in the morning?

With her heart beating in time to her quick steps, she walked halfway around the pond, then stepped into the thick woods that blocked the park entrance. She found a trail that led her in the general direction of Shannon Boulevard and the unknown vehicle. As she pushed her way through brambles and brush, a squirrel chattered at her from the branch of a tall oak tree, and she recognized the raucous cry of a crow flying overhead. A titmouse called softly, and his mate answered. Nothing seemed amiss, yet she found herself looking over her shoulder, startled by any sound she couldn't immediately identify.

Voices. She stopped, listening, all systems on full alert. Low, indistinct, but definitely human voices somewhere nearby. Cautious now, Jeannie padded along until the trees thinned into a clearing dead ahead. Instinctively, she slipped in behind the trunk of a sprawling oak tree. Something told her to watch and listen before marching up there.

At least a hundred yards from where she stood, she saw a gray mini-van parked at the northern edge of the woods, its back doors wide open. Even as she watched, a man in a dark business suit jumped to the ground. He carried what looked like a square box, about the size of a large book, and he was heading straight toward her. She shrank back, but the man stopped in the middle of the clearing and began to move around slowly, holding the box straight out in front of him. What on earth was he doing?

A second man stepped out of the van, then a third, this one holding a camera. They walked over to the first man and squatted down close to the ground. From this distance, Jeannie couldn't see them clearly, but they seemed to be examining the ground. Leaning forward, she tried to get a better view. If only she had brought binoculars.

"Get back, you little fool!"

The hoarse whisper brushed against her ear just as a hand clamped over her mouth, silencing the scream that had already risen from her throat. She was pulled back against a hard male body, both her arms pinned to her sides by an arm that felt like a steel band. Terror gripped her. She couldn't see her captor; she couldn't scream. She couldn't move her upper body but she could kick, and that's what she did, hard and fast.

"Settle down, you little wildcat! I'm not going to hurt you."

Sure, and puppy dogs can fly! She raised her right foot again.

"Jeannie, for heaven's sake, calm down!"

That voice. Denis? She lowered her leg but didn't relax.

"If I take my hand away, will you promise not to yell?"

It *was* Denis! Her head thumped against his chest as she nodded her assent.

His hand slid away and he loosened his hold on her, but he didn't let go, and maybe that was a good thing. Her legs had turned to jelly sometime in the last thirty seconds, and her heart felt like a sledgehammer working overtime.

"What are you doing here?" she hissed, turning.

He held one finger to her lips, cautioning her to speak softly. "Same as you, checking out the park," he whispered, and added, "Sounds carry out here."

She hated to admit it, but he was right. This wasn't the time or place for discussion. Later, she promised herself, he would have some fancy explaining to do.

"What do you make of that?" she asked, pointing toward the van.

"Beats me, but I'm going to find out. Wait here while I slip around to the other side and come up behind them."

"No way!" she said. "I was on my way over there when you barged in."

"Hold it right there!"

They both swung around and stared into the grim face of a man leaning against a nearby tree. Jeannie had never seen him before, nor was he one of the men she had spotted near the van.

"Who are you?" Denis demanded.

Reaching inside his jacket, he pulled out a small leather case and flipped it open. "Ron Siegel. Federal Agent." He tucked the case back into his pocket.

"Are you with them?" Denis indicated the men in the clearing.

"That's right. We're doing an official government survey. Either of you have a security clearance?"

"Just a minute, mister," Jeannie said, stepping forward. "This is a public park. Since when do we need a security clearance here?"

"Since five o'clock this morning."

She muttered a word that made Denis raise an eyebrow. Siegel didn't flinch.

"I don't know about you," she said, turning to Denis, "but I want to see what's going on over there. I don't think this guy has the right to keep us out."

She hadn't taken two steps when Denis grabbed her arm. "Think again," he said quietly.

She followed his eyes and watched Siegel as he unbuttoned his suit coat and slid his hand underneath. Very casually, he let the hand rest on a prominent bulge on the left side at his waist. Jeannie swallowed hard. "Is that what I think it is?"

Denis nodded. "I'd say so."

"Listen to your friend, Miss. He seems like a sensible fellow."

Meaning she wasn't. That rankled. Jeannie considered herself one of the most reasonable people she knew. She took a closer look at this man. Medium height, a little overweight with thinning brown hair, he had a completely unremarkable face, one that would blend into any crowd. Which could be a very useful talent in certain lines of work.

Not liking it one bit, she went with her better judgment. "Okay, we're leaving. For now," she added, under her breath. Denis' hand, which still gripped her arm, tightened.

"I said I'm going." Turning around, she started back toward the trail she had followed into the woods. "But you haven't seen the last of me," she shot back over her shoulder.

Denis came right along behind her, practically walking up her heels in his hurry to get out of there. "You're really something," he muttered.

"What's that supposed to mean?"

"What were you trying to do back there, get yourself killed?"

Jeannie stopped in her tracks and whirled around. Denis ploughed right into her.

He reached out to steady her. She shook him off. "Aren't you overreacting just a bit, Doctor?"

"I don't think so. I figured we didn't need to wait around until he pulled the gun."

"You're joking!"

"No joke, Ms. MacLeod." Denis' lips tightened into a thin straight line. "That man meant business."

"That man was bluffing." She hoped. She needed to believe it.

"Are you always this stubborn?" He looked down at her with eyes that had turned a smoky green in the muted sunlight. *Smoky and sexy.*

Her senses had suddenly fine-tuned. She felt his hands ease up to her shoulders. Another inch or two, and he would wrap her in his arms. She swayed toward him.

"Siegel's still watching, Jeannie."

She jerked away, mortified that she had practically thrown herself at this guy.

They walked back down the trail in silence, Jeannie cursing the luck that had brought Denis barging in on her scene. Left alone, she might have figured out what those guys were up to. Now she had two puzzles, what interest the U.S. government had in Crossland Park and why Denis Earley had decided to check it out. He didn't believe in her UFO theory--did he? Now that she thought about it, she realized he had never expressed an opinion one way or another. No, not possible, but why else would he come here? The more she thought about it, the more she knew she really wanted this man's acceptance. Well, only one way to settle the issue. She would have to risk telling him what she was doing. Just the thought gave her a sinking feeling in the pit of her stomach, but she knew she was going to do it.

When they crossed the ball fields and came to the grassy area on the southeast edge of the park where South Street met State, Denis turned to face her. "Where did you park?"

Jeannie pointed behind her. "State Street. I found a hole in the shrubbery over there."

Denis rubbed his hands together and shifted from one foot to the other. He looked like he had something to say but couldn't quite make up his mind.

That did it. Jeannie hated tiptoeing around, trying to second guess someone. Better to speak up and know exactly where you stood, even if it wasn't where you wanted to be. With that thought firmly in mind, she faced Denis, her arms folded in front of her. "We need to talk."

He nodded. "You're right. This isn't getting me any-where."

"Getting you--what are you talking about?"

"Come now, Ms. MacLeod. Give me some credit. Surely you know why I'm here this morning."

"In case you don't remember, Doctor, that was the first thing I asked when you attacked me back there in the woods. If I knew the answer, I wouldn't have asked. You said you were checking out the park. That doesn't tell me a thing."

He had a most expressive face. Fascinated, she watched the tiny pucker between his thick blond brows lengthen and deepen. His eyes, which she had already seen both golden and smoky, now turned a deep murky gray, the color of a stormy sea. "You're either the world's best liar or a total innocent, and so help me, I can't figure out which."

"This is the most ridiculous conversation I've ever had," Jeannie snapped. "What would I lie about?"

"How about the reason for all your snooping around? Do you deny that you're looking for so-called evidence to support your UFO theory?"

"Of course not. I'm trying to help Loren."

"Help him? Is that what you call it when you pump him full of ridiculous ideas that will only confuse an already troubled man? It looks to me like you're more interested in a sensational story, whether it's true or not."

Stunned by his accusation, Jeannie's mouth dropped open, and she stared at the angry man in front of her. Well, she sure knew now what he thought about her ideas. She wouldn't have to worry any longer about telling him what she'd been doing. He'd already figured it all out, tried her and condemned her.

They glared at each other for several seconds. The more she thought about what he had said, the angrier Jeannie became. "I don't know what you imagine I've told Loren," she said stiffly, "but I haven't talked to him in over a week. As for what I've been doing, if you had given me a chance, I was going to tell you about my investigation."

"That's what--"

"Investigation, Dr. Earley, as in 'a systematic examination.' Whether you care to accept it or not, UFO's are and have been the subject of numerous scientific investigations. They are a legitimate subject for study, an acknowledged unexplained phenomenon, that any *reasonable* person would like to see resolved."

"I'm not--"

"As for Loren's case," she went on, as though he hadn't said a word, "I can show you documented proof that my ideas about Post-Traumatic Stress Syndrome are absolutely sound."

"Listen, Jeannie, I--"

"However, since you've already decided that I am a horrible person, who would hurt someone who has been like a brother to me." Her voice caught, but she plunged ahead.

"I doubt you have the guts to look at anything I would recommend."

She heard Denis calling her name as she ran toward the shrubbery, but she didn't stop or look back. Where was that opening? There! Scooting down, she crawled through to the sidewalk on State Street. Thirty seconds later, her car made a U-turn, headed back to Benton.

* * *

DENIS could have chased her down, but he didn't see that another confrontation at this point would accomplish anything, at least not anything positive. Maybe he could have made her angrier but that didn't seem likely, since she'd already looked ready to pop a cork.

Scowling at this turn of events, he tried to figure out what had gone wrong. He sure hadn't expected such a violent reaction when he confronted her with his suspicions. Hell, he didn't think she had it in her. He'd pegged her as mild-mannered and soft-spoken. She was that, all right, with a hidden core of fire that he'd accidentally tapped into. Not an unpleasant surprise, he decided, just unexpected.

He walked slowly toward the South Street entrance, still seeing the very real hurt on Jeannie's face when he mentioned using Loren to get a sensational story. No way she could have feigned such a reaction. It just wasn't possible. He had accused her unjustly, which left him worse than embarrassed. He just might have dug himself a hole he'd never climb out of.

* * *

WHEN she finally calmed down enough to think again, Jeannie decided Denis Earley had done her a favor.

He'd shown his true colors. She now knew he was no different than most other people she met. Anything he couldn't see or hear, touch or smell, simply didn't exist in his narrow world. Okay, she could accept that, as long as she didn't have to deal with him. As far as she was concerned, the man was a total washout.

She leaned on the steering wheel, gripping it hard with both hands, trying to ignore the hollow feeling her decision had left in the pit of her stomach.

* * *

WHAT am I doing here? Shivering, Jeannie huddled down beside the shrubbery just inside Crossland Park, the same shrubbery she had squeezed through that morning.

She had parked in a secluded spot near the Shannon

Boulevard entrance, hoping to get in that way. Not only was the gate locked, but a barricade had been stretched across the road with barbed wire on top of the fence. The park was closed in on three sides, which had left her no choice but State Street.

And she was freezing, in spite of her lined bomber jacket. Leave it to her to pick the coldest, darkest night of the year to play Nancy Drew. Not real smart, except she'd had a feeling, ever since this morning, that whatever Ron Siegel and his cohorts were up to, it had nothing to do with a government survey as he'd claimed. And something told her if she wanted to find out the truth, she'd better get here soon.

So she had sneaked in shortly after midnight on a night that held promise for the first snow of the season.

Her icy fingers wrapped around the plastic flashlight in her jacket pocket. Switching it on, she stood up and looked as far as the narrow yellow beam allowed. She appreciated the comfort of the light, but it made her feel vulnerable, too, pointing out her whereabouts to anyone who happened by. If she hadn't felt such a strong sense of urgency, she would have waited for a clear night with moonlight, but she had made her decision. Stepping carefully, she moved into the grassy area that led to the ball fields.

Guided only by a thin shaft of light, Jeannie walked as quickly as she dared. Within minutes, she had circled the duck pond and reached the edge of the woods. She felt her stomach shift uneasily. Was there was any other way?

There wasn't. Not if she wanted to find out what Siegel had been so anxious to hide.

With the help of her light, she found the trail between two towering pines that she had followed this morning. The woods closed in around her.

The air in here felt thick and damp and the silence unnerved her, yet she welcomed it, knowing it meant safety from unseen night creatures. She tried to steel herself against the fear she felt and yet still remain alert. Shivering, she walked as fast as she dared along the narrow path. It seemed to take forever, but eventually the woods thinned and the clearing lay straight ahead.

A wave of relief swept through her as she shone her flashlight into the open area. Now all she had to do was check around, and then check out fast.

As she stood at the edge of the woods, staring across the patch of grass her light cleared, Jeannie felt a strange sense of *deja vu*. The opening itself couldn't have been more than fifty or sixty feet across, quite unremarkable, except the entire area had been cordoned off. She shone her light on the barrier, a wide strip of plain white plastic tape. No, not plain. As she moved the light along the strip, she saw that every fifteen or twenty feet, it was stamped with the words: "Property of U.S. Government." What struck her as eerily familiar, however, was the eight or ten-foot area in the center of the clearing, covered by an army green tarp.

"And I'll bet I know exactly what's under there!" Jeannie said softly.

She ran to the clearing and jumped the tape. Leaning over, she lifted one side of the covering, which had been staked down at the corners, and shone her flashlight inside. She still couldn't see very well, so she squatted down and held her light underneath.

Brown grass! Probably burned, just like what she'd found at Barb's house. She would bet her next paycheck on it. Why would the government cover up a circle of burned grass? Why would they lie about what they were doing here? And threaten someone who wanted to check it out. There had to be a very good reason. Like national security?

Certain she had stumbled onto a gold mine, Jeannie laid the flashlight on the ground with the beam pointed toward the tarp. Then she stretched out on her stomach and reached under the covering.

She wanted a sample of this grass, something she could

have analyzed and compare with what she'd found in the other circle. Grabbing a handful of the brown blades, she shoved them in her pocket and took a second bunch. Satisfied, she rocked back on her heels and saw the feet, two shoes on the ground no more than six inches away.

Run! But her body refused to respond. Only her eyes moved, inching slowly up the pants-clad legs to the bottom of a jacket.

A hand touched the back of her neck and squeezed hard.

Jeannie crumpled into darkness.

6

"JEANNIE, can you hear me?"

The voice, faint and very far away, sounded like an echo through a long, long tunnel. *Not important. Sleep.*

"Jeannie, please. Wake up!"

Louder now. She knew that voice.

"I'm calling an ambulance."

"No." The word slurred out through lips that refused to move.

"That's right. Come on, baby. Snap out of it."

She tried to shake her head, but her neck hurt.

"Not...baby," she managed, and opened her eyes.

A steady light close by and something hazy further off filtered through the darkness. Dark and cold. Where was she? The park!

Ignoring the pain in her neck, she sat up and found herself nose to nose with Denis Earley, his rugged features outlined by the glow of his flashlight. Without thinking, she blurted, "Not you! You didn't--"

He shook his head. "No, I didn't. You'll have to find yourself a different bad guy this time."

She knew that. Deep down, she knew Denis would never hurt her, although he sure turned up at odd times and places. She'd have to think about that later.

"What happened?" he asked.

"Someone--I saw his shoes. He did something to my neck. I passed out." She wasn't making much sense, but she didn't care. She was hurt and cold and she wanted to go home.

Denis leaned over, his face so close she could see the worry line between his brows, so close she felt his warm breath on her face. "Can you walk?"

"Yes, I think so."

Gripping her under the arms, he helped her to her feet. The ground and Denis tilted at a crazy angle. Instinctively, she grabbed his coat and held on till the world stopped spinning.

"Better?"

She nodded as the one word, a mere whisper in her ear, sent deep shivers rippling through her that had nothing to do with the near-freezing temperature. They started walking, and that's when Jeannie noticed where she was, or more precisely, where she wasn't. The hazy light she'd seen earlier came from a street light about seventy yards away, yet she remembered only darkness in the woods.

There were no woods here.

She stopped short and looked up at Denis. "Did you bring me here?"

He shook his head, and she saw the puzzled look on his face. "I found you on the ground back there. I didn't dare move you. I'm still not sure."

"No, not that. It's just--"

He groaned. "Let me guess. You went back to the clearing."

"Well, yes."

"That means somebody went to a lot of trouble to get you here." He tightened his grip around her shoulders. "I had a feeling you might go back. That's why I came here tonight. When I found your car parked over on Shannon, I won't tell you what I thought."

Jeannie could pretty well imagine. She was beginning to think maybe she should have taken a few extra precautions. Not that she would admit it.

"When I saw the barricade and the barbed wire, I figured you didn't get in that way, so I came around here and found you on the ground near the shrubbery." For just a second, he pulled her even closer. "You're a damn lucky woman. Let's get out of here."

Denis didn't want her to drive, but since she couldn't leave her car parked on the street all night, he finally relented. "I'll be right behind you," he said, as she slid in behind the wheel. "If you feel dizzy or anything, just pull over."

"You don't have to do that," she objected. "I'm fine now. The walk cleared my head."

"I'm coming." His voice left no room for argument. "And remember what I said."

"Yes, Doctor." She gave him a half-smile through the closed window and started the engine. *Worrywart.* But she didn't really mind. It made her feel, well, special, to think he cared enough to worry and to check on her tonight. She might still be lying out there in the park if he hadn't come along. Shivering, she turned on the heater. The clock said one-twenty. Another hour or two on that cold ground could have meant real trouble. As Denis put it so bluntly, she was damn lucky.

With no traffic to speak of, they made it to Benton in fifteen minutes. Jeannie turned the corner from Manley and drove slowly down Parsons Street, the same as she had done hundreds of times before, although she'd never before had a small red sports car follow her up the driveway in the wee hours of the morning. She opened the old-fashioned, swinging garage doors and drove her car inside.

"You need an automatic door opener," Denis said, following her through the small entry into the kitchen.

"I've thought about it." Just like she'd thought about a

new roof, plumbing repairs, a new dishwasher, and a dozen more things a fifty-year-old house needed. Some day, after she earned fame and fortune as an investigative reporter on a major newspaper, she would retire in Benton and fix up her parents' old house. Sure, she would. She couldn't even check out a public park at midnight without getting caught. Some investigator.

Incredibly weary, she wanted nothing more than a couple of aspirin and her bed. Her head ached, she was cold and shivery, and she had to figure out a way to get rid of Denis without hurting his feelings.

But first, she needed to sit down. Had the kitchen grown larger? That chair looked awfully far away....

Two strong hands grabbed her and guided her across the wavering room. "Head down."

She didn't want to, but Denis was already pushing her head down between her knees. In just a minute, she would argue with him.

He held her till the world stopped spinning. When she opened her eyes, he eased her back in the small wooden chair, still holding her hands as he sat down. "Better?"

Nodding, she said, "You knew that would happen, didn't you?"

"I expected a reaction sooner or later. Yours took longer than most." He smiled. "You're a strong woman, Jeannie."

"So I've heard."

"But everyone needs a break. Tell me where to find the coffee and I'll put it on."

She started to object but gave up. Denis had done okay so far, and a hot drink sounded heavenly. "First cabinet on the right, next to the sink."

He puttered around the room like someone comfortable in a kitchen. Who was this man who had stepped into her life and so quickly become a part of it? Was he married? No, Barb would have told her. Divorced? Did he have family here in Oklahoma? She knew he cared about Loren and Barb, and he seemed to care about her, too. She followed his tall, lean body as he set two steaming mugs on the table. He had broad hands with sturdy, blunt-tipped fingers, a worker's hands, yet graceful, too. She watched him ease one cup toward her, fascinated by the springy blond hair covering the back of his hand and the tops of his fingers. Would it feel coarse or smooth if she reached over and touched it?

As though reading her wayward thoughts, Denis came around behind her and lifted her long dark hair.

She froze. "What are you doing?"

"Checking to see where that creep hurt you." His fingers, as strong and sure as she had imagined, gently probed the base of her neck. "Was it here?"

She jumped and nodded, as a sharp pain sliced through her head.

"No wonder you passed out," he muttered. "That's quite a bump." He moved his fingers gently. "Did you know you have a scar here? No, two. What happened?"

"Nothing I remember," she said, and returned to a more immediate problem. "Who do you think was out there, Denis? Siegel, or one of his buddies?"

His hand stopped for a second, then resumed its slow steady massage. "You think Siegel did this?"

"Well, yes. Don't you? I mean, who else?"

"Almost anyone. Face it, Jeannie. Crossland Park at midnight, well...."

His voice trailed off, but his meaning was clear. She had set herself up for trouble by going into the park alone. Since she couldn't disagree with that, she held her temper and disagreed with his conclusion.

"Siegel knew I wasn't happy about leaving this morning," she said, thinking aloud. "You figured out I'd go back. Maybe he did, too. Since he didn't want anyone to see what they were doing this morning--"

The grass! She reached into her jacket pocket and

brought out nothing.

"No!" she wailed.

"Did I hurt you?" Denis asked quickly.

Ignoring him, she stood up and pulled both pockets inside out. Carefully, she brushed them onto the table. Two pieces of lint and half a peanut rolled out. Nothing else. "It's gone. Someone took my grass."

"Your grass? What are you talking about?"

As calmly as she could, Jeannie explained how she had plucked several handfuls of burned grass from under the tarp and put them in her pocket so she could have them analyzed.

"You wanted to have some dead grass analyzed?"

Put that way, it did sound bizarre. She could tell Denis was doing his best to keep his voice neutral, strictly professional, probably the tone he saved for seriously disturbed patients. How could she explain something she knew he was unwilling to accept?

She couldn't, but maybe she could show him. Rubbing her neck--it had started aching again--she turned to face him. "Denis, I know what you think about UFO's, but please, hear me out before you jump all over me."

He nodded. "Sure. Go ahead."

"First of all, I want to help Loren, and I would never do anything deliberately to hurt him. Second, I truly believe that my UFO theory, as you call it, deserves serious consideration or I wouldn't pursue it. Third, yes, I would like to get a story out of this--this situation. I believe it has great potential, but I will never sacrifice Loren or anyone else for a story. I really hope you believe that." She waited, anxiously searching his eyes for reassurance.

Again, he nodded. "I believe you."

Relieved, thankful, and very sure they had just passed a huge hurdle, she squeezed her eyes shut and breathed a quick thank you. When she opened them, Denis was smiling. "But I still don't understand the dead grass."

"I know, but I'm going to ask you to be patient with me and do me a favor. Can you meet me at Loren's house tomorrow, about ten o'clock?"

"In the morning?"

"Yes, in the morning." She detected a teasing note in his voice. "Believe it or not, I usually work during the day and sleep at night!"

"I guess I can manage ten o'clock."

"Good. Barb has a doctor's appointment, so we won't have to disturb her."

"Should I assume I'll understand everything after tomorrow morning?"

"Uh, not exactly." Jeannie crossed her fingers behind her back. "Are you busy next Friday night?"

"Are you asking me for a date, Ms. MacLeod?"

"I'm asking you to go to a meeting with me."

"What kind of meeting?"

Keeping her fingers crossed, she blurted, "The Oklahoma Chapter of the UFO Research Association."

Denis rolled his eyes. "Good grief, woman!"

"Please?"

He jammed both hands into the front pockets of his jeans. "Why?"

"Because I think we might learn something worthwhile. We won't stay if they turn out to be a bunch of kooks."

"By whose definition?"

She ignored that question. "It's in Oklahoma City at seven-thirty."

"I can't believe I'm even considering this," he muttered.

"You'll do it?"

He threw up his hands. "Okay, okay. I'll go! On one condition."

Jeannie watched his eyes turn that stormy gray and followed his long legs as they took him across the floor in two strides. Instinctively, she backed up and bumped into the table. Wary, she said, "What condition?"

"That you kick me out of here right now, before I do something we'll both regret." But even as he said the words, he opened his arms.

Without thinking, purely on instinct, Jeannie stepped forward.

"On second thought," he murmured, "I wouldn't regret a thing."

His lips closed over hers, and she felt herself flowing into a deep sea filled with feelings she had only dreamed of till now.

This is what I've missed. This is what I want.

Denis pulled away, his breathing harsh, his hands not quite steady. "Ten o'clock tomorrow. Loren's house."

A few seconds later, Jeannie stood alone in her kitchen. Two cups of cold coffee waited on the table.

* * *

HE shouldn't have come. He wouldn't have come if he hadn't been dazzled last night by a pair of midnight blue eyes and an innocent charm that had knocked him off balance.

Driving up Loren's long winding driveway, he parked behind Jeannie's car. He could see her head bent over as she worked on something. A story?

Denis had already decided what he would do. He'd go along with whatever she showed him this morning, listening to her explanations, no matter how absurd, and then, only then, he would tell her that as a man of science, he simply couldn't accept her beliefs in phenomena that defied logic, reason and the laws of physics. He got out of his car and walked up to the driver's window of the white compact. Her head turned. She smiled, and her whole face lighted up.

That smile stunned him. Sure, they had kissed last night, a dynamite kiss that he'd finally decided was nothing more than reaction to a highly charged situation.

But he was wrong. He felt Jeannie's smile deep inside,

touching a part of him he thought he had locked away forever.

She opened her door and the moment passed, leaving him to wonder what was going on.

"Hi!" She glanced at her watch. "I'm glad you're on time. I have another appointment in an hour. Shall we get going?"

Had he misread her after all? He watched her walk quickly across the grass, her deep pink jacket and skirt neatly outlining the rounded curves of her hips. A business outfit, he told himself, hardly provocative, but his body didn't seem to know that. He definitely had not misread how he responded to this woman. As for her smile, well, he didn't know what to think about that. Coming back to Tulsa was supposed to simplify his life. He didn't need complications, and that's what Jeannie was. One big puzzle. Hell, every time he saw her, they argued, but his body didn't seem to get the message.

She stopped at the southeast corner of the house and glanced over her shoulder. "Are you coming?"

Breaking into a jog, he caught up with her before she reached the corral.

As they walked toward the woods, she turned around several more times.

"Looking for something?" he asked.

"Dicey. She usually takes her guard duties very seriously and stays close by when no one is home."

"She's probably hot on the trail of a rabbit. By the way, where are we going?"

"That way." She pointed straight ahead, into the deepest part of the woods.

"Have a heart!" he protested, looking down at his well-buffed wing-tip shoes. "I didn't wear my hiking boots."

Jeannie grinned and kept walking.

That's when Denis noticed her bright purple tennis shoes. "Nice color scheme," he drawled. As he expected, her face turned a shade of pink that closely matched her suit.

But she recovered fast. "My Girl Scout leader didn't say we had to match, just be prepared. I keep these in my car." Then she did something Denis didn't expect at all. She reached for his hand. "Stick with me, and I'll try to keep you out of the thick stuff."

Again, that flash of awareness when their hands touched. Did she feel it, too? But the color had faded from her cheeks, and once again she appeared cool and calm. Desirable. He tightened his hand in hers.

They made their way into the thickest part of the woods, till gradually Denis felt himself climbing a steady slope. "Are you sure you know where you're going?" he called. His slick, leather-soled shoes kept sliding in the underbrush.

Still leading the way, Jeannie stopped and waited for him to catch up. "This hill leads to a small clearing. We're almost there."

"Right. And we're--"

"Shh. Listen. Do you hear that?"

They stood perfectly still. Gradually, Denis became aware of a soft rushing sound, the only sound he heard, he realized. Sometime in the past minute or two, without his even noticing, the woods around them had stilled. Except for that one, soft, continuous hum, he heard nothing. "What is it?"

"A waterfall. Come on. Right up here."

As they climbed, the trees thinned, and finally they stood at the edge of a small clearing. Sure enough, a small waterfall, no more than three feet high, spilled over into a dry creek bed.

"Very nice." For the life of him, he couldn't imagine why Jeannie had brought him all the way up here to look at a waterfall.

"There's more." Again she reached for his hand, and they

jumped the small gully together. "There." She pointed to the wide area all around them.

Denis studied the clearing. "This is what you wanted me to see?"

"This is it."

He saw a large stretch of grass, perhaps forty or fifty feet, giving way gradually to thick woods as far as the eye could see. Nothing unusual. No giant rocks or hidden caves. "I give up. What am I missing?"

"Look at the grass."

"I'm looking."

"Anything unusual?"

"Some of it looks dried out, burned maybe."

"It *is* burned. So was the grass under the tarp in Crossland Park."

Denis raised one eyebrow. "So?"

"So, I think that's pretty strange." She walked over to the burned area. Kneeling down, she took a metal tape measure out of her jacket pocket and held it at the edge of the brown grass. "Will you bring this to the other side?"

"You're measuring the grass?"

"That's right. I think it's a perfect circle. I want to be sure."

Denis shook his head, but he took the tape and set it at different spots around the fringe of the circle, finally ending up where he'd started. He rocked back on his heels and looked up at Jeannie. "Well?"

She slid the tape back in her pocket. "I was right. Nine feet, two inches all the way around."

"Which proves?"

"It's a perfect circle, just like I thought."

"That's not--what are you doing now?"

Down on her hands and knees, she broke off blades of brown grass and slipped them into a small envelope. "I want to have this analyzed. Too bad they got my grass samples from the park. I wanted to compare them."

Talk about one track! Smiling, Denis said, "You don't think it could have fallen out when you hit the ground?"

"Nope. Someone removed every little blade. I want to know why."

"And you think this stuff will tell you?"

"It might. Sure wish I had a Geiger counter."

"You're kidding!"

Standing up, she stuck the envelope in that oversized purse she lugged around, then jammed her hands in her pockets and slowly walked the outer edge of the circle. "Sure is quiet here," she commented.

Denis followed her. "I noticed that." When she didn't respond, he couldn't resist one small jab. "Surely you have an explanation."

She shrugged. "A couple."

That did it. He took three giant steps and stood in front of her, blocking her path. "How about telling me what this is all about, Jeannie."

She sighed. "All right. That's why I brought you up here." She looked straight into his eyes. "Promise me you won't laugh. You don't have to agree with me, but don't laugh."

He held up one hand and crossed his heart with the other. "Promise."

That got a smile out of her. She started down the hill, and he fell into step beside her. "Have you ever seen anything like that circle back there? A picture, or anything?"

"Never," he replied promptly, which was true enough. He had a pretty good idea what she was leading up to, but only because he had put two and two together.

"Well, I have, but only in pictures. Till now. It's called a landing trace, and it's often found near the site of an alleged UFO encounter."

"Back to that again," Denis murmured.

Jeannie nodded. "Back to that."

He had to ask. "Doesn't it bother you, sticking your neck out for such a wild theory?"

"Don't some of the bizarre things we've come across bother you?" she countered.

"With a little time and patience, every one of those bizarre things, as you call them, could be logically explained, without resorting to visitors from outer space."

"Is that so?" Jeannie squared around and glared at him. "You know, Doctor," she said, putting just a little too much emphasis on that last word, "I get tired of people with no idea of what they're talking about who make sweeping generalities they can't back up. They pick the most obvious or socially correct position and jump in head first. Talk is cheap, Doctor. How about some proof?"

Denis grinned; he couldn't help himself. "You want me to prove that a UFO did *not* land up there?" he asked, pointing back up the hill.

He had to give her credit. She didn't back down an inch. "That's right, and while you're at it, go ahead and find out what's causing the mysterious lights over Crossland Park, what the government is hiding there, and what's wrong with Loren. Oh yes, don't forget to explain the light that followed his car and why he lost an hour out of his life a few weeks ago!" With that parting shot, she jogged off down the hill.

Talk about hot! It was almost a shame to take advantage of her in such a state. Almost. Swallowing the laugh that threatened to bubble over, Denis took off after her.

"Are you serious?" he asked, matching his steps to hers.

"What's that supposed to mean?"

"Do you really want me to prove that we haven't been visited by UFO's?"

Jeannie stopped short. "You won't even try."

"Backing out already?"

"No! I just don't think you care enough to bother. I'm looking for the truth, remember? Maybe with two of us looking, we would find it a little faster."

It would be fast all right, Denis agreed. It shouldn't take long to discredit a flaky idea like flying saucers landing in the woods. "Okay, you've got a deal," he said, grabbing her hand.

She looked surprised but didn't pull away. Encouraged, he slipped his fingers between hers, enjoying the feel of her soft, smooth palm. In fact, he wouldn't mind feeling more than just her hand.

Maybe, once they finally laid this fantasy of hers to rest, he could do that. Maybe then they could put their time to better use.

* * *

"JEANNIE, thank goodness you came. What would I do without you?"

Enveloped in her sister's embrace, Jeannie did a fancy juggling act to keep the pizza box she held from tipping over. "Take it easy, Sis. This is priceless cargo you're messing around with."

A thin smile crossed Barb's face as she backed away. "Double pepperoni, right? Can you believe Buddy had only two snacks after school so he'd have room for at least half of it?" Shaking her head, she absently held one hand against her stomach. "That oldest kid of mine must be having a growth spurt. I don't know where he puts all the food he consumes."

Jeannie set the red and white checkered box on the table and her overnight case on the floor, then took a long look at her sister. "He must be doing all the eating in the family. Have you lost weight, Barb?"

"Since when does a pregnant woman lose weight?" she answered quickly.

Too quickly. "What did the doctor say yesterday? Is everything okay?"

"Everything is fine. They did an ultrasound, and the

baby looks perfect."

"But you still don't know if it's a boy or a girl?"

"I told her I don't want to know. As long as we have a healthy baby, I'd rather be surprised. But I have a feeling it's a girl." Again, her hand moved over her flat stomach, a protective gesture that Jeannie remembered.

No. She wouldn't even think about Barb's first pregnancy. She had mistaken an innocent gesture, something perfectly normal for any expectant mother, that's all. And yet, her sister did look tired, her pretty face drawn. "How's Loren doing?" Jeannie asked abruptly.

"He's difficult." Barb's mouth tightened. "Like tonight. He's known about this faculty reception for weeks, but I just found out about it this morning when I ran into Rose Timmons at the grocery store. I called you right away because I knew we ought to show up. You know how uptight Dean Timmons gets about these things, but I hate dragging you out in the middle of the week to baby-sit. Loren should have told me."

Alarmed now, Jeannie watched her sister's agitation rise till she was literally wringing her hands. "It's no big deal," she soothed, putting an arm around Barb's shoulders. "I like spending time with my favorite nephew. By the way, where is he? He usually sniffs out the pizza as soon as I come in the door."

"He's in the den. Some new TV show." She glanced at the clock. "What is that man doing? He's been getting dressed for a half hour!"

"Have you seen Denis lately?" Jeannie asked, trying to distract her sister.

"He's called a couple of times, and I've tried to get Loren to go by and talk to him, but you know how stubborn my husband can be."

She knew. In his own quiet way, Dr. Price usually did exactly what he wanted to do.

"Barb, have you seen my cufflinks?"

At the sound of his voice, both women turned toward the hall. Loren stood in the doorway, his white shirt unbuttoned and hanging over his pants, his hair still damp and tangled from his shower. He looked straight at Jeannie, but she might as well have been invisible. She knew he didn't see her, and of all the little disturbing things she had seen and heard in the past five minutes, this was the worst. Loren looked detached, out of focus, and that scared her. It scared Barb, too. Jeannie saw the flash of panic in her sister's eyes as she hurried across the room and took Loren's arm.

"We'll be back in a minute," she called over her shoulder. "Why don't you set up the TV trays in the den and get some drinks out of the fridge?" Her voice trailed off as she hustled her husband upstairs.

Jeannie picked up the pizza box and followed them down the hall as far as the stairway. Then she slowly turned left into the family room and headed toward the den.

7

"JUST a few more minutes, Aunt Jeannie. Please?"

"Buddy, it's after nine o'clock. You've already fallen asleep twice over that book, and your mom and dad should be home any time. We'll both be in big trouble if you're not asleep when they get here."

"Grownups don't get in trouble," Buddy grumbled, but he rolled over, punching the pillow several times for good measure.

Smiling, Jeannie picked up the super heroes comic from the floor where it had fallen out of Buddy's hands, then she reached over and switched off the bedside lamp. "Good night, big guy," she said softly, ruffling her nephew's thick hair.

"Aunt Jeannie?"

"Mm-hmm?"

"Could you leave the bathroom light on?"

"Sure, sport. 'Night."

A big sigh. "G'night."

As she passed the bathroom, Jeannie reached around the corner and flicked the switch, then closed the door halfway. This was something new. She couldn't remember Buddy ever wanting a night light before. Probably just a phase he was going through, although he seemed kind of old to be scared of the dark. But then, what did she know about kids? She crossed the hall into the guestroom she always slept in when she stayed here. Unfortunately, this room was next to the bathroom. With her door open so she could hear Buddy if he needed her, she would have a night light, too, although tired as she was tonight, she doubted it would make a difference.

She hurried through her nightly routine, not even taking time for the leisurely bath she usually enjoyed. Must have been all that fresh air out in the woods this morning, she decided sleepily, pulling the warm down comforter up to her chin. As soon as she thought of the woods, a full color picture of Denis' rugged face flashed into her mind. Her eyes popped open and all her senses went on full alert, just as though he was right there beside her.

Uh oh! Wrong analogy. Picturing the handsome doctor lying with her in Barb's antique, four-poster bed most definitely would not put her to sleep. Besides, she had already spent too much time today thinking about the man. Reluctantly, she pushed the image away. Such a shame, she thought, as her heavy lids again covered her eyes. He would have made a delicious dream.

She came awake suddenly and completely, but it took her eyes a minute or two to adjust to the darkness.

Dark? When she went to sleep, her room had been filled with the soft half-light from the bathroom. Had Loren and Barb already come home and turned it off? What time was it? Strangely reluctant to move, Jeannie managed to open her eyes just enough to see the digital clock. Twelve-twenty-one. Relief rushed through her. They *were* home. That explained the light.

Thump! The hard knock on the other side of the wall, right by the door, brought her straight up.

Thump! The second blow sent her back down under the covers, all the way down, till she was nothing but a shaking mound in the middle of the bed. After two or three more thumps, none apparently any closer than the first, she cautiously inched her way up till her eyes and nose peeked out. Lights had come on in the hall and the master bedroom, and a tall figure stood outlined in her doorway. She swallowed hard. "Loren?"

"Are you all right, Jeannie?"

Thank goodness! "I'm fine. What is going on? What's that noise?"

"Noise?"

"That thump in the wall. Don't tell me you didn't hear it."

"Oh, the noise. You heard it?"

"Of course, I did. What was it?"

Barb appeared in the doorway beside her husband. "Everything okay in here?"

Jeannie felt like pounding the wall herself in frustration. "No, everything is not okay. Will one of you tell me what's going on?"

Barb put her arm around Loren and tried to nudge him back to their room. "We've, uh, had a problem with mice lately. They get in the walls."

"A ten-pound mouse? Come off it, Barb!"

"I don't hear anything now. Whatever it was, I guess it's gone."

"Thank goodness!" Loren muttered, running his fingers through his hair. "Let's go back to bed."

"See you in the morning," Barb called over her shoulder, as she and Loren took the few steps back to their room. They closed the door behind them.

"Mouse, shmouse! Even a rat wouldn't make that kind of noise."

Jeannie jumped out of bed and closed her own door, none too gently. If Buddy hadn't awakened with all that commotion a few minutes ago, she probably didn't need to worry about him. And if that thing, whatever it was, started thumping on the wall again, maybe it would be polite enough to knock before it opened her door.

* * *

SCARED. So scared. Six-year-old Jeannie crouched in the dark place with Mama and Barb. Something was outside, and if they weren't quiet, it would come and take Mama away. It might take all of them. Jeannie didn't like the dark place. She began to whimper.

"Sh-h!" Mama whispered and held her closer. "If we're quiet, maybe they'll go away."

Jeannie knew better. Something awful was going to happen. She could feel the darkness, heavy and black, all around her, could smell the strange sweet smell of the dark place. She squeezed Mama's hand tighter. So quiet in here, but they were coming closer. She could feel them coming.

Jeannie moaned in her sleep, her body rigid with fear.

Suddenly, Mama's hand tugged away from hers. "No!" Mama moaned, but still she moved toward the door.

Jeannie tried to hold her back, but something had glued her body to the spot. Nothing worked, not her hands or feet, not even her eyes or mouth. Terrified, her heart pounding frantically under her tee shirt, she watched Mama disappear through the door.

"No-o-o!"

Her cry echoed through the room, and Jeannie shot straight up in bed for the second time that night, her hands clutching the twisted sheet. She blinked. Every light in the room blazed brightly. How did that happen? She remembered the dream, the first time she'd had it in years, but it hadn't changed. It never did. And it still scared her silly, just like it did twenty years ago and all those times between.

She would get up any minute now and turn off the lights.

"Jeannie! Was that you?" Barb burst through the doorway. "It sounded like someone dying. I checked on Buddy, but he's still sound asleep. Loren, too, even with all the lights on. That must have been one potent sleeping pill he took."

She's babbling, Jeannie realized, reaching for her glasses. Not only that, Barb's huge and bright eyes, seemed to fill her face. She was spooked, just like Jeannie. Had she been dreaming, too, or had something else happened? Like the lights?

Jeannie managed to extricate herself from the tangled covers and picked up the robe she had draped over the foot of the bed. "I don't know about you," she said, carefully knotting the sash on her old plaid bathrobe, "but it's going to take me a while to get sleepy again. How about a cup of hot chocolate?"

"I don't--"

"Come on, Barb. Like old times. Remember how we used to sneak downstairs after Mom and Dad fell asleep? We'd make a pan of hot chocolate and fill our mugs half full of marshmallows."

"Then we'd sit on the couch with the lights out and the TV on low and watch scary movies." She shuddered. "I sure don't need that part."

"Me neither, but a hot drink sounds great. I wonder if we really fooled Mom and Dad," she mused, tucking her arm in Barb's as they walked down the stairs.

"Probably not, but it was fun thinking we did."

Jeannie felt around for the kitchen light. The whole downstairs was pitch black, not like the second floor. Who had turned on all the lights up there? As she watched Barb huddle into a chair, looking small and miserable and scared, Jeannie knew the lights were only part of the problem. Something here was terribly wrong. But first things first. She opened the refrigerator and took out the milk.

A few minutes later, they moved to the living room. With the TV humming softly and its hazy glow sliding around the room, they sat on the couch, clutching steaming mugs of chocolate in both hands. The bone-chilling terror from her dream had eased, and now Jeannie shifted all her attention to Barb, who still looked shaken. "Want to tell me about it, Sis?"

"I wish it would just go away," she mumbled.

"What are we talking about?"

"These things that keep happening. Weird stuff...." Barb's voice trailed off and her hands began to shake.

Jeannie put her mug on the coffee table, then carefully set Barb's down. She took her sister's icy hands in hers and began to rub some warmth back into them. "Like the lights?" she prompted.

Barb sighed. "The lights and the noises in the wall. Loren says it's nothing, it'll go away, but I know he's scared, too. He thinks he's responsible," she whispered.

"Why should he think that?"

"Because nothing happens unless he's in the house, then, well, all hell may break loose. It's getting to all of us. Even Buddy's edgy, and I know it's not good for the baby." She pulled away. "You saw what went on tonight, and that's just part of it. The phone rings and no one is on the line. Or else all we hear is a bunch of garbled noise that makes no sense. Sometimes Loren knows who is ringing before he picks up the phone."

Jeannie shivered. ESP? She'd never known her brother-in-law to be that sensitive before. "What else?"

Barb started pacing. "Footsteps. Upstairs. We all hear them when we're down here. No one is up there. We've checked half a dozen times, yet we hear someone walking upstairs. It's like our house is haunted." She sat down again, her arms folded tightly in front of her. "There! I said it. Do you think I'm crazy, Jeannie?"

"Definitely not! And neither is Loren."

"Then what's wrong with us? Why are these things happening?"

Jeannie reached for her sister's hands again. "I don't know for sure, but I can make a guess. When did it start?"

"Two or three weeks ago."

"After Loren saw that light at Crossland Park?"

"Well, yes, I guess so. Why? You don't think--oh God, Jeannie! You're not still going on about UFO's, are you? Now that is crazy!"

"No worse than what's been happening here."

Staring at her sister, Barb said, "You really believe it, don't you?"

"I believe there are things in this world science can't explain. I believe paranormal phenomena exist, yes. And I don't believe that's crazy." She turned to Barb. Somehow, she had to get her sister to accept the possibility of what she was saying. She had to give her something to hang onto. "Barb, if I give you a book by a very credible person, explaining what I'm talking about, will you read it?"

"You won't leave me alone till I do, will you?"

Jeannie grinned. "You said it."

"Then I guess I'll read it."

"Good. That's a start. Here's something else. I'm going to a meeting in Oklahoma City tomorrow night. I may have something more after that."

"Do I dare ask what kind of meeting?"

Jeannie explained. Then added quickly, "Denis is coming with me."

That got Barb's attention. "How did you manage that? I didn't think he was, well, into that sort of thing."

"He's not, but I can be pretty persuasive."

"You're telling me." But she smiled. "Do you see him very often?"

"Not really. We've talked a few times. How about Loren?" she asked, changing the subject. "Has he talked to Denis yet?"

"They played a round of golf the other day, but that's hardly a professional consultation. Loren's scared," Barb said softly. "So am I."

What could Jeannie say? She knew Barb was thinking

about her baby and the horrors of her last pregnancy. Would it happen this time? Was her sister strong enough to go through that kind of ordeal again? No wonder she was scared. Both she and Loren had good reason to be. Finally, Jeannie said simply, "We'll figure this thing out, Sis." She hoped she was right.

Barb hugged her. "So, let's talk about you," she said brightly, picking up her mug. "That must have been some dream you had. You sounded like you were in agony."

Jeannie decided later there must have been something in the chocolate that loosened her tongue. Or maybe it was just the comfortable room and her sister's sympathetic ear that made her blurt out a secret she had kept for twenty years. Whatever the reason, she told Barb all about the dream that had plagued her most of her life, and with the telling, the terror eased, at least for the moment.

"Something must have really scared me when I was little," she offered, "but I can't imagine what. Do you--"

Her voice broke as she saw her sister staring at her in shock.

"I don't believe it," Barb whispered.

"Believe what?"

"You just described my dream."

"You're kidding!"

"I'm serious. I've had a dream like yours for years. We're hiding under the eaves upstairs. Did you ever tell Mom about this?"

Jeannie shook her head. "I've never told anyone till now."

Barb laughed, a quick mirthless laugh. "I guess it doesn't matter. This is just one more weird happening. Maybe eventually we'll get used to them and nothing will bother us any more."

"What do you mean?"

Barb leaned back against the couch cushion, her eyes closed. The TV droned on, and shadows from the screen danced around the room. "I'm not as brave as you," she said. "I had to tell someone about my dream, so I told Mom. I was nine or ten." She opened her eyes. "Do you know what she told me?"

Jeannie held her breath as she shook her head.

"I've always thought this was the strangest coincidence. Now, well, I don't know what to call it."

"Barb--"

"Okay, okay. When I told her my dream, Mom got this real funny look on her face. For a minute, she didn't say anything, then, real soft, she said, 'Sometimes I have a dream like that, except Jeannie's not there. It's just you and me, Sissy, and we're hiding in the garage. I hold on to you real tight, but I know it's no use. You pull loose, and I watch you fly right through the garage door."

Jeannie stared at her sister. *Shared dreams? Impossible!*

And yet, it had happened. Sure, there were differences, but the significant details of all three dreams were the same.

Barb walked slowly across the room to turn off the TV. "I don't know about you, but I've had more than enough excitement for one night." She added, "It might be a good idea to keep this dream stuff to ourselves for now. What do you think?"

"I think you're right." She certainly wouldn't be telling a certain young doctor, who would have a field day analyzing three-way, mother-daughter dreams.

* * *

JEANNIE had mixed feelings about this trip to Oklahoma City with Denis.

If only she knew what they were getting into. Suppose these UFORA people turned out to be a bunch of flakes? That would pretty well destroy any credibility she might have established for her UFO theory. On the other hand....

She smoothed the soft folds of her favorite watch plaid

skirt and leaned her head back against the sofa, trying to relax. Kenworth jumped into her lap. Absently, her hand stroked his thick yellow fur. Too late to worry now. She'd been through all this before, several times, and besides, she'd already committed herself. Her eyes popped open. Maybe that was the problem. She had committed herself to spending the whole evening with Denis. Not that they had a date. This was strictly a business engagement.

She looked at her watch for the third time in five minutes, then turned around and pushed the curtain aside. They should have done what she wanted. She would have picked him up on her way through Tulsa, but no, he'd insisted on coming to Benton. So, where was he? He said he'd be by around five o'clock. That was ten minutes ago. She didn't want to be late. She hated being late.

Headlights appeared down the street and a few seconds later, his little sports car parked in front of her house. Well, that settled one question. No way would she spend three hours cramped up in that toy.

She already had her hand on the doorknob when the bell rang. Kenworth, brave feline that he was, took off like a shot for his safe place under her bed.

"Sometimes I wonder about you, Ken," she mumbled, opening the door.

"Sorry, I'm not Ken."

She started to laugh, but the sound caught somewhere below her throat and took her breath away. No, Denis took her breath away. Lean, yet solid, he filled the doorway. She knew, if she wasn't careful, he could fill her heart as well. What was there about this man that touched her as no one ever had before?

"Jeannie?"

She came back with a start and realized she'd been gawking at him. "Hi, Denis. I'm ready. Come on in while I get my coat."

He followed her into the living room. "Who's Ken?"

"My cat." Picking up the coat she had draped over the couch, she held up her keys. "My car is bigger."

"Okay." He plucked the keys out of her hand, then took her coat and held it for her.

"I don't mind driving," she said quickly.

"But you don't mind if I do either."

"Well, no." Maybe she should, being a liberated career woman, but she didn't. Smiling, she shrugged into her coat. Somehow, in the past few seconds, the evening had taken on a whole new meaning. "Are you always this sure of yourself, Dr. Earley?"

Leaning over, his lips brushed her ear. "Always, Ms. MacLeod."

Shivering, Jeannie grabbed her purse and forced her wayward thoughts back to business. "I hope I'm around when you have to eat those words!"

"I hope so, too. Let's see, ten years from now? Twenty?"

She was sure Denis knew exactly what she was talking about. "How about three months?"

Outside, Denis turned the key in the front door. "Want to make a bet on that?"

"Uh...sure. Why not?"

"What are you willing to wager?"

Reckless now, Jeannie declared, "You name it!" Then hoped she hadn't just thrown away a whole paycheck.

Again, Denis surprised her. "How about a real date? At least four hours together. No arguments allowed. Winner's choice."

Oh Lord! Her fertile imagination immediately conjured an image of what Denis might choose. Soft music, candle-light, and a king-sized bed waiting.

He wouldn't. He might.

A wave of heat filled her face, and she practically flew to the car sitting in her driveway.

He waited till she settled in and buckled up. "So, how about it?"

"You sure are persistent!"

He grinned. "So I've been told."

"Okay! I'll bet that three months from now I have solid, acceptable evidence to support my UFO theory."

Denis took his right hand off the steering wheel and slowly pumped hers up and down. "You're on," he said. Then leaned over and lightly touched his lips to hers.

Several minutes later, Jeannie realized the car had turned onto Columbus Ave., headed toward the Expressway. She wished she could remember how they got there.

Thankfully, Denis chose not to pursue the subject of their date, and gradually she relaxed as they made their way west toward Oklahoma City. They talked about this and that. Mostly--Jeannie realized later--about her dreams, her ambitions, her family, which eventually brought them around again to Loren and his problems.

"Something really strange is going on," she said, after telling Denis what had happened at her sister's house the night before. "Loren seems to be the focal point, but it's affecting Buddy and Barb, too." She turned to face him. "Can't you do something to help them?"

"First, Loren has to agree to therapy," Denis replied quietly, "and so far, he hasn't. Why don't you and Barb work on him, keep after him to come in and talk to me. I don't know what else to suggest."

Jeannie sighed. "You're right. There's nothing else we can do."

He reached over and wrapped his broad hand around hers. "It'll work out. You'll see. Loren is tougher than he looks."

Jeannie nodded and hoped Denis was right. She tried to get him to talk about himself, but he seemed preoccupied, deep in thought. After half a dozen single syllable responses to her questions, she gave it up and turned on the CD player. Maybe some Big Band music would lighten his mood.

* * *

THEY had already reached the outskirts of the city when Denis realized Jeannie was awfully quiet. He took a quick peek out of the corner of his eye and grinned.

She was sound asleep with her head wedged between the seat and the window. Lucky for him. Engrossed in Loren's problems, he'd been sorting through twelve years of clinical experience trying to come up with an answer. He hadn't been very good company. Too bad she hadn't turned the other way. He wouldn't mind having her all soft and sleepy, leaning against him.

Damn. He almost went past his exit. In one smooth motion, he eased the car into the right lane and shot off down the ramp. Only then did he allow himself another quick look at the woman who had talked him into this crazy trip. All in all, she looked normal and pretty fantastic, with her dark lashes fanning out on her face. As usual, she had pulled her thick brown hair back at the nape of her neck, fastening it with a silver clip. It had worked its way around till it spilled over her left shoulder and arm. His fingers itched to work through those long strands and along her neck, to turn her face toward him and taste her full red lips.

The sign for Bainbridge Street loomed directly ahead, and Denis muttered a colorful oath as he hit the brake and turned left.

Jeannie blinked and sat up. "Where are we?"

"Almost there. You really conked out."

She yawned. "Sorry about that."

"You must have needed the sleep." He chuckled. "You're kinda cute when you're sleeping."

Jeannie made a face and turned her back to look out the window as they drove into the Bainbridge East Library parking lot.

* * *

THE north wind swirled around them, catching the building's heavy glass door and forcing Denis to lean all his weight against it so Jeannie could slip inside.

Thoroughly chilled just from the short dash across the lot, she stood inside the door, shivering in spite of her lined coat and woolen skirt. Her feet felt like two blocks of ice inside her brown leather pumps. Why hadn't she dressed in slacks and boots like any sensible person coming to Oklahoma City in November? She knew the wind never stopped blowing out here on the plains.

"I haven't felt anything like this since my undergraduate days in Norman," Denis grumbled, blowing on his hands to warm them. "The wind chill out there must be close to zero." With just a sport jacket and no topcoat, he'd underestimated the weather, too.

She looked around the lobby. "Let's find the meeting room. Maybe they'll have a coffeepot on."

They located the UFORA group in a room at the very back of the lobby. Jeannie quickly scanned the fifteen or twenty men and women of all ages talking quietly in small groups, and breathed a sigh of relief when she didn't spot a single antenna waving anywhere.

"Jeannie, it's good to see you."

"Hello, Dr. Kendrick." She smiled at the white-haired professor. "I'm glad I could make it." And very glad to see a familiar face. "I'd like you to meet a friend of mine, Dr. Denis Earley. I hope you don't mind that he came, too."

Kendrick shook Denis' hand. "Not at all. We're always glad to welcome guests. What is your field, Dr. Earley?"

"I'm a psychologist."

"Then you should find tonight's program interesting. Our speaker is a psychiatrist from Dallas, Dr. Mia Andrews. Perhaps you know her?"

"No, I don't."

His reply was curt, almost rude, and Dr. Kendrick raised an eyebrow in surprise.

"Denis has just moved back to Tulsa from the East Coast," Jeannie explained quickly. She and Kendrick talked for another minute or two before he excused himself, saying the meeting was about to begin.

"Your hostility is showing, Doctor," she murmured, as they made their way toward two empty seats in the middle of the room.

"Yeah, I know."

Frowning, she slid into her seat, then turned toward Denis at the very moment he looked at her. Their noses practically touched. Before she could even think about moving away, he said softly, "I'm sorry, Jeannie. It just suddenly hit me where I was and why these people are here, and well, I just lost it for a few seconds. Don't worry. It won't happen again."

She couldn't stay mad after such a sincere apology. The truth was, she understood exactly what he meant. If anyone had told her a few weeks ago that she would attend a meeting of UFO enthusiasts, well, she would have laughed. She smiled to let him know she accepted what he said, then turned her attention to the podium at the front of the room where a young man, probably in his early twenties, had picked up the microphone. Jeannie leaned over and took a notebook and pen out of her purse. She hadn't asked permission to tape the meeting, but she didn't want to miss anything either.

Dave Wallace introduced himself as president of the Oklahoma City chapter of UFORA. He conducted a ten minute business session, then immediately turned the meeting over to their guest speaker.

Trim and blonde, Dr. Mia Andrews had a pleasant face that crinkled often into well-worn laugh lines. "Thank you, Dave, for those flattering words," she said, looking relaxed and smiling at her audience. "I appreciate the opportunity to address a group such as this, a group that is knowledge-able about the UFO abduction phenomenon, a 'speaker-friendly' group, you might say. When I stand in front of many audiences--civic clubs, community groups, my own colleagues in the medical fields--I am looked upon as an anomaly. 'How did you get into this crazy business?' they ask. 'You look so normal.'"

Her words brought smiles and nods and a few chuckles from the audience, and a general shuffling and shifting, as people settled in for the next hour or so. Jeannie felt herself relax, although Denis, she noted, didn't move a muscle. He sat with his long legs stretched out in front of him and his arms folded across his chest, looking slightly bemused, slightly bored, yet all his attention was on the woman at the podium.

"The answer," Mia Andrews continued, "is simple, yet so very complex, I am still wrestling with the consequences of what happened twelve years ago.

"A colleague at the hospital where I'm on staff referred a patient to me, a young mother with severe insomnia. Her doctor could find no physical basis for her problem and thought I might be able to help her. Eventually, through an exploration of the deeper realms of this woman's consciousness, we uncovered an amazing story of a lifetime of alien contact and abductions."

By this time, Mia Andrews had completely captivated her audience. Jeannie sneaked a look at Denis. He still hadn't moved an inch. For the next thirty minutes, Dr. Andrews spoke about her gradual involvement with other men and women who told stories so similar to the young mother's experiences that they agreed down to the most minute details.

These "experiencers," as they were called, had no contact with each other, nor was there any media source at the time to provide the details they reported. Realizing that she needed more information in order to help these people, Dr. Andrews had become involved with UFORA.

She spoke of numerous UFO sightings in Texas,

witnessed by hundreds of people including civilian and military pilots and local law enforcement officials. Her workload had increased as more and more people came to her telling of their abduction experiences. She mentioned physical exams, sometimes painful, conducted by the aliens. Finally, she talked about physical evidence, the scars left by these exams.

"She's gotta be kidding!"

Jeannie gasped and froze. The voice beside her wasn't loud, but in that room, where you could have heard a pin drop, nobody could have missed it. Several people turned and stared. Out of the corner of her eye, Jeannie saw Denis' mouth tighten into a thin line.

Dr. Andrews continued without missing a beat. "The first abductee I worked with, the young mother, insisted that what she'd been experiencing were dreams. Even after several sessions of hypnotic regression, when I myself became convinced we were not dealing with dreams, she refused to admit the abductions were real. Until the day she came into my office for an emergency session.

"She described a 'dream' the night before in which she was taken into a craft and subjected to several medical procedures, including something done to her right leg. Ladies and gentlemen," Dr. Andrews said softly, "I can't even begin to describe the horror I saw in that woman's eyes when she lifted her skirt and showed me her right leg. This is what I saw."

She held up a black and white slide, an enlargement of the shin area of a human leg, and pointed to a circular, scoop-like depression between the knee and the ankle.

"The scar on the woman's leg was fresh, although it showed no evidence of bleeding. It was half an inch in diameter, three-eighths of an inch deep. It looked exactly like a punch biopsy, except this woman had never had a biopsy. Nor did she have the scar when she went to bed the night before. But she definitely had it when she woke up that morning."

Dr. Andrews looked out over her audience. "Sometime that night, without her consent or even her knowledge, someone or something put that scar on my patient's leg. She could no longer deny what she'd been fighting for so long. Her 'dreams' had become a frightening reality."

8

THE room erupted. Several dozen voices buzzed with comments, conjecture, and some wild speculation on Dr. Andrews' last words.

Jeannie said nothing. Something about that picture bothered her. She wished she could see it again, but Dr. Andrews had laid it on the podium. Her talk concluded a few minutes later, and the audience immediately broke into small groups.

"Jeannie?"

She turned and took Allen Kendrick's outstretched hand.

"I'd like you to meet Dr. Andrews. Mia, this is Jeannie MacLeod, a newspaper reporter from Benton, and Dr. Denis Earley from Tulsa."

Behave yourself, Denis. The words jumped into Jeannie's mind, and she sure hoped Denis was tuned in. She shook the woman's hand. "It's a pleasure, Dr. Andrews. I found your talk fascinating."

"Thank you, Ms. MacLeod. That's a good way to describe my work and the whole abduction phenomenon."

"Dr. Earley is a psychologist," Kendrick said. "He has just moved back to Tulsa from the East Coast."

"Where on the coast, Dr. Earley?"

"Arlington, Virginia."

"I'm familiar with Arlington. Do you know Alex MacGregor?"

Denis frowned. "Alex is a good friend. How do you know him, Dr. Andrews?"

Careful, Denis.

"We met at a conference in Richmond last year. I was very impressed with the success he's had using hypnosis therapy."

"Alex has become quite an expert in the field," Denis said tightly.

Jeannie couldn't keep quiet any longer. "Dr. Andrews, I'm curious about that picture of the young woman's scar. May I see it again?"

"Why, yes. I believe I put it back in my purse. Here it is."

Jeannie held the slide and stared at it. "Something about this...." She shook her head. Something about the picture bothered her, but she couldn't figure out what or why.

"Perhaps you have seen a scar like that before?" Dr. Andrews suggested.

An image began to form in Jeannie's mind. A scrape, no, a scoop. Round and deep. *What's wrong with your leg, Barb? Does it hurt?*

I don't know what it is, but we won't tell Mama, okay?

I think we should, Barbie.

No! I'm not supposed to tell. Promise, Jeannie.

"I promised," Jeannie whispered, still staring at the picture.

"Promised what?" Denis asked.

"Not to tell about the scar."

"What scar?" Three voices spoke at once.

She remembered now. "Barb. Barb has a scar like that picture, on the back of her leg. I haven't thought about it in years."

"An interesting memory," Dr. Andrews commented.

"No big deal," Denis declared. "You and your sister

were probably playing somewhere you shouldn't and she cut herself. Nothing mysterious about that. Most kids have scars on their legs."

"I guess, but--"

"But nothing!" Denis put his arm around her shoulders. "You're worse than a dog worrying an old bone. No wonder you drive your editor crazy."

That brought a laugh from everyone. Grinning, Allen said, "I hate to change this fascinating subject, but I have a question for you, Jeannie. How would you like to go on a fact-finding trip to Washington?"

Still thinking about the scar, she blinked and tried to shift gears. "Who me?"

"I don't see anyone else around here named Jeannie."

"You're serious?"

"Absolutely. Next Wednesday and Thursday I'll be in D.C., meeting with our national director and several top UFO researchers, as well as a congressman who has cleared the way for me to get into a number of government files on UFO's. I could come back empty-handed or--"

"Or you could get some very interesting information." Her mind took off in a new direction. What an opportunity to dig out the real facts, which she would need if she were to write an in-depth article. "You really wouldn't mind if I tag along?"

"I'd appreciate your company. With me opening the right doors and your reporter's nose digging up facts, no telling what we'll come up with."

Jeannie could already feel the adrenaline flowing like it did when she got hot on the trail of a really good story. This was it, her big one. She knew it, as sure as she knew she had to make this trip to Washington.

Should she do it?

Could she live with herself if she didn't?

Quickly, she put out her hand. "You've talked me into it, Dr. Kendrick."

"Good!" He smiled as he pumped her hand. "I'll give you a call in the morning and let you know about the flight."

"If I didn't have a full schedule next week, I'd invite myself along," Dr. Andrews said. "I want to hear everything when you get back, Allen."

Denis just rolled his eyes. He couldn't think of a more worthless way to spend two days, hot on the trail of flying saucers. But it was obvious Jeannie and the other two didn't feel that way. While Kendrick reeled off a list of people he planned to see, Mia Andrews and Jeannie hung on every word. At least she had forgotten about that scar. What a crock. Yet she actually believed Barb had one just like it. Showed you how a skillful speaker could pull in a crowd and have them believing everything she said.

He watched a man ease past several people, headed toward them. Medium height. Brown hair.

"Damn!"

Jeannie followed Denis' eyes. "What's he doing here?"

Ron Siegel nodded to Allen Kendrick. Then turned to Dr. Andrews. "Good talk, Doctor. These folks enjoyed it."

Frowning, the psychiatrist said, "And you didn't, Mr. Siegel?"

"On the contrary, I find it fascinating that so many of your patients claim strange encounters. Has that happened in your practice, too, Dr. Earley?"

"As a matter of fact, I've never had a patient who said he was abducted by aliens," Denis said shortly.

"Interesting. Don't you agree, Dr. Kendrick?"

Allen's eyes narrowed. "That's your opinion, Siegel, which I don't find interesting at all."

"Too bad. Many people do." His eyes moved slowly from one person to the next.

He gave Jeannie the creeps. She wished he would leave, but he seemed in no hurry to move on. She still believed he was the one who had attacked her in Crossland Park, no matter what Denis said.

Finally, he settled on Jeannie. "Have you enjoyed your evening, Ms. MacLeod?"

"How do you know our names?" she demanded.

He shrugged. "I make it my business to stay informed."

"That must keep you pretty busy. Have you been keeping late hours, say, after midnight, since you came to Tulsa?" For just a second, she could have sworn she saw a flash of anger in his eyes, but then it was gone and he regarded her steadily.

"I take good care of my health, ma'am. I hope you do the same." He nodded to the rest of the group, and then casually walked off into the crowd.

Scowling, Jeannie said, "That guy leaves a bad taste in my mouth. Who is he anyway?"

"One of our government's finest." Kendrick's voice dripped with sarcasm. "Where did you run into him?"

She told him about their encounter in Crossland Park. "If he's the best we have, this country's in big trouble. Who does he work for? CIA? FBI?"

Kendrick shook his head. "I doubt it. When he first started showing up at our meetings last year, I put out a few feelers. So far, no one has claimed him. Personally, I think he's a lot more specialized than we'll ever know."

"You think he's part of some super secret project?" Denis asked.

"I think so."

"Black budget?"

"Possibly. There have been rumors."

"Wait a minute. Back up here," Dr. Andrews said. "You've lost me. What is a 'Black Budget?'"

"Isn't that the hidden funding for super secret projects?" Jeannie asked. "Stuff so secret the government doesn't even acknowledge its existence?"

Kendrick nodded. "So secret its budget gets tucked in with someone's else's appropriations. No records, no project. Unfortunately, it works all too well."

"I've never figured out what kind of project is so secret the government has to hide it from itself." Denis smiled. "I know they do it, but it sounds more than a little paranoid to me."

"You're right," Kendrick agreed, "but it happens all the time, and they get away with it. It happened back in the sixties with certain mind-control projects and in the early days of the stealth project. And it's going on now with the investigation of UFO's."

"Which brings us back to Ron Siegel," Jeannie said.

"Right. For years, the government has been saying UFO's pose no threat to our security and they have no official interest in them. That's hogwash, as all of us here know. If there's no official interest, why have they left a fifty-year paper trail of classified documents, some of which are finally being released through the Freedom of Information Act?" Kendrick sighed. "In another ten years, maybe someone will get around to explaining people like Siegel and exactly who they're working for."

"And why," Mia Andrews murmured.

Kendrick nodded. "And why. In the meantime, we plod along, trying to figure out the answers on our own."

"And hope Siegel and company don't try too hard to stop us."

"Fortunately, there are those in authority who don't appreciate the secrecy any more than we do. I'll introduce you to a few of those next week, Jeannie."

"I'm looking forward to it." She promised to call Mia when she returned from the trip. Then, after circulating for another twenty or thirty minutes, she and Denis left.

This time, he didn't object when she offered to drive. "I'm bushed," he admitted, settling into the passenger seat and closing his eyes. "But if you get sleepy, just give me a nudge. I wake up fast."

Jeannie had hoped they could spend the ride talking about the meeting, but maybe it was better this way.

Turning out of the parking lot, she glanced over at Denis. He had pushed his seat all the way back and stretched his long legs under the dash. With his eyes closed, his face looked relaxed, peaceful even, but she doubted that much had changed inside. Even with all they had heard tonight, he probably still thought she was chasing saucers and little green men!

She knew better. The people she had met tonight had impressed her deeply. They weren't kooks or phonies. These were serious researchers looking for the answers to big questions. Are we alone? Who is out there? Why won't someone tell us the truth?

Jeannie meant to find the truth. Just like UFORA, she had come up with tantalizing bits and pieces. Loren, with his missing time and strange happenings, was one of those pieces. Ron Siegel, whoever he was working for, was another.

As her car moved east on the Expressway, she looked up through the windshield into the winter sky. As far as she could see, hundreds of stars dotted the inky blackness.

What else is out there? Who else that I can't see, can't even imagine?

* * *

ALLEN had booked seats for a seven-thirty flight from Tulsa on Wednesday morning. Even with the layover in St. Louis, they should arrive in Washington at noon Eastern Time. Like a six-year-old waiting for Santa Claus, Jeannie had stayed awake most of Tuesday night, her mind clicking off lists, things to do, things she should have done.

At three-fifteen, she had jumped out of bed to check whether she'd really packed her robe in the suitcase Barb had insisted she borrow.

"Can't have you looking like a redneck Okie on her first flight," her sister had said yesterday, smiling as she rummaged in the back of her closet for her own stylish weekender.

"Oh really? What would you call me?"

"Don't you dare put yourself down," Barb scolded. "You may not be a world traveler, but you'll never be a redneck."

"Even though I've never gone any farther east than Little Rock? And except for a couple of high school trips to Dallas, I've hardly been out of Oklahoma?"

"So, you're a late bloomer. Nothing wrong with that." She sat down on the edge of her king-sized bed. "I'm so glad you're doing this, Jeannie. I had my chance with my modeling career before Loren and I married. Now you're finally beginning to spread your wings. I worry about you living all alone in that big old house." Before Jeannie could protest, she said, "What does Denis think about you taking off on a cross-country jaunt?"

"Not much, I'm afraid. Mostly because of what I'll be doing."

"There is that," Barb agreed. "What do you expect to find in Washington?"

"A story," Jeannie replied promptly, dusting off the suitcase. "A really big story. And eventually, the answers to some puzzling questions. I want to help Loren, Sis."

"And you think this UFO stuff will do that?"

"Yes, I do." She sat down beside Barb and put an arm around her shoulders. "You should have heard some of the things I heard at the UFORA meeting. Totally weird, but believable."

An image of the slide Mia Andrews had shown at the meeting flashed into her mind. Should she mention Barb's scar or the disturbing flashback Jeannie herself had experienced that night?

"Do you really think Loren had an encounter?" Barb asked with a shiver.

"I think something happened to him at Crossland Park," Jeannie replied carefully. "Don't you?"

"I guess. I don't like to think about it."

"Then don't. Let me do the thinking and the checking, but there is one thing you can do, both you and Loren." She turned Barb around to face her. "Promise me you'll try to get him to talk to Denis, and not just on the golf course or over a few beers at the club."

"You mean a professional consultation?"

"Exactly. He might do it, if you go with him." She expected an argument, but it didn't happen.

"I'll see what I can do. I'm worried about him, Jeannie, and the baby, too." Barb's voice had dropped to a whisper, and as she did so often these days, she laid one hand protectively on her stomach.

That's when Jeannie decided not to bother her sister by dredging up old memories of an incident that happened years ago. Most likely, the scar on Barb's leg didn't mean a thing. Maybe it had even disappeared. More important, she didn't need anything more to worry about now. Jeannie knew for a fact her sister hadn't gained a single pound since she became pregnant, and that wasn't good--another reason Jeannie had been tossing and turning all night. She had to come up with something soon that would help Barb. Sure, she wanted that story, as much as she'd ever wanted anything in her life, but not as much as she wanted to help her family. Lying back in her bed, she turned out the light. Maybe this trip would help her do both.

* * *

THE silver jumbo jet climbed into a cloudless sky at 7:33 a.m. Like the gentleman he was, Allen refrained from any comments about Jeannie's fingernails attaching to the armrests or her eyes glued to the seat belt sign straight ahead. He didn't even tell her she was missing the impressive Tulsa skyline rapidly shrinking below them. Instead, he talked easily about himself and his family, his involvement with UFORA, and what he hoped to accomplish on this trip. Together they went over the materials in his briefcase, with Jeannie taking pages of notes. By the time the plane approached St. Louis, she had a good feeling for the information they would try to track down in the next two days. When they finally landed at Washington-Dulles Airport, she felt like any seasoned traveler looking forward to several days of business meetings in the nation's capitol.

An oversized mini-van left them at their downtown hotel. As she headed toward the front desk on the far side of the spacious lobby, she caught a glimpse of herself in a gleaming mirror and couldn't help wondering if this trim young woman with her smart-looking tweed suit and expensive luggage could possibly have traded places with the real Jeannie MacLeod. Somehow, standing in this elegant room among men and women of all sizes, shapes and colors, speaking languages she had never heard before, the idea didn't seem at all impossible.

An hour later, Jeannie tightened her grip on her over-sized purse and stepped out of the yellow cab in front of a white stucco building in the heart of Washington's embassy district. While Allen paid the driver, she turned and twisted, trying to take in everything at once. Ms. Typical Tourist, she thought, but she didn't care. Her country's history surrounded her on all sides, and she might not have the chance to see it again, at least not any time soon. She watched several brightly-colored flags atop nearby buildings flapping in the stiff breeze and realized she didn't recognize a single one. Definitely time to bone up on her world history and geography.

Allen took her arm and they hurried along the shrubbery-lined walk that led to the stucco building's main entrance. "We may have time for a little sightseeing after this meeting," he said, smiling. "If John doesn't have us over-booked."

"I hope he does," Jeannie said quickly, as they walked through the lobby. "That's what we're here for. Although I'm afraid this trip will whet my appetite just enough so I'll have to come back soon and see it all."

"Make it in the Spring," Allen advised, "when the cherry blossoms are in bloom. My wife and I came here on our honeymoon. There's nothing quite like it. Dr. Earley would probably make an excellent guide," he added as they headed toward the elevators.

Jeannie opened her mouth to inform him in no uncertain terms that Dr. Earley did not figure anywhere in her future plans, but Allen had already changed the subject, giving her a few more details on their meeting with John Fraser. She decided she must have been mistaken. Allen was reminiscing, not matchmaking.

Still, when they walked into the UFORA Director's office, her thoughts had turned into a curious jumble of cherry blossoms, orange blossoms and UFO's.

"Allen, good to see you again! And this must be Ms. MacLeod."

Jeannie almost winced aloud as Col. John Fraser, USAF (Ret.), gripped her hand. Straight, stiff and tall, he looked every inch the military man. His steel gray hair was still cut *regulation* style, and Jeannie had no doubt he could still wear his Air Force blues without straining a single button.

"Col. Fraser," she murmured, thinking she should check her tingling hand for broken bones.

"Call me John." With a grin, he added, "The Air Force hasn't actually disowned me yet, but I'm afraid I'm a bit of an embarrassment to them. They prefer to pretend I don't exist."

"Because of your involvement with UFORA?"

"Exactly, although it's not quite as bad now, since the government no longer denies the existence of UFO's and simply claims they pose no threat to national security. Which is pretty absurd, since the damn things regularly breach secure air space and abduct citizens right under our noses."

He chuckled and Jeannie relaxed a bit. The well-worn

laugh lines in his face made him appear much less formidable.

"But don't get me started on that business or we'll never get anything done today." He glanced at his watch. "We have an appointment with Representative Howe at three, so I should have time to brief you on a couple of ongoing cases involving the government and also some of the latest information released under FOIA."

"Freedom of Information Act?" Jeannie pulled up a chair and dug into her case for a notebook and pen.

"Right. It keeps dribbling in, bit by bit. One of these days, maybe we'll get lucky and they'll give us one of the missing links to the puzzle. As you've probably discovered, Ms. MacLeod, this is a time-consuming and frustrating business."

"So I've noticed." A sudden thought popped into her mind. "John, have you ever heard the name, Ron Siegel?"

"Siegel. Sounds familiar, but I can't place him."

Briefly, Jeannie described her encounters with the man.

"I'll do some checking and get back to you," Fraser promised. "Now let me tell you about the latest can of worms we've opened up at DIA."

For the next hour, Jeannie listened to Fraser and scanned dozens of government files, completely immersing herself in the subject of UFO's. She took a few notes, but mostly she just read and allowed the magnitude of the government's involvement to sink in. "I had no idea," she said several times, shaking her head. "They've lied to us for over fifty years! If we can't believe our own government, who can we trust?"

"No one," Allen replied promptly. "This whole field is ripe with paranoia and with good reason. Last week, a senior CIA official told me the Agency has no active research into UFO's. When I showed him the FOIA document I'd just received that flatly contradicted him, he simply repeated, straight-faced, what he'd said. It's frustrating as hell. By the way," he added, glancing at his watch, "we need to get on over to the House Office Building."

Flipping through several more of the photocopied sheets, Jeannie suddenly stopped, as her eyes scanned one page. "I think I may have something here."

Allen leaned over her shoulder. "That's an old one: 1951."

"Old, but interesting. It says here that Sgt. Virgil Owens of Tulsa, Oklahoma, took some 16-mm footage of several flying discs that followed his car while he was en route to a new duty station in Colorado. When he arrived the next day, he was ordered to hand over the film to his C.O. It was returned three weeks later with a note explaining the sighting as 'birds in flight.' No further comment." She looked up. "Yet it was stamped 'Secret' and just released last year. Makes you wonder what was on that film."

Fraser shrugged. "It probably got buried in the paper-work shuffle. Doesn't seem especially significant to me."

"Maybe, maybe not." Jeannie walked over to the copy machine and ran the single sheet through. "At least I know now that someone from Tulsa had a sighting in Oklahoma way back near the beginning of the UFO era."

"I'm sure he's not the only one," Fraser said, "but there's probably no way to follow up on it after all this time."

"You're probably right, but--"

"Got a feeling on this one, Jeannie?" Allen asked quietly.

She swung around and found him studying her. "Yes, actually. It may be nothing, but I just think I should look into it."

"Then go for it," Allen said. "In this business, we need all the help we can get. That includes women's intuition."

"And the cooperation of Congress," Fraser added, picking up his coat. "Let's get going before Representative Howe changes his mind about helping us."

The rest of the day and the next passed quickly with several more meetings. Jeannie and Allen spent every free minute poring over copies of released government documents. By the time they were once again in the air Thursday evening, Jeannie was exhausted, yet exhilarated.

Her life was changing. She could feel it and it felt good. She had just taken a trip she would never even have dreamed of just a few months ago. She had met and talked with government officials and U.S. Congressmen, and she had a suitcase crammed with official documents concerning an elusive phenomenon that had thoroughly captured her imagination.

What's more, conceding that she was now a seasoned air traveler, Allen had graciously relinquished his window seat so she, Jeannie MacLeod from Benton, Oklahoma, could spend the next few hours scanning the night sky, studying the stars, wondering what else was out there, and why she wasn't one of those chosen to see.

* * *

THE hickory logs had finally caught and a cozy fire filled the wood-burning stove perched on the hearth at the far end of the living room.

Warm and comfortably drowsy, Denis pushed away the remains of his sandwich and settled back in the old, red leather Morris chair, his eyes closed. Immediately, an image of Jeannie formed in his mind, Jeannie in her bright pink suit, tramping through the woods at Loren's house last week. Her long dark hair swung as she walked, and her soft warm hand rested in his.

Had the temperature in the room suddenly risen ten degrees? His eyes flew open. Damn. He had it bad. All he had to do was think about the woman and his hormones went into overdrive.

Not yet ready to relinquish this particular train of thought, he took a deep breath and relaxed, letting his mind drift. He'd missed her these past few days. What with work and her trip to Washington, he hadn't seen her since last Friday. Her plane should be getting in to Tulsa soon. He'd offered to meet her, but she was enjoying her independence and politely declined. Thinking how very prim and proper Jeannie could be, Denis felt a smile touch his lips. That thought led quite naturally into the kiss they'd shared. Nothing prim about that. Deep down this lady had a hot streak she didn't even know about.

Deep in his fantasy world, he ignored the phone till the third ring. By the time he picked it up, his answering machine had clicked in.

"Denis? I thought you weren't there."

He recognized the soft voice on the other end right away. "Hi, Barb. I guess I dozed off there for a minute."

"Oh, I didn't think you'd be sleeping this early."

"I wasn't. How are you doing?"

"Okay. I--"

"Barb? Are you okay?"

"Yes...no."

She spoke the last word so softly Denis almost missed it. "Is it Loren?" he asked.

"Yes." Again, just a whisper.

"What can I do?"

"I don't know. He just fell asleep. I finally persuaded him to take a sleeping pill. He's exhausted, but he can't sleep."

"I see."

"Denis, I hate to ask this--"

"Barb, I want to help."

"Can you--would you come to the airport with me? Jeannie's plane comes in at nine-fifteen. We could talk on the way."

Denis didn't hesitate. "When should I pick you up?"

"There's no need for you to drive all the way out here. I'll come into Tulsa--"

"Let me do this, Barb. How long?"

"Half an hour?"

"I'll be there."

"Thank you, Denis. Jeannie will be glad to see you."

Would she? He wanted to think so, but right now helping Barb and Loren was first on his mind.

* * *

EVEN before he pulled into the driveway, Barb had the front door open. Huddled into an ankle-length coat with a fuzzy scarf around her head, she walked quickly to the passenger side of his car and slipped inside.

"You didn't even give me a chance to do my gentleman thing and open your door," Denis said, smiling.

"I know you're a gentleman." Barb snapped her seat belt in place. "So, how's everything?" she asked, brightly.

Denis backed down the sloping drive and turned onto Bentonville Road. "Everything's fine at my end of town. Tell me about Loren."

She seemed to shrink into the seat, her arms folded tightly in front of her. For a few seconds, she didn't speak, then her words came out faint and hesitant. "He's changed, Denis. I don't know my husband any more."

"How has he changed? What's different?"

"Everything," she whispered. "He doesn't eat, just picks at his food or sits and stares across the room without touching a thing. He has headaches and he's losing weight, and God knows, he can't afford that. He doesn't sleep. I hear him wandering around the house at all hours of the night."

"Does he have any idea why he can't sleep?"

"Oh yes, he knows why. He's afraid."

"Of what?"

"His dreams. Can you believe that? Loren has never been afraid of anything in his life, and now he can't sleep because he's afraid he'll dream!"

Mentally noting everything she said, Denis asked, "What does he dream about that's so frightening?"

"Black pools of water."

Startled, Denis took a quick look at his passenger. She sat stiff and unmoving, staring straight ahead at the highway.

"He's afraid of drowning in pools of black water. Where he came up with that, I don't know. We don't even have a pond near the house."

"Anything else?"

Barb hesitated. "Well, there's the round room."

"Round room?"

"A few nights ago, he dreamed he was locked in a round white room. He woke up screaming and thrashing around in bed. His heart was racing and he was gasping for breath. I-- I thought he was having a heart attack. He sat up the rest of the night."

"Has he seen a doctor?"

She shook her head. "You know how stubborn he can be. He says it's just nerves and he'll get over it. I wish I could believe that but...."

Her voice trailed off, leaving only the muffled hum of highway traffic between them. Denis, too, wished he could believe the "just nerves" theory, but a dozen years of professional experience told him no. Something was very wrong with his old friend. He had suspected as much when he observed Loren's erratic behavior at Buddy's party nearly three weeks ago and again on the golf course last week.

PTS. Post Traumatic Stress. The symptoms fit, just as Jeannie had pointed out not so long ago. Only the trauma was missing, no matter what she said. Still, it wouldn't hurt to ask. "Can you think of anything that might have precipitated these symptoms, Barb? Has anything happened to Loren recently that could have upset him this much?"

"You mean, besides the light that followed him into

Crossland Park last month?"

Yes, besides that. But he was curious. "What do you think about that?"

"Well, I--you know, it does make me wonder," she replied thoughtfully. "Loren was an hour late coming home that night, and he can't account for that time. It's very strange, especially since he started acting, well, weird, right after that. Jeannie thinks there's a connection."

Denis smiled. "Your sister has a vivid imagination. What do you think?"

"I guess I haven't decided yet. It is strange though, and so are the lights and those noises we hear, only when Loren is around. Nothing like that ever happened before."

"I remember Jeannie saying something about lights and noises."

"Did you believe her?"

"Well, I--"

"Do you believe me?"

"Yes, I do," he assured her. "I just don't think we have to look to the paranormal for an answer to Loren's problem."

"Jeannie's not so sure about that." Barb sighed. "I don't know what to think any more. I just know that Loren is really troubled about something, and it's driving us both crazy."

Her voice caught on the last word, and Denis could almost feel the worry and fear that had her strung so tight. If she, and Loren, too, didn't get help soon, they could both be in serious trouble.

"Can you get Loren into my office tomorrow?" he asked abruptly.

"For a consultation?"

"If he'll agree to a professional visit, at least he's acknowledging that he needs help. That's the first step."

Barb nodded. "We'll be there. You know, Jeannie told me the same thing."

"She did?" That was a surprise. Since when did Jeannie

agree with him about anything?

"That's right. I think you've impressed my little sister, Dr. Earley." She reached over and touched his arm. "You impress me, too. You're a good friend, Denis."

Easing over to the right lane, Denis steered his car down the off ramp to the airport. "I haven't done anything yet, Barb. I'm not making any promises."

"I know, but at least you care enough to try. That helps a lot."

Maybe. But Denis knew they were in deep water here, and in spite of Barb's kind words, he just hoped he could swim well enough to keep them all afloat.

* * *

"THERE she is. Over here, Jeannie!"

Walking through the gate at Tulsa Airport, Jeannie heard her name. Then saw two arms waving frantically over the crowd that had gathered.

"Looks like you have a welcome committee," Allen said, grinning. "At least I have my car waiting for me."

"I was only expecting my sister. I guess Loren decided to come, too."

She stopped in her tracks as she realized the man standing beside Barb wasn't Loren. What was Denis doing here? Had something happened? Even as her concern grew, however, she recognized another feeling stealing over her. She was happy to see him, so happy she couldn't take her eyes off him. Like a parched woman, she drank in every inch of him and had to force herself not to run down the people around her on her way through the gate where he waited. She felt like she was seeing him for the first time, and yet she knew him well, those eyes that shone like rich green quartz, the strength in his square-cut jaw, the kindness in his lean face.

He smiled at her, and she had to fight an almost irresistible urge to throw herself into his arms.

Tearing her eyes from him, she turned to hug her sister. "Barb! Thanks for coming. Hi, Denis," she added, shyly.

"Hello, Jeannie. Welcome home."

"Thank you." She looked around. "Loren?"

"He conked out early tonight," Denis said quickly, and Jeannie knew she'd have to settle for that till they were alone in the car.

Finally, thirty minutes later, after the usual ordeal of baggage claims, Jeannie settled into the front seat of Denis' car. She tried to relax, but that was impossible with Denis just three feet away.

As soon as they got onto the freeway, she turned around to Barb, who had insisted Jeannie ride up front. "How's Loren doing?"

Her sister's face contorted, and Jeannie knew what she would say without even hearing the answer. "He's--oh, God, Sis. He's worse than ever." She fumbled in her purse for a tissue and sat with it pressed against her face while she looked out the window.

Jeannie squeezed Barb's hand and turned back to the front seat. "Have you talked to him yet?" she asked Denis.

He shook his head. "I didn't know how things were until tonight. Barb told me they would come to my office tomorrow."

"Can you help him, Denis?"

For several seconds, he didn't answer, and she simply stared into the blackness outside, watching the headlights of dozens of cars swell and fade behind them. It was a clear night, seasonally cold. It would have been a beautiful night if all was well in her little world.

"Without knowing what the problem is," Denis said finally, "I probably shouldn't offer an opinion, except I know Loren and I still think he's as steady as they come. So, yes, I think I can help him." He glanced over at Jeannie for just a second.

"I have a feeling you're about to qualify that opinion,"

she murmured.

"You think right. I need you to help me, Jeannie."

"Why do I think I'm not going to like this?"

Denis sighed. "That's probably right, too, and I wouldn't ask if I didn't think it was the best thing for Loren. I want you to promise me you won't say a word to him about UFO's, mysterious lights, missing time, or any of the other things you've been investigating. Give me a chance to get to the bottom of this situation first. Will you do that?"

She wasn't surprised. She'd figured that Denis didn't take her ideas seriously, but still she'd hoped.

She would just have to work harder. She knew there was a connection between what Loren had seen and his strange behavior, and somehow she would prove it. She would give the doubting doctor proof he couldn't deny, no matter how much he wanted to.

"I'll do what you want, Denis," she replied, "but I won't stop looking for answers, the real answers."

He reached over and took her hand. "I didn't expect you to."

His hand dwarfed hers. It felt wonderful. Terrific. Sensational. And he would probably yank it away when he heard her next question. "Will you do something for me?"

"If I can."

"Oh, you can." How could the heat from one hand possibly travel through her so far, so fast? "When the truth comes out--and it will--will you accept it?"

Without hesitation, he replied, "The truth is what will help Loren. He'll know it when he hears it, and so will I."

Satisfied, Jeannie said, "That's all I ask."

Denis eased his fingers between hers, and they stayed together all the way to Benton.

9

"'MORNING, Barb. Loren, good to see you!"

As they shook hands, Denis immediately noted Loren's cold clammy palms, a sure sign of his anxiety. And he looked terrible. His long lean face seemed pinched and sallow. It was obvious he wasn't eating or sleeping well.

"Is this a good time?" Barb asked. "We're not disturbing you, are we?"

Denis opened the front door wider. "Time is the one thing I have plenty of. As you can see, business isn't exactly booming around here."

Loren walked past him into the hallway. "You mean I'm your first patient?"

Typical Loren humor, yet Denis got the feeling his friend wasn't joking. Shutting the door behind them, he said, "You're my first visitors of any kind since I moved to Tulsa."

Barb shook her head. "I'm really sorry about that. With everything that's going on, I'm afraid we haven't been very neighborly."

"You've been great," Denis assured her, following them into the foyer.

"Very nice." Loren's eyes took in the intricately carved woodwork and paneled wainscoting that lined the hallway.

"Your taste has improved since our apartment days in Norman."

"Don't remind me." Denis groaned.

"If I remember right," Barb commented, "that place was a good example of Early American Junkyard. Very unique."

Denis laughed. "That's a kind way of putting it. I still have a lot of work to do here, but it already feels like home. I've picked up quite a few antiques over the years, and now I have plenty of room for them."

"Room for your office, too. What made you decide to work out of your home?" Barb asked, glancing into the front parlor that was still stacked high with boxes. "Did you do that in Washington?"

Denis gave a short laugh. "Hardly. My former practice was what you might call 'professionally correct'. The right location, right associates, right patients. Everything to enhance my rising career. I had it all for a while, but it didn't work out, so now I'm trying to make this place as different as possible. I'm starting out small, and I plan to keep it that way."

"Simplifying your life," Barb said, nodding. "I can relate to that." She poked her head into an open doorway. "This must be your office. You've done a nice job, Denis. I'd love to see it all when you've finished."

"You will. We'll have a party as soon as the place is presentable."

"Any spooks in here?"

Denis swung around to face Loren. His friend stood at the foot of the elegant oak staircase that split the entrance hall and spiraled up both sides to the second story balcony. With his head tipped back, Loren stood perfectly still, staring at nothing.

"No spooks," Denis assured him. "Do you see something up there?"

"I just thought you might see shadows, hear noises or

something. It's a pretty old house." His voice became faint as his eyes focused somewhere in the distance.

Behind his back, Barb caught Denis' eye and gestured, as if to say, "See, I told you so."

Denis nodded. Once, not so long ago, he would have felt confident of his ability to help his troubled friend, as he'd helped so many others. But that was before Eric.

Quickly, firmly, Denis closed that door. Loren needed him and at least he could try. "Barb, why don't you wait for us in the parlor? Help yourself to the TV, magazines, whatever. We may be a while."

She nodded and gave Loren's hand a reassuring squeeze, then disappeared into the front room. Denis clapped a hand on Loren's shoulder and they walked toward his office.

He had decorated this room himself, and he liked the results. A simple room, long and somewhat narrow, with soothing blue-gray walls and coordinating drapes, he had crammed it full of the old books he'd been collecting for years. Bookshelves completely covered the north wall and much of the one adjoining, and a huge fireplace of black and white Italian marble faced his old oak desk, a relic from a nineteenth-century schooner. A small table, leather couch, and several chairs completed the furnishings. Denis ushered Loren past the couch to the oversized leather chair next to the desk. Pulling up his own chair, he forced himself to wait quietly, hoping Loren would choose an opening.

He didn't. He sat in the easy chair with one long leg crossed over the other, apparently relaxed, but Denis could see his hands clenched into fists under his tightly folded arms. He was concentrating hard on some point behind the desk.

Denis cleared his throat. "Barb tells me you haven't been sleeping well. What's going on, Loren?"

"Damned if I know."

For the second time in ten minutes, his friend's words

knocked him completely off balance.

"Don't look so surprised. You're the shrink. You're supposed to tell me what's wrong."

"After you give me something to work with."

Loren slumped down in his chair. "Sorry. I know that. I just never expected to be sitting on this side of your desk, but right now I'm ready to try anything."

Denis grinned. "Thanks for the vote of confidence."

"Sure. Anytime." He looked at Denis, and they both laughed.

"Okay, now that we have that settled, let's get down to business. Talk to me. Tell me what's been happening, how you feel, what you think. Anything. Everything."

"Everything? You promise not to think I'm crazy?"

"Loren, I know you're not crazy. Now, shoot."

They talked for well over an hour. Actually, with Denis prodding, Loren talked, probably more than he ever had at one time in his life, except during a lecture. Denis knew they had never carried on such a lengthy conversation, not even while they shared an apartment years before. He listened carefully for any small detail that might explain Loren's present behavior, but aside from a few common childhood fears, his friend seemed to have led a happy and uneventful life, until a few weeks ago when all hell broke loose. Seemed. That was the key, Denis felt sure. Something, perhaps even the bright light in Crossland Park, must have triggered a painful memory that Loren had successfully suppressed for years, one he was still suppressing.

"It's frustrating as hell," he muttered, resting his elbows on the desk. "If I knew what the problem was, I'd tell you, Den, but I honestly don't have a clue."

"I realize that." Denis regarded him thoughtfully. "How would you feel about hypnotherapy? I've found it can be a successful shortcut to breaking through a stubborn memory."

"Hypnosis?" Loren straightened up, a deep frown

settling on his craggy face. "Isn't that kind of drastic?"

"Not at all. Actually, it's pretty standard therapy."

"I don't know. I've never put much stock in that sort of thing."

"What sort of thing do you mean?"

"You know, all that paranormal stuff."

"Me neither," Denis replied promptly, "but there's nothing mysterious or otherworldly about hypnosis."

Loren's frown deepened. "I don't like the idea of going into a trance. I want to have control of what I say and do."

"You will." Denis leaned forward. "Hypnosis is simply a state of focused concentration. I'll help you relax, causing your memory to sharpen. No more, no less. The result is, you may be able to remember certain incidents, long forgotten, that have contributed to your anxieties. Hypnosis is an excellent tool. I recommend that we use it."

Loren didn't look convinced. "Isn't there something else you can do?"

"Not a heck of a lot. We can talk some more and maybe ease some of your fears, but we need to find the underlying reason for them. Hypnosis is the quickest and easiest way I know to access that information."

"Then I guess I don't have much choice."

"There's always a choice, Loren. I won't try to force you into anything."

"But you'll give me a good push in the direction you want me to go. You always could sell a straw hat to an Eskimo, Earley."

Denis grinned. "Does that mean yes?"

"I suppose."

"Great! How about tomorrow morning? Same time, same place."

Loren untangled his long legs and stood up. "If you say so. You're the doctor."

* * *

DENIS stood in the doorway watching Loren as he backed his car out and headed down the street, disappearing around the corner. Barb sat close to him, and Denis could almost hear her words, encouraging, comforting. Thank goodness Loren had this intelligent, loving woman to support him. Without her, Denis' chances to help his friend would be even slimmer.

He closed the door and walked into the living room. Suddenly weary, he sat down in the chair and closed his eyes. Would hypnosis work? He wanted so much to ease Loren's pain, but he just didn't know. Times like this, he missed having a partner, someone to believe in him the way Barb did Loren.

He thought of Jeannie, with those deep blue, thoughtful eyes. She'd be working now, maybe chasing down a story somewhere in Benton, maybe sitting at her desk at the newspaper office.

Denis jumped out of his chair and ran up the stairs to his bedroom. Grabbing his keys off the dresser, he took a quick look in the mirror and then dashed downstairs headed for the garage. He wanted to see Jeannie. More than that, he needed to talk to her, and he refused to analyze his need. For once, he would go with his gut feelings and figure out the *why fors* later. Right now, he had the time and the inclination and that was sufficient.

He slid into the front seat of his car and turned on the CD player. He was in the mood for something upbeat. As the powerful engine came to life, mellow music wrapped around him. Denis settled back to enjoy the short ride to Benton.

* * *

"CAN I come in?"

Jeannie's head turned and her hands slipped off the keyboard. "Denis! What are you doing here?"

He eased around the corner into her cubicle and settled

himself on the corner of her desk. "Taking you away from work. Do you mind?"

A deep breath slowed down her galloping heartbeat, then she pressed a couple of keys and the computer screen went blank. "I don't mind."

"Am I interrupting something important?"

"That depends. Eddie thinks it's big news."

"What is it?"

She grinned. "The monthly feature on the Benton Garden Club. I still have to do the Music Club and the Thespian Society. And--" Pausing, she glanced at her watch. "I have five minutes to get to the Wagon Wheel Restaurant to interview an Indian artist who's speaking at the noon Lions meeting."

"Good grief. Your boss is a slave driver."

Shrugging, she said, "He didn't bother to re-assign anything while I was gone, so I'm playing catch-up. I'll get it done eventually." Her curiosity got the best of her. "Did you come here for something special?"

"I thought we might do lunch, but I guess that's out, since you have an appointment."

A wave of disappointment, completely out of proportion to the situation, washed over her. "I'm really sorry, Denis. I'd love to have lunch with you."

His golden green eyes lit up. "You would? Then let's do it. Can someone cover the Lions Club for you?"

"Nobody's here but Eddie."

"Who is this Eddie anyway?"

"Eddie Barnes. The editor."

"Would he?"

She rolled her eyes. "You're dreaming."

"Yo, Jeannie!" A dark-skinned young man, his long black hair tied back in a ponytail, stuck his head into her office. "Working hard?"

"Isn't this your day off, Billy?"

He shrugged. "Got work to do."

An idea was forming in her mind. "Billy Whitecotton, this is Dr. Denis Earley."

Jeannie looked from one to the other as they shook hands. "Billy, how would you like to interview Wayne Allen?"

"Right." A scowl crossed his smooth face. "I already tried that, remember? Eddie said I'm not ready yet, even though I'm Cherokee, too. And an artist."

"I think you'll do a fine job," Jeannie said, casually reaching behind the desk for her purse.

Billy's eyes grew bigger. "You do? I will?"

"Yes, you will," she assured him. "Hurry up and get over there. They'll give you lunch, too."

"Hey, cool."

"And for heaven's sake, don't let Eddie know."

"Right. Thanks, Jeannie!" he called back over his shoulder. "I owe you one."

Denis wrapped one arm around Jeannie's shoulder and hugged her. "You are one devious lady, did you know that?"

"Just taking advantage of the situation," she replied, but she had to admit she felt good. No, great. Like a kid playing hooky, not that she'd ever played hooky.

The phone rang. She picked it up and wedged the receiver against her ear. "Jeannie MacLeod here."

"Ms. MacLeod, this is Mrs. Thacker at the Riverside Nursing Home. I've spoken to Mr. Owens, and he would like to visit with you. When can you come by?"

Virgil Owens. The man whose name appeared on the government document she had copied in Washington. Not knowing whether he was dead or alive, she had made half a dozen phone calls that morning and finally located him in a Tulsa nursing home. She had left her name, asking him to call. Now here he was, wanting her to visit. "When would be a good time, Mrs. Thacker?"

The voice on the other end of the line hesitated a

moment, then dropped to a confidential half-whisper. "Actually, right now would be good. He's having one of his good days today, if you know what I mean."

Jeannie didn't know, but she could guess. When she called the home that morning, she had learned that Mr. Owens had a debilitating spinal atrophy that had paralyzed his legs and would eventually prove fatal. He had no immediate family and was battling depression, but on his good days, he enjoyed visitors. "I could be there in thirty minutes. Can I see him then?"

"That would be perfect. I'll tell him to expect you."

"Thank you very much, Mrs. Thacker. I appreciate your help." Thrilled with her good luck, she hung up the phone and found herself staring at Denis Earley's puzzled face.

"Why do I get the feeling I've just been stood up?"

"Oh, Denis, I'm sorry!" How did she get herself into these predicaments? "Maybe. Would you like to come with me?" Quickly, she explained about Owens and the movie he had taken in 1951.

"Why are you so anxious to talk to him?" Denis asked. "His sighting was explained, so it's no longer 'unidentified.'"

"Explained by the government. Sometimes their reasoning gets pretty creative. I'd rather hear what Owens says. We won't stay long, and we can stop for lunch on the way back to Benton."

"Promise?"

His deep green eyes locked on hers and took her breath away. His voice, deep and just a bit husky, sent a shiver to the very tips of her toes. She heard herself whisper, "I promise." At that moment, she would have promised this man anything.

"Good. Let's go before Eddie comes in checking up on you."

Still mesmerized, she automatically flicked the computer's power switch. Then reached for her purse, only to find it hanging over her shoulder.

Chuckling, Denis took her hand and guided her toward the front door.

* * *

"MR. Owens, I'm Jeannie MacLeod." Smiling, she leaned forward and grasped Virgil Owens' outstretched hand.

The wizened old man, hunched into a wheelchair, surprised her with his steady, firm grip. "Glad to meet you, Ms. MacLeod."

"Please call me Jeannie. And this is Dr. Denis Earley."

"Doctor."

Jeannie settled down on one of the brown vinyl sofas pushed against the wall in the nursing home lounge. The whole room had been decorated--if that was the right word --in shades of brown and tan. A pair of ancient drapes hung crookedly at the room's one window, and the wall-to-wall carpeting, stained in some spots, threadbare in others, had faded to a neutral non-color. The room even smelled old, and yet, in spite of this evidence of the home's decline, Virgil Owens appeared neat, well-groomed and cheerful. "I appreciate your agreeing to meet with us, Mr. Owens."

He gazed at her intently. "Don't get many visitors these days. Can't afford to turn 'em away." He turned to Denis. "What kind of doctoring you do?"

"I'm a psychologist, Mr. Owens."

"Good! I've had enough of the other kind. What can I do for you folks?"

Smiling at the feisty old man, Jeannie said, "Mr. Owens, I recently came across your name while researching some old documents in Washington. I believe you spent some time in the Army."

"That's right. Spent the last two years of the War in Europe, then stayed on for another hitch." His eyes narrowed. "What did you find that had my name on it? I didn't do nothing special."

Jeannie took the copy she had made in Col. Fraser's office out of her bag and handed it to Owens. Muttering as he read, he looked it over carefully before giving it back. "What do you want with something that happened almost fifty years ago?"

Again, Jeannie reached into her purse, this time taking out a small white business card, which she gave him. "I'm a reporter for the *Benton News and Sun*, Mr. Owens, and I'm working on a story about UFO's. I realize this was a long time ago, but I'm talking to anyone from the Tulsa area who has seen any kind of unidentified objects."

"You believe in them things?"

"I--" She looked at Denis. He was watching her closely, obviously very interested in her answer. Okay, she didn't mind clarifying her position. If he couldn't handle it, then so be it. "I believe something real is causing the sightings and the other happenings," she said slowly. "I don't understand that 'something.' I'm not sure even our scientists can understand or explain it, but I do believe it's real."

Owens nodded. "I've thought about it a lot, and that's pretty much how I feel."

Good. At least somebody agreed with her. "Can you tell me what happened that day?"

"Sure can. I've never forgotten it. Don't expect I ever will. Or what happened afterwards either."

The old man hitched himself up in his chair. "I was driving to my new duty station at Fort Lewis, right outside Colorado Springs. It was late October, 1951. I'd made it as far as western Kansas, and I had my old Chevy wagon floor-boarded. That part of the country was wide open back then, no traffic, no speed limits.

"A little after noon, I looked up over the horizon--there weren't no clouds or haze--and I noticed the strangest thing I'd ever seen. Looked like five silver discs moving across the sky, northeast to southwest. I was a camera buff back then, and I'd just bought a 16-mm camera. I had it right there in the car with me, so I stopped to get some footage. I knew I was seeing something real unusual, and I wanted proof, so nobody could laugh at me for seeing things that weren't there." He shook his head. "I got my proof, all right, for all the good it done me."

"What do you mean?" Jeannie asked.

"They took the best part of the film, that's what I mean."

"They? Who?"

"The Army, that's who." Owens fidgeted in his chair, trying to find a comfortable spot. "When I got to Fort Lewis, I took the film to the lab and developed it. Couldn't hardly believe what I saw. Them five discs showed up bright and clear. I held the camera real still so their speed could be calculated, and I had no doubt it would be faster than anything our planes could do. Then came the best part. I caught one of those guys shooting straight out of formation, and zap! He disappeared."

"Disappeared?"

"Yep. The durn thing just blinked out, then all of a sudden, about thirty seconds later, it showed up again. That's the part they took. I done what I thought was right, giving that film to my C.O., and they stole the best part." His voice rose and so did the color in his sallow cheeks. Even after all these years, the subject of this film apparently still affected the man deeply.

Trying to calm him down, Jeannie spoke slowly, keeping her voice soft and even. "Mr. Owens, do you still have that film?"

"'Course I do. You don't think I'd lose track of something that important, do you?"

"I'm sure you wouldn't," she replied, smiling.

"You know, I like you, Miss, uh--"

"Jeannie."

"Miss Jeannie. You and the Doc here, too, even though he don't say much."

She had to cough to keep from laughing aloud, and from

the corner of her eye, she saw Denis trying hard to cover a grin. "I like you, too, Mr. Owens," she assured him.

He leaned forward and whispered confidentially, "You and the Doc got one of those movie projectors?"

"I don't--wait a minute. Mom had one. I'll bet I can find it somewhere in the house."

"Good. You want to see my film?"

"I'd love to see it, but I'm afraid I don't have the projector with me."

"Shucks, that's no problem. I know an honest face when I see one. You'll bring it back. Which film do you want?"

"Which one?" Jeannie stared at him. "I thought you only had one."

Owens' voice dropped even lower. "That's what I let everyone think. The Army brass made me mad when they cut out those frames, then they wouldn't admit they done it. So I never told anyone about the copy I'd made. They might of doctored up one film, but I kept the other one, and it's got everything on it."

10

"THAT old guy is really something!"

Jeannie paused, with her sandwich halfway to her mouth. She and Denis had stopped for a late lunch at a deli east of Tulsa. "Can you believe he never told anyone about that second film in all these years?"

"I sure can," Denis replied. "He's a wily old fellow. I'll bet he keeps that staff hopping."

"You know he does. Everyone seems to like him."

"They treat him well. That place doesn't have a lot of money, but the residents seem well cared for. I talked to some of them and several of the staff."

"So, that's what you were doing while Virgil and I went to his room for the film." Jeannie had guessed as much. She was beginning to realize that Denis was a very caring man. He hid it well, with his jokes and light-hearted banter, but deep down he took other people's problems seriously.

"You never did tell me why you're so anxious to see that film," Denis said. "I mean, it's--"

"Almost fifty years old. I know that, but it's one more piece of the big puzzle, and the whole subject has me hooked. If I can get enough material, I'm going to put together a comprehensive article, maybe even a series."

"For the Benton paper?"

She nodded. "With the option to go national."

Denis finished his sandwich and settled back in his chair. "Getting pretty ambitious, aren't you?"

"And about time. When I took this job, I never planned to stay with it forever." She leaned forward, suddenly anxious for Denis to understand. "I love journalism," she said, "and believe it or not, I'm really grateful to Eddie for giving me the chance to learn all I have. But I'm ready to move up, and I think this story could do it for me."

He didn't say a word, and Jeannie felt her excitement draining away. Maybe he didn't care about her job or what she wanted. Or about her. Had she misjudged him that badly?

"When you talk about a story," he said finally, "you're not thinking of including Loren, I hope."

Relief. And disappointment. He cared, but he didn't understand. He still thought she could use Loren.

Disappointment quickly turned to anger. How dare he think such a thing! Slamming down her napkin, she almost tipped over her chair as she stood up. "If that's all you think of me, Dr. Earley, you'd better take me home. Somebody might see us together. And that could be bad for your reputation and your business." She ran through the dining area and out the door, letting it slam hard behind her.

Darn the man anyway. She had never met anyone so thick-headed and likable! She stomped down the walk toward the parking lot. That was the worst part of this whole confusing business. The guy was obtuse and completely lacking imagination. She couldn't stand him, right? Wrong. When he looked at her, she melted. Plain and simple, he was driving her nuts. Needing a quiet corner to vent her frustrations, she yanked on his car door. He'd locked it.

"Damn, damn, damn!" Pounding her fists against the sturdy metal, she imagined herself pummeling Denis' broad solid chest.

"Feel better now?"

She whirled around and came face to face with that very part of his anatomy she'd fantasized about just a moment ago.

"Actually, yes," she admitted stiffly. "It's been a long time since I've had a tantrum. It was...refreshing."

Not trusting herself to look into Denis' face, she stared straight ahead, concentrating her attention on the intricate pattern of his deep blue sweater. Alpaca, she thought. Very expensive. Very soft. She could almost imagine the fine wool brushing her skin as she buried her face in that fuzzy warmth. Mesmerized, she watched his chest move in and out, faster and faster. "You're laughing," she accused him.

"I can't help it," he chuckled, opening his arms wide and wrapping them around her. "You're adorable, Jeannie MacLeod. Did you know that?"

Oh no! It was happening again. She couldn't even see him this time, but she had already lost herself in feeling. The plush sweater, soft and warm, just as she'd imagined; his strong arms holding her, his lips....

God, his lips. Full and firm, they found hers. She was drowning in the sea of sensations that flowed through her, drowning, yet gloriously alive for the first time ever.

"Jeannie?"

"Hmm-m?"

"Let me open the door." His words floated past her ears as he eased her aside and fumbled with the lock.

She jumped and scrambled into the car. The door slammed behind her. Back to reality.

Denis slid in beside her and pushed down the door locks. He leaned toward her. "Where were we?"

Jeannie sat straight up in her seat. "Making a public spectacle of ourselves."

"Is that what you call it? I'd say we were making a momentous discovery." He touched her chin and turned her face till their eyes met. "Look at me, Jeannie."

She didn't dare, yet she couldn't stop herself. Somehow, she had lost all control where this man was concerned, and that just couldn't be. She never lost control.

"Jeannie?" He sounded puzzled now. "Are you angry with me?"

"Yes. No. I should be, but...." She sighed, as his face moved closer. "Denis, I--"

"Shhh. Just one more, sweetheart."

Did she hear that right?

Their lips met again. Just this once, she promised herself, and gave in to the wonder of his kiss.

"You are really something, woman." His husky whisper brushed her cheek and she shivered.

"Cold?" he murmured, pulling her against him.

The way she felt right now, she doubted she would ever be cold again, but she didn't say it. She just let herself drift slowly back to earth after that glorious high, then she gently inched away till they no longer touched. Now she could think. Maybe. Tucking back a stray strand of hair, she looked straight ahead, breathing deeply. "Denis, this has all been very nice--"

"Nice? You call that kiss nice?"

"Well, I--"

Denis gunned the engine, and the little car shot backwards. "Nice is a peck on the cheek from your brother-in-law," he growled. "What we did was hot, terrific, dynamite, but definitely not 'nice.' Got that, Ms. MacLeod?" He whipped the car around a corner and peeled out into the traffic with a screech that would have done any hot rod proud.

Jeannie hadn't buckled the seat belt, and she ended up straddling the console between them. "You're mad." she said, and couldn't believe the catch in her voice or the sudden burning behind her eyes. Ridiculous! So what, if the man's kisses got an A+ rating? She'd been kissed before and quite thoroughly, thank you. Scrambling back to her seat, she buckled up and carefully kept her eyes anywhere but on the driver.

Pretty soon, Denis slowed the car down to just ten miles over the speed limit. "I'm not mad at you, Jeannie." The words came out with a sigh, as though he was weary.

She turned around cautiously. "You're not?"

"I'm impatient, that's all, and you're cautious." He shrugged. "We'll work it out."

"Work what out?"

"Whatever there is between us."

"I'm not sure that's wise. Denis, we've been thrown together in an unusual situation. We both want to help Loren, but we don't agree on how to do it. In fact, we don't seem to agree on anything."

"Oh, I think we do. Didn't you find me pretty agreeable back there in the parking lot?"

"That's not what I'm talking about."

"Then you did find me agreeable?"

She threw up her hands. "You are the most impossible man I've ever known. But maybe we can at least get one thing straight. Whatever else I do, please believe that I will never write about Loren or anyone without his permission. Does that satisfy you?"

"Sounds good to me."

"Great. And now that we have that settled, maybe you can help me come up with a good story to tell Eddie when he finds out I gave Billy that interview."

* * *

WHEN Denis dropped her off at the *News and Sun* office a little after three, Jeannie assured him she had everything under control, no problem. After all, the tale they had put together was basically true. Billy did need the experience, and she had been working on a story. Okay, so it wasn't an assignment, but she could handle that. And she would have, if Eddie hadn't decided to work today instead of taking off at noon like he usually did on Fridays. He looked up just as she sauntered past his office.

"MacLeod!"

Uh-oh. The royal summons. She backed up and poked her head in the door. "Did you want to see me, Chief?" Watching the red band of heat creep up his neck, she wondered for the umpteenth time what imp prompted her to aggravate her boss this way. Probably the same one that kept urging her to put a little spark in her life.

"Nice lunch, MacLeod?" Eddie held up his arm and studied his watch.

"Uh, pretty nice."

"I'm a nice guy, so I won't even ask where you've been for the past three hours, but I expect those club reports on my desk before you leave today."

"Sure thing, Boss."

His face turned blotchy, a sure sign of imminent explosion. "And be damned sure Whitecotton's copy is perfect. And accurate."

"Yes, sir." She gave him a thumbs-up and escaped to her own cubbyhole. With a sigh, she set her purse on the floor under her desk. Besides her tape recorder, notebooks, pencils, pens and other assorted paraphernalia, the carryall now held Virgil's film. Jeannie wanted nothing more than to go straight home, dig out her mother's old movie projector, and see exactly what the old man had recorded so many years ago, but she had at least two hours work ahead of her before she could do that. Come to think of it, she wouldn't even get home till eight or nine o'clock. Barb was expecting her for supper tonight. With another sigh, she decided she'd better fortify herself. Grabbing her "Reporters Are People, Too" mug, she headed down the hall toward the coffeepot.

* * *

"THAT was a great dinner, Barb." Jeannie laid down her

napkin and smiled at her sister, who sat beside her at the dining room table.

"You always did like my chili," Barb said, sipping her tea. "I could give you the recipe, but you probably wouldn't bother to make it, not for just you, all alone in that old house. It's a wonder you don't shrivel up and fade away out there. I worry about you, Sis."

Jeannie shook her head. "You're a great one to talk. You hardly even touched your dinner. I thought pregnant women ate for two."

"That's an old wives tale. Besides, I had a late lunch."

"So did I, and I still ate twice as much as you."

Barb changed the subject. "Let's take our drinks out to the living room. There was a good movie on TV at eight. Loren and Buddy are probably already watching it."

"Is it that late? I should get going."

"For what? So you can curl up in bed alone with some weird book?" She emphasized the *alone*. "Now, if you had a date, say, with a certain, good-looking young doctor...."

"Actually, I have a movie to watch at home," Jeannie said quickly.

"Which one? Do you have it with you? We can all watch it here."

"Not this one. It's a home movie. I have to hunt up Mom's old projector to show it. You don't remember where she stored it, do you?"

"Matter of fact, I do, and you won't be watching your movie at home."

"I won't?"

"Not unless you take the projector with you," Barb replied with a smug smile. "I borrowed it from Mom a few years ago and never returned it. We can all watch your movie right here."

Jeannie hadn't planned on an audience, but she hated to appear secretive, so she helped her sister drag the old projector out of a closet and into the dining room. "Let's not bother Loren and Buddy," she said, when Barb suggested the living room. She had noticed her brother-in-law dozing on the couch, and she really didn't want to disturb him, not after promising Denis she wouldn't mention UFO's with Loren around. She knew he hadn't been sleeping well, either, and he'd looked exhausted at supper. Barb had mentioned that he had another appointment with Denis, too, tomorrow morning, and Jeannie figured he needed all the rest he could get.

"What's going on?" Buddy wandered into the dining room and plopped down on the floor. "Is this one of those weird movies of you and Mom when you were kids?" he asked, watching Jeannie thread the projector.

"Kind of like that," she said, smiling, "except we're not in it."

"Who is?"

"No one that I know of."

"What good's a movie without any people?"

"Maybe no good at all. Maybe real interesting. Let's watch it and see." She turned down the dimmer switch, then flicked the projector to the *forward* position. "This was taken in western Kansas in 1951," she explained, as the blank wall across the room lighted up.

At first, they saw nothing but a frame full of hazy sky-- pale gray, blue, then gray-blue.

"Bo-ring!" Buddy commented.

"Quiet, monster," Barb said, sharply. "If you don't like it, leave."

He scowled but kept quiet.

Pretty soon, the camera focused on the horizon. Now Jeannie could distinguish patches of sparse grass, what looked like miles of fences, and in the distance the brownish horizon, outlined against a clear blue sky. Then suddenly, she saw it, a single row of silver spots at the top of the frame. "There! Do you see them?"

Barb moved in closer. "I don't see anything."

"I do." Jumping up, Buddy ran to the wall and pointed to the silver spots. "See? There they are. Cool! What is it, Aunt Jeannie? UFO's?"

"It's sure not birds," Jeannie declared.

"I see it now," Barb said. "Somebody said that's birds? No way."

Jeannie agreed. As the footage rolled through the projector, the silver spots got bigger and closer, although not close enough to make out any detail. Then, without warning, one of them shot off to the right and disappeared.

"Man, did you see that?" Buddy exclaimed. "Where did it go?"

"I'm not sure." Puzzled, Jeannie continued to watch the remaining discs. "Wait a minute. There it is. I see five of them now." She shook her head. "How did that happen?"

A few seconds later, the same disc shot off again, but this time, the focus was on that one alone. The camera followed the silver spot for several seconds till it simply blinked out. When the camera moved back to its original position, the sky was empty.

"Turn that thing off."

"Loren!" Jeannie gasped.

"Turn it off!"

Jeannie flicked off the projector just as Barb reached for the light switch. The room brightened, and three pairs of eyes settled on the tall figure in the doorway. "What's the matter, Loren?"

Barb moved toward him but he waved her back, his eyes still fixed on the wall where the movie had shown.

"I hate those things."

"You hate them?"

"Yes. They--" He ran the back of his hand across his forehead. His fingers came away glistening with sweat.

"I don't know." He slumped into the nearest chair, cradling his head in his hands.

Barb knelt down beside him. "What is it, Loren? Tell me

what's wrong."

"I don't know. Something...." He paused and looked up. "God, I'm tired."

He looked totally drained and so did Barb. Buddy looked totally confused. He'd never seen his parents like this.

Jeannie made a quick decision. "Barb, why don't you and Loren go on upstairs and get a good night's sleep? Buddy and I will clean up down here."

"You don't mind?" She was still holding Loren's hand.

"Not a bit."

"Will you stay?"

Jeannie heard the hopeful note in her sister's voice. "I'll stay," she promised. "You two get going and get some rest." She put an arm around her nephew and gave him a hug. "Looks like you and I get KP duty, Bud. Think you can handle it?"

He shrugged. "Guess so."

"Good. Say good-night and we'll get it on." Jeannie smiled at her sister. "If we decide to make brownies, we'll save you a couple."

Buddy's eyes brightened. "Brownies! Oh boy! G'night, Mom. 'Night, Dad. Come on, Aunt Jeannie. Let's get those dishes done."

It was close to midnight when Jeannie crawled into bed. What a day. Many more like this one and she'd be gray-headed by the time she was thirty. After her bath, she had checked on Buddy and found him sprawled across his bottom bunk, breathing deeply. Across the hall, the master bedroom was dark and quiet, the door closed. Hopefully, Barb had calmed Loren down so he could get some rest.

With a deep sigh, she slid down under the thick comforter and closed her eyes. Immediately, a picture of Denis' rugged face clicked on in her mind. He did not look happy. Her eyes popped open, banishing the image, but as soon as she closed them, there he was again. She shouldn't have shown that film. She should have--darn! She'd never get to sleep this way. If she had been home, she would probably get up and work at the computer for an hour or two, but she couldn't do that here. Maybe there was a good movie on TV, something light and funny that would lull her to sleep, or at least distract her mind from a certain, very attractive doctor. She clicked on the remote. The small TV perched on the dresser opposite her bed came to life, and she finally settled on an old Doris Day movie with lots of music and light-hearted banter.

Several minutes passed. It was a good movie, one of her favorites, but she couldn't seem to concentrate on the screen. She kept listening....

The grandfather clock downstairs struck once, twelve-fifteen. Other than that one gong, she heard nothing, yet she felt the silence. What a dumb idea. You can't feel silence. But she had, once, the night of Buddy's party. The stillness that night had been thick, oppressive, almost tangible, and frightening. Jeannie shivered and pulled the covers back up to her chin.

From the corner of her eye, she caught a glimpse of the window on the east side of the house. The drapes had been drawn, but the window seemed unnaturally bright. Was there a full moon tonight? She couldn't remember, but the whole room was brighter now. It must be the moon.

The TV crackled. Slowly, almost against her will, Jeannie turned her head. The screen had changed to black and white snow. She thought about changing the channel, but she didn't want to move.

She stared straight ahead at the screen.

The TV blinked and the picture came back. Jeannie looked toward the window. It was dark, just like the rest of the room, except for the TV.

She stretched and groaned. She must have dozed off and dreamed that awful bird dream, where the ugly things surrounded her and held her down. Once of them had scratched the back of her neck and her leg.

Tired. So tired. Her body felt heavy and she ached all over. Should she get up for an aspirin? Too much trouble. She wanted to sleep. Her eyes closed and she sighed deeply. Just before drifting off, she heard the loud crack of rifle fire and the thunder of horses' hooves from the western movie playing on the TV.

* * *

"BARB, I don't think this is such a good idea." Jeannie looked out over Denis' wide front lawn and wondered again how she had let herself get talked into coming here this morning. "You should have let me stay with Buddy instead of sending him to Todd's house. Why don't I go on home and let you and Loren--"

"Jeannie, you promised." Barb took her sister's arm and urged her up the front steps. Loren walked on her left side, looking as reluctant as Jeannie to keep this appointment.

"That was then. This is now. Suppose Denis thinks I'm butting into his business?"

"Why would he think that?" Barb asked. "You're family. We want you here, isn't that right, Loren?"

He nodded absently. "That's right. Misery loves company."

Barb reached up and rang the bell.

Almost immediately, the door swung open. Too late to back out now. Denis must have seen them drive up.

"Loren, Barb, good to see you. Jeannie, this is a surprise."

"Barb asked me to come," she explained quickly.

"I see."

From the scowl on his face, he didn't see at all, but keeping up a steady stream of small talk, he didn't give her a chance to say more. He hung their coats in the hall closet, then led them into the living room. "Barb, why don't you and Jeannie make yourselves comfortable here. I'm not sure how long we'll be. Sometimes a hypnosis session can last a couple of hours."

"I want them with me."

Denis' eyes narrowed. "You're sure about that?"

Loren shoved his hands in his pants pockets. "I'm sure. Whatever comes out of this, I don't have any secrets from Barb."

"And Jeannie?"

He shrugged. "Don't ask me why. I just feel like she ought to be there."

Jeannie didn't miss Denis' frown. Surely, he didn't believe she had planned this, that she wanted information for her story.

"Whatever you want, Loren," Denis said abruptly. "We'll do whatever makes you comfortable." Carefully avoiding Jeannie, he led the way to his office.

* * *

"LOREN, the first thing we're going to do is concentrate on your breathing."

Fascinated, Jeannie watched Denis work with her brother-in-law, who sat in the recliner in front of the desk. Denis had drawn the drapes, and the only light in the room came from an old-fashioned Aladdin lamp on the corner of the desk. The only sound was the soft whir of the tape player recording the session.

Jeannie and Barb sat on the couch ten feet away on the left side of the room. Denis had warned them both not to concentrate on his instructions to Loren. "I don't know how susceptible either of you is to hypnosis, and I don't want you going under, too."

They had laughed and assured him they were in no danger of doing that, but he told them it could happen easily, without their even being aware of it. "Believe it or not, everyone spontaneously enters into trance every day, even several times a day. These situations are not usually called hypnosis, but that's what they are. Daydreaming or intense concentration on a book or a movie are also spontaneous hypnotic states.

"So, if you feel yourself listening hard to what I'm saying to Loren, shift your eyes around the room. Resist any urge to close them."

Jeannie smiled. "In other words, distract ourselves."

"Exactly."

For a moment, she thought he might say something more, but he turned abruptly and walked back to his desk. "Okay, Loren, I'm going to help you relax. Close your eyes, not too tight. That's right."

They worked on his breathing. "Each time you breathe out, feel yourself relax. Release your stored-up tension, your anxiety. When you breathe in, you relax even more."

As he instructed Loren to breathe in and out, in and out, Denis' deep voice took on a soothing rhythm. "Now you're going to see yourself relaxing. Visualize your muscles. Feel them letting go. First, your face muscles. Every inch of your face feels relaxed. Now your jaw, your neck and shoulders, your arms. Everything feels light and loose. Feel the tension drain from your back and stomach muscles, from your legs. Your whole body is sinking deeper and deeper into the chair."

His voice droned on. Jeannie felt herself unwinding. He had a wonderful voice, deep and soft.

"Jeannie!"

She jumped, as Barb hissed in her ear, "Stay awake!"

"I'm fine," she protested.

"Then keep your eyes open."

Jeannie stared at her sister. She hadn't closed her eyes, had she? She would know if she were falling asleep, wouldn't she? She shivered as she turned her attention back to the two men.

"Imagine a bright white light at the top of your head, inside your head." Denis continued talking to Loren, bringing the light down into his body, letting it spread slowly into every nerve, every cell, bringing him into a deeper and deeper state of relaxation. "The light now fills your whole body. Slowly, ever so slowly, it surrounds you, envelops you."

Jeannie admired the man's skill. Within ten minutes, he had her high-strung brother-in-law sunk limply into his chair, totally ignoring his surroundings. And he had her fighting to keep from joining him.

Denis leaned forward, his elbows on his desk, all his attention on his patient. "Loren, I'm going to count backward from ten, very slowly. You will hear only my voice. With each number, you will sink deeper and deeper. By the count of one, you will be in a deep state of relaxation. Ten. Nine. Eight."

Jeannie managed to distract herself while he counted. She watched Denis roll out his chair and carefully move it next to Loren, who now lay back in the recliner totally at ease, his eyes closed, his head lolled to one side. She fidgeted, tapped her fingers, looked around the room, and breathed a sigh of relief when Denis finally finished counting.

He settled back in his chair. "How do you feel, Loren?"

"Relaxed. Very relaxed."

"Good. What else are you feeling today?"

"Uh, slight headache. Not too bad today."

"Tell me about this headache."

"It, uh, feels like a sinus headache. Tight. Uh, here." He rubbed his forehead. "And here. Achy." His fingers moved down to the bridge of his nose. "My nose is stuffy. Uncomfortable." He sighed, and his hand dropped to his lap.

"Do you have this type of headache often?" Denis asked.

"Pretty much, the last few weeks."

"And before that?"

"No. Just recently."

Nodding, Denis made a notation on his desk pad. He

couldn't remember Loren complaining of headaches back in their college days either. "Do you remember when you had the first of these sinus headaches?"

"I--not exactly."

"Can you give me a rough idea of when you first felt them?"

"I'd rather not talk about that," Loren said firmly. He sat up straighter and folded his hands together tightly.

Bingo! He was on to something now. Denis jotted down a few more words. "Is there some reason you don't want to talk about that first headache, Loren?"

Squirming around as though trying to get comfortable, he mumbled, "Makes me--makes me nervous."

"I see." Denis leaned back in his chair, considering his options. He had a strong suspicion he was on the right track here. He just had to get Loren to follow it. "I want you to relax now," he said softly. "Next time you breathe out, you will feel so relaxed you just sink down into that chair."

"Mm-hmm." Loren sighed and settled back in the recliner.

"When you breathe in, you take in energy from the air. You're recharging yourself. For every breath in, you have to breathe out, and that's when you relax."

"Okay."

"Breathe in and out, in and out. You're getting very relaxed, sinking deeper and deeper into that chair." Denis watched Loren's breathing become slow and even. His head flopped to one side. "You're doing fine. How do you feel?"

"Good. Very relaxed. Best I've felt in a long time."

"That's great. Now I want you to go back. Go back in time to the day you had your first sinus headache. Tell me about that day, what you see, what you feel."

"Uh, it's Friday. I'm at the College. Just two classes, so I spend time at the library, researching a paper. I go home at four-thirty and take Barb and Buddy out for supper. We talk about the baby. Buddy's really excited about his new brother or sister. I'm worried about Barb, but she tells me everything is fine. Sure hope she doesn't have trouble like the last time.

"I leave the house again at six-thirty and go back to the College for my seminar. Buddy says he'll wait up for me and we'll have a cribbage game."

So far, he had mentioned nothing unusual, no crises, not even a confrontation of any kind that might bring on a headache. Nor had he given a date, but since Barb was pregnant, Denis figured he must be describing a Friday sometime in October.

"Driving down the highway." Loren balled his hands into fists, and his voice dropped even lower. Denis leaned forward to catch every word.

"Almost missed my exit. Something--something doesn't feel right. I lock my doors. Moon's real bright, right over my car. Crossland Park. Maybe I can turn there." Again, Loren squirmed in the chair, his head moving from side to side. "I--I want to get away from that light!"

He'd heard this before. Denis recognized the story as the same one Loren had told the night of Buddy's party.

"I turn into the Park and follow the road till it stops. That light--it followed me. God, I'm scared! I sit there and wait."

His voice actually quivered, and Denis had no doubt Loren was experiencing something very frightening, although whether or not it was real, he didn't know. "What are you waiting for, Loren?"

"I--I just wait."

"What happens next?"

"The light, it's--I start my car and drive away. Barb is waiting for me at home."

"What time do you get home, Loren?"

"It's--" He frowned. "That's strange. It's ten o'clock. I should have been home an hour ago."

That was the one thing Denis didn't want to hear. Could Loren actually have slipped into some sort of fantasy that night? If not, Denis had to consider Jeannie's explanation for the time lapse, and he wasn't ready to do that.

"Loren," he said quietly, "you can relax now. You're among friends and you're safe. Nothing can hurt you."

Loren sighed. "Yes."

"Now, while you are relaxed and safe, I want you to go back again to the night you stopped in Crossland Park. The moon was very bright. Tell me what happened while you sat in your car."

Immediately, Loren stiffened. "The light--not the moon. It's getting bigger, brighter." He twisted in the chair and lashed out with both arms. His face contorted into a look of pure terror. "Oh God, no! They're coming!"

11

"WHAT'S wrong with Loren?"

Catching Denis' frown and the quick shake of his head, Jeannie grasped her sister's arm and urged her back to the couch. "Shh. It's okay, Barb. Let Denis handle this. He knows what he's doing." But she didn't take her eyes off the two men across the room.

Neither did Barb. "Is he dreaming? What is going on?" she hissed.

"I think he's reliving something that happened to him," Jeannie replied. Her heart thumped madly as she watched Denis calm his patient. This was it, the breakthrough she'd been waiting for. Loren had seen a UFO the week before Buddy's party and now, under hypnosis, he was about to describe his experience.

"You're fine, Loren," Denis said, softly. "Very relaxed. Breathe deeply in and out, in and out. Each time you breathe out, you relax more and more. Good. Go back now to the night in Crossland Park. The light is over your car. What do you see? What do you feel?"

"The light covers my car. The light pulls me--pulls me from my car." Loren jerked up straight. "I don't want to go! I'm walking--no, floating down a ramp. God, I'm scared! They keep telling me, 'Don't be afraid. We won't hurt you.'

But I know they will!"

Barb grabbed Jeannie's hand, and they both strained to hear what Loren was saying.

"We're in a big round room. Cold in here." He shivered and hugged himself tightly. "They help me onto the table."

Barb looked at Jeannie and shivered, too. Her sister's face was white, completely drained of any color.

"Who helps you?" Denis asked. "Is someone with you?"

"Eyes. Big black eyes, like pools of black water, staring at me." He shuddered again. "Damn them anyway! I hate them! They take--take. No! Don't do that!" Gripping the arms of the chair, Loren strained forward, agony written all over his face.

"Relax," Denis said quickly. "I'm going to count to three. On the count of three, you will ease back in your chair, totally relaxed. One. Two. Three."

Slowly, Loren sank back into the cushions.

"Good. You are very relaxed now. Tell me what you see, what you feel."

Beads of sweat broke out on Loren's upper lip. He appeared to be pushing against invisible restraints. "I can't move! They're doing something to my nose. They say they won't hurt you, but they do. Don't do that!" He groaned in obvious pain, and then relaxed. "They put something in my nose, way up in the sinus cavity."

Denis scribbled on his pad. "Who did this to you?"

"Same--same ones. Always the same."

"What do they look like?"

"Small. Four, five feet. Big heads. Gray. Gray all over. Big black eyes. Weird eyes. They look at you and you know what they're thinking."

"Mental telepathy?"

"Not exactly. Something with those eyes."

"What happens now?"

Loren ran his tongue over dry lips. "They examine me, like a physical exam, but it's a black machine. Big, real big.

They run it over my body, close to my body." He sighed and seemed to sink down in the chair. "Going down the ramp, back to my car. I start driving home."

* * *

AFTER the hypnosis session, Denis spent another thirty minutes in his office talking to Loren alone, then with Barb.

Talk about feeling like a fifth wheel! Jeannie paced the living room while she waited, wishing she had her own car so she could get to her office and her computer. She wanted to write up Loren's session before she forgot some of the details. What she wouldn't give to have a copy of Denis' tape, but she didn't dare mention that yet, not until she knew he accepted what had happened to Loren as fact and not some fantasy his mind had conjured up. She had no intention of using the material until her brother-in-law gave his permission, but she wanted to have it to compare with the other cases she planned to pursue. She'd been thinking about calling Allen Kendrick and Mia Andrews about collaborating with her on a story or a book, and this afternoon seemed like a good time to get started.

She walked to the doorway again and glanced down the hall. What was taking them so long?

The office door opened and Denis strode into the hallway, his arm draped over Loren's shoulder. Barb held her husband's right hand. All three were smiling. "Now, don't forget, Loren," Denis said. "Nobody said your problems will go away overnight. You may experience a temporary reprieve, then find the symptoms have come back. You need to talk this out, and that means getting together again, possibly quite a few times."

"That's fine with me, Den." Loren grinned broadly, something Jeannie hadn't seen in weeks. "If you can make me feel this good, I'll come back every week, every day."

"I didn't do it," Denis said quickly. "You did. Be sure you keep that in mind."

"I will." Loren punched his friend lightly on the arm, then looked toward the living room. "Jeannie? Are you glad you came now?"

"You know I am." She fell in step as they walked toward the front door. "I take it you're feeling better?"

"A hundred percent better. I can't get over it. You'd think I'd be freaked with some of that stuff that came out, but I'm not. I don't like what I remembered. I feel used, violated even, but at least now I have some sort of explanation."

"Loren, remember what we talked about," Denis cautioned.

"I know, I know. But I can't help feeling that I'm on the right track here. What do you think, Jeannie? You're the one who believed all along there was something strange going on, with those lights in the yard and the way Dicey got so spooked that night." He shook his head. "This whole business is spooky as hell, but fascinating." A thought struck him. "Maybe I should read up on some of this stuff. Jeannie--"

"No." She and Denis spoke together. "I don't think you should read about anyone else's experience, Loren," she said quickly. "The less you know about what has happened to other people, the more credible your accounts will be."

Denis nodded. "I have to agree, although my concern is that you can easily clutter your subconscious mind with extraneous material."

Loren grinned. "Since that's the first time I've heard you two agree on anything, I guess I won't indulge my curiosity."

Denis hung back and walked with Jeannie to the car. Keeping his voice low enough that Loren and Barb wouldn't hear, he said, "Promise me you won't read too much into what you heard this morning."

She stopped and stared at him. "What's that supposed to mean?"

"Just that we don't know what we're dealing with here."

"Are you saying you don't believe Loren?"

"I'm saying we shouldn't jump to conclusions."

"That sounds like the same thing to me."

"Not at all." Denis took her hand and slid his fingers between hers. "I know that Loren believes what he said this morning."

"But you don't?"

"Sometimes the mind can create what it needs to hear."

"In other words, he could be fantasizing."

Denis shrugged. "Could be."

"What about the other hundreds, thousands of people who report the same experiences? It seems to me a mass fantasy of that proportion is a scarier possibility than believing these abductions actually take place."

"I don't know about anyone else," Denis said, stiffly. "Loren is my first patient to report seeing a UFO."

Jeannie stopped a few feet from the car. "You are the stubbornest, most infuriating man I have ever met," she declared between clenched teeth. "Maybe you're the one who should do some reading. It's a big, wonderful, mysterious world out there, Dr. Earley. I think it's about time for you to wake up and look at the stars, stretch your mind a bit. You may be surprised at the wonders out there just waiting for you to see them."

She swung around, but before she could stalk off, Denis caught her around the waist and turned her to face him. "Did anyone ever tell you you're cute when you're mad?" Then right there, in front of Barb and Loren, he slanted his firm lips across hers and kissed her.

* * *

SATURDAY, November 21
During his hypnosis session with Dr. Denis Earley, Loren Price spontaneously regressed to a recent close encounter of the fourth kind, a CEIV, during which he claimed to have been abducted by extra-terrestrials. The

encounter, as he described it, obviously terrified him, and he re-lived this terror during the regression. Dr. Price has no conscious memory of his abduction, although he remembers driving into Crossland Park (Tulsa) that night, apparently influenced by a bright light that "followed" him, then hovered over his car. The next thing he consciously remembers is driving home and arriving there an hour late.

Since the night in question, Dr. Price has been troubled by insomnia, recurrent nightmares, sinus-type headaches, and mysterious paranormal happenings in his home.

During the regression, he described several small gray beings who conducted a physical exam using a large black machine that "scanned" his body. He also re-lived an intrusive procedure on his nose, with something placed deep into a sinus cavity. This painful procedure obviously terrified him.

Jeannie's fingers came to a sudden halt on the keyboard. She looked up, then cautiously turned her head and looked around. Imagination. She couldn't have heard anything, not at this hour. The presses had stopped, and the last worker left the Sun Building over an hour ago. At eleven-thirty, hers was the only office light still burning, although peering into the hallway, she could see the dim glow of night lights spilling over from the front room. Being alone here hadn't bothered her before, not till she stopped typing and noticed the stillness that had settled over the building.

She had never worked this late before, and she wouldn't be here now if Eddie hadn't pounced on her when she showed up this afternoon. The State Police had cornered an escaped convict in downtown Benton, and Eddie wanted her to cover it. By the time she got back, wrote up the story for the Monday edition and grabbed a burger at Mack's Diner, it was after nine o'clock. She'd spent another couple of hours sorting through notes and organizing material, including this morning's hypnosis session, everything she had gathered for her article or book on UFO abductions.

Somewhere down the hall, she heard a creak. She turned around again. When the sound didn't repeat, she went back to her computer. Buildings creak, she told herself. Everything's fine. But she didn't feel comfortable. Five more minutes and she could leave.

"Good evening, Ms. MacLeod."

Jeannie jumped as though she'd been shot.

Ron Siegel stood in the doorway, as calm as if he had just strolled into the building during normal business hours. "Working rather late, aren't you?"

She opened her mouth, but no sound came out.

"You're not usually this quiet, Ms. MacLeod." His voice seemed to bounce around the silent room.

"What are you doing here?" The words came out in a quivering, half whisper.

"Talking to you, obviously."

"But the building is locked. You broke in."

"A minor detail." His pale face and small dark eyes remained expressionless.

"Minor? The police won't think it's so minor!" Something about this man made her so mad she forgot all about being scared and reached for the phone.

"Don't."

Her finger was still on the "nine" button when she looked up. He hadn't moved. His face could have been carved out of marble, except for his eyes. They glared at her, daring her to complete the call.

Slowly, she set the receiver back in its cradle. Her mind and heart racing, she never took her eyes off him as she inched her fingers back onto the keyboard. Whatever this man wanted, he probably wouldn't hurt her, not when she could identify him. But if she had something he wanted, say, a certain computer file, what would stop him from taking it, then denying he'd done it?

Siegel wasn't a tall man, no more than five-six or seven, and she was betting that he couldn't see her hands behind the computer monitor.

As her fingers slid into position, she continued to keep eye contact. Just a few more seconds. She clicked the mouse once, twice. Her document disappeared and the main menu lit up the screen. She breathed again. At least he wouldn't know what she'd been working on.

He took two steps into the room and stood directly in front of her, his legs apart, his hands clasped loosely in front of him. He wore the dark blue suit Jeannie had come to think of as his uniform, and his right hand stayed within easy reach of the slight bulge under his coat. She had no doubt what caused that bulge. The guy wasn't big, but he was calling the shots here. Still, it wouldn't hurt to let him know he hadn't completely cowed her.

"What do you want, Siegel?" Good. Her voiced sounded almost normal.

"We need to talk."

"I'm listening."

"You would be wise to do just that. We think you should get out of the UFO business. It's a dead end, a losing cause. You're wasting your time."

"Is that so? Seems to me you're going to a lot of trouble for something that's a lost cause."

"Believe me. It is."

Suddenly, Jeannie was angry, deep down to her toes fighting mad. She pushed back her chair and stood up. Siegel stiffened, but Jeannie didn't care. She didn't get angry very often, but when she did....

"Now you listen to me, Siegel." She spoke softly and distinctly, enunciating each word. "I don't like being told how to do my job, and I don't like being threatened."

She saw the spark of anger in his eyes and knew she should shut up now and leave well enough alone, but dammit, she was tired of his cat and mouse game. Drawing herself up to take advantage of every one of her sixty-seven inches, she heard the words spill out of her mouth as though they had a life of their own. "I don't know who you work for, Mr. Government Agent, but I do know you're mighty interested in UFO's, no matter how much you deny it. For all I know, our government may be working with those little gray monsters, helping them abduct innocent citizens.

"Besides that, I don't like bullies. So take yourself back to whatever super-secret, super-sneaky agency you crawled out of and tell them to leave me alone."

"I'm sorry you feel that way, Ms. MacLeod."

Calm, reasonable words, but Jeannie felt their icy edge slice right through her. Nor did she miss the tiny tic beating rapidly in Siegel's left temple. The man was furious. Suddenly drained, she gripped the edge of her desk for support.

Siegel's hand moved slowly and came to rest at his side.

Jeannie drew in a sharp breath. He wouldn't....

"You'll be hearing from us." He spun around--the phrase *about-face* shot through her mind--and disappeared down the dark hall toward the back of the building. Jeannie didn't doubt that he had a key to fit that door, and any other he wanted to open.

She sat back down. She wouldn't think about what had just happened, not yet. With shaking hands, she copied her latest data onto the diskette that held all her Tulsa Lights files. Five minutes later, she was driving down Main Street with her doors locked and her shoulder bag--with the disk and Virgil Owens' film--tucked under the seat between her legs.

She still hadn't allowed herself to think or react, but she could feel fear bubbling just beneath the surface, waiting to erupt. She kept checking her rear-view mirror, but so far had seen no sign of anyone following her. She was afraid to stop and equally afraid to go on home to her empty house. Siegel could be waiting anywhere.

What should she do?

Shuddering deeply, she felt the car swerve over the center line. Luckily, Benton streets were nearly deserted at midnight on Saturday nights. She managed to jerk the car back into her own lane, but she knew she wouldn't make it home at this rate. Turning sharply, she screeched into a brightly lit parking lot on the south side of the highway. Danners Country Store stayed open twenty-four hours. Nobody would bother her here.

A few minutes later, she pressed herself into the phone booth outside the store and dialed Information, although she didn't remember making a conscious decision to place this call. "Dr. Denis Earley. In Tulsa."

She got the number, then disconnected. She had dialed three digits before her mind went blank. She started all over again, this time writing down the number before she dialed. Her watch said twelve-fourteen. Would he think she was crazy, calling at this hour? He was probably sound asleep. What could he do anyway? He was twenty minutes away.

A deep shudder tore through her. She wanted to talk to Denis. She needed to--

He answered on the second ring. "Dr. Earley here."

This time it was relief that washed through her. No voice had ever sounded so good. "Denis? It's me, Jeannie."

"Jeannie?" His voice was thick, fuzzy. "What's the matter?"

"I saw Siegel."

Denis' voice sharpened abruptly. "Are you okay?"

"I'm--Yes, I'm fine."

"You don't sound fine. Are you home?"

"I was at the office. I drove to Danners, on the highway. Siegel broke in while I was working."

"Bastard!"

"Denis, I--I'm afraid to go home." There. She said it. She had to bite her lip to stop the trembling.

"Jeannie, I want you to stay right where you are. Wait in one of the booths at the front of the store, where the clerk can see you. Siegel's not there, is he?"

"No. I don't think he followed me."

"Good. Don't leave the store. I'll see you in fifteen minutes."

She heard a click, then the dial tone. Slowly, she hung up the phone and walked into the store. Fifteen minutes. She hoped he didn't get a ticket.

He made it in thirteen and a half, which included running two red lights on the west end of Benton. Jeannie's white car sat in front of the small convenience store. Denis pulled up right beside it.

She was watching for him just inside the front door. He didn't stop to think. He simply wrapped his arms around her and held her. She was shaking. Still holding her with one arm, he led her to a booth and slid in beside her. "You're freezing." He rubbed her icy hands between his. "How about some coffee?"

She nodded, and a few minutes later, they were both nursing steaming cups of sweetened coffee. A permanent hazy layer of smoke hung close to the ceiling, and from a tape player under the counter, a country singer bemoaned his faithless lover.

"Only thing missing," Denis mused, pointing to his cup, "is a jigger of good brandy."

"Is that one of Dr. Earley's famous, old-fashioned remedies?" Jeannie asked, sipping steaming coffee from a plastic cup.

"That's right. Guaranteed to perk up any damsel in distress."

She let out a long sigh. "You do seem to have a habit of rescuing me."

He knew she was thinking of the night he'd found her in Crossland Park. "Twice isn't a habit, but maybe you should leave well enough alone. I might not be around the next time."

"Denis, I--" She looked up from her cup. "Thank you for

coming," she whispered.

Could he drown in the deep midnight blue of her eyes? Like two tiny whirlpools, they tugged at him, pulling him closer, closer.

His eyes closed and their lips touched. Soft and sweet, she was everything he had ever wanted and never had. She swayed toward him, and even through several layers--his shirt and sweater, her blouse and wool blazer--he felt the rounded softness of her breasts against his chest. Desire exploded and filled him. He wanted this woman. He needed her. She was unique, special. "Jeannie," he murmured, burying his face in her long dark hair. "You must think I'm terrible, coming on to you when you're upset."

"Shh." She laid a finger against his lips. "Don't say that. Don't even think it. You don't see me pulling away, do you?"

"No, but--"

"But nothing. I wanted you to kiss me. It was the best thing you could have done. I was scared and now I feel better. A kiss fixes everything. Don't you remember your mom doing that when you were little?"

Denis scowled. He wasn't sure he liked his kiss being compared to a mother's.

"You know," Jeannie continued, "I don't have any idea what you were like as a little boy. You know a lot about me, but you never talk about yourself."

"Not tonight." He had no intention of rummaging around in the dusty corners of his childhood and young adulthood. "Tell me what happened at your office."

He thought she might not give it up, but finally she said, "You win, this time," and proceeded to give him a detailed account of her run-in with Ron Siegel.

"That bastard!" Denis said again. "I thought he was more of a nuisance than anything, but now I'm not so sure."

"That's the way I feel," Jeannie agreed. "He's a bully, and I'm not sure how far he'll go. When he left, I definitely felt threatened. Just how interested is he in the work I'm doing? Does he know or suspect what data I have, and if he does, how far will he go to get his hands on it?"

"Maybe it's not so much what you're doing as the fact that you're messing around with the subject at all. Sounds crazy, I know, but--"

"Not really. If the government knows more than it's saying and has been concealing information and misleading the public about UFO's for the past fifty years, then they sure don't want anyone else digging around and finding out the truth, especially someone like me."

"You mean the press?"

She nodded. "The *Benton News and Sun* may not be big, but what happens if something I write gets picked up by one of the news services? Or a major network? That could get messy."

"If Siegel wants what you have, why didn't he just take it tonight when he had the chance?" asked Denis.

"Like I said, he's a bully. He'll make sure his dirty work can't be traced back to him. A sneak attack in the park at night is more his style."

Denis didn't reply. Deep in thought, he sat drinking his coffee. Abruptly, he set down the empty cup. "Let's go."

"Go where?"

"To Tulsa. You know the way to my place. I'll follow you in my car."

"What are you talking about? I'm not going to Tulsa at this hour. It's almost one o'clock in the morning!"

"Jeannie, be reasonable. You can't stay at your house tonight. What if Siegel comes back?"

"I'll call the police."

"What if he gets into your house and you don't have a chance to call? You said he didn't have any trouble letting himself into your office building."

Exasperated, she threw up her hands. "I'll barricade my doors!"

"And what if--"

"Denis, I've had a long day. I'm dead on my feet. All I want to do is crawl into bed, my own bed, and sleep for ten hours straight. I admit I was scared when I called you, and I really appreciate your coming here in the middle of the night, but I can't go home with you."

"Why not? He won't look for you in Tulsa, and besides, I have an excellent alarm system in my house. If Siegel comes snooping around, we'll know it and have time to get help."

"I refuse to be scared out of my own home."

Damn, she was stubborn. Denis ran his fingers through his hair. Out of the corner of his eye, he saw the clerk watching them warily. Reaching for Jeannie, who had scooted to the far end of the booth, he said, "Okay, we'll do it your way."

"We will?"

"Yes, we will." With his hands on her shoulders, he urged her out of the booth. "Go ahead and drive home. I'll be right behind you."

"You're going to follow me home?"

"Right. And them I'm going to follow you into your house and crash on your couch. If Siegel decides to pay you an after-hours visit, he'll have to get past me first."

There was no arguing with the man. Bull-headed, arrogant, bossy, and a few other choice adjectives came to mind as she drove home, but Jeannie didn't have the energy to deal with them--or him--tonight. Let him crash, as he called it, at her house. He's the one who would lose the sleep. However, she did suggest he sleep in a bed, not on the couch. "This house has four bedrooms," she said, showing him through the first floor. "Why waste them? Besides, the couch isn't long enough for you."

He finally agreed, as long as he could stay downstairs, just in case Ron Siegel decided to come calling.

Two o'clock. Three o'clock.

Jeannie groaned and scrunched her feather pillow into a lopsided ball. She shouldn't have had that coffee. No, admit it. Her problem wasn't one cup of coffee. It was the man in the next room. She should have insisted he take the guest-room upstairs. Not that it would have made any difference. She doubted that one floor between them would have stopped her from thinking about him, or wanting him. She stretched out her leg, and her foot touched the bundle of fur rolled up in a ball on the far side of the bed. Kenworth didn't move. He certainly wasn't going to lose any sleep, just because she tossed and turned all night.

"Males," she muttered. "They're all alike." She flopped onto her back. Take the one just two thin doors away. While she lay here wide awake wondering why he didn't continue what he had started in the booth at Danners, he was probably dead to the world. Why did he have to be such a gentleman? Big help he'd be if Siegel showed up.

Her mind wandered a bit further. Had he simply stretched out on top of the bedspread? Or had he stripped and slid in between the cool sheets? She groaned again, imagining herself snuggled up to Denis' smooth, warm back. A delicious warmth spread through her whole body and her eyes slowly shut.

* * *

JEANNIE awoke the next morning to a room bright with sunshine, no cat, and the delectable aroma of coffee to remind her she wasn't alone in the house. She had just swung her feet over the side of the bed, when she heard a soft knock on her door.

"Room Service. Are you decent?"

She grabbed her robe. "Come in."

Bare-chested and barefoot, Denis wore his slate-gray Dockers low on his hips. Which answered her question from the night before about how he'd slept and triggered her very active imagination all over again. Grateful for anything to distract her wayward thoughts, she accepted one of the steaming mugs he held. "Mm-m, perfect."

"I hope you don't mind that I made myself at home," he said, sitting on the edge of her bed. "As soon as I walked into the hall, Ken told me it was time for breakfast."

"I know, and he's loud and not very subtle. I've decided we'll never agree on what is a respectable breakfast hour." Trying to ignore the nearly naked man sitting not more than two feet away, she took another quick swallow of coffee. "Did you sleep well?"

"Sure. No problem. How about you?"

"Okay." *Liar. Tell him the truth. That you couldn't sleep, knowing he was so close and yet so far away.*

"Jeannie?"

She didn't move.

"I was lying."

She looked at him.

"I wanted to come in here last night. I almost did, several times, but I couldn't."

"Why not?" she whispered. "I wanted you."

"I wanted you, too, but not like that, not after what you went through last night. I would have--" His words halting, he set his mug on the night stand and rose. As he paced the floor with long impatient strides, his left hand massaged his neck.

Jeannie put her cup down, too, and sat with her hands in her lap. "You would have what, Denis?"

He eased himself onto the bed, close, but careful not to touch her. "You don't know me, Jeannie. You don't know anything about me."

Anguish, hurt, and other emotions she couldn't even begin to identify had etched themselves into his rugged face, and Jeannie could no more stop herself than she could stop breathing. Reaching up, she gently traced the worry line between his brows. "I know you're a good man, a caring man. I know you would never deliberately hurt me or anyone else. And I care about you very much. What more do I need to know?"

"Ah, Jeannie." He took her in his arms and held her. "I would have felt like I was using you, and I know what that does to a person, to be used and discarded, like so much trash." Looking deep into her eyes, he said, "I'll never do that to you, Jeannie. I promise you that."

"You're talking about your wife?" she whispered.

He nodded. "It wouldn't have hurt so much if I hadn't loved her. That is, if the grand passion of youth--a one-sided passion, at that--can be called love. Hell, it doesn't matter. I thought I loved her." He looked at Jeannie uncertainly. "Are you sure you want to hear this?"

"I'm sure."

"Right. Well, I grew up in Tulsa. Dad's a surgeon. He's retired now, but he was well-known in this part of the state. Mom helped his career along as a professional volunteer doing good works. I was an unexpected surprise who disrupted their lives when they were in their late forties. I always figured they didn't quite know what to do with me. They love me, I suppose, in their own way, but they sure don't know how to show it. I managed okay till I got in high school, then I rebelled against them and everything else. Believe me, they put up with a lot. By the time they shipped me off to college, they made it plain I was to shape up and do what was expected of me, which meant following in Dad's footsteps.

"By that time, I'd figured out my antics were hurting myself more than anyone, and I probably would have done what they wanted if they hadn't pushed so hard. So I compromised. I had a great time at OU and kept my grades acceptable, but no more. If Loren hadn't take me under his wing my sophomore year, I'm not sure what would have happened, but I wouldn't be what I am today.

"He showed me what determination can do for a person. He'd grown up in California, in a bunch of foster homes, and he was determined to make something of himself. He came to OU on full scholarship and worked damn hard. I really admired him. He was the brother I'd never had, and he felt the same way about me. He knew I'd never see eye to eye with Dad, so he convinced me to get out of Oklahoma. He badgered me till I applied to Georgetown's graduate program and then said, 'I told you so' when they accepted me. Loren stayed here and got his doctorate in history. I went to D.C. and got mine in psychology. And I met Suzanne. She was beautiful, rich, and spoiled, and I fell for her hard."

Denis sighed and reached for Jeannie's hand. "At least, I can talk about it now. For years, I kept everything inside and let it fester. A psychologist friend of mine finally convinced me to talk it out before it burst open and buried me. I've always been grateful to Alex for helping me see what I was doing to myself.

"Anyway, I thought Suzanne was everything I could ever want in a woman, and I asked her to marry me. Her father is a Senator from South Carolina and our wedding was the social event of the season in Washington. I was twenty-four, working on my doctorate. Life was wonderful for six months. It took me that long to figure out why she had married me."

His hand tightened in hers. "Go on," she murmured.

Staring straight ahead, he said woodenly, "I was her plaything, a convenient pawn in her great scheme. I would get my doctorate and go into private practice in D.C., catering to the problems and psychoses of the rich and influential. She thought my income would nicely supplement her trust fund, allowing her to live the life she wanted. I soon found out that life didn't necessarily include me.

"Her first affair hurt, but I wanted to put it behind us and go on. She agreed, and for the next two years, I believed we might work things out, although I still didn't want the kind of practice she had planned for me. I liked the idea of working in a hospital clinic. I wanted to help people, not just make money. In time, I thought she would come around to my way of thinking.

"I was wrong. The night I got my degree, I told her I couldn't do what she wanted me to, and she told me she hadn't been sick with the flu the week before. She had gone to a private clinic and aborted her six-weeks fetus. And maybe, just maybe, it was mine."

12

HORRIFIED by such callousness, Jeannie whispered, "I'm so sorry, Denis."

He shrugged, a kind of "that's life" gesture. "I left that night. The story broke the next day, and before the divorce went through a few months later, I seriously considered murdering several city reporters. In their zeal to get every last detail about the Senator's family, they made my life hell."

No wonder Denis was less than enthusiastic about reporters, and overly cautious about a romantic involvement. Still thinking about his ex-wife, Jeannie said, "I can't imagine coping with such a betrayal."

"It wasn't easy," he replied, "but my practice helped. By that time, I had associated with a large clinic, doing the kind of work I like. And I had the boys."

"The boys?"

A faint smile touched his lips. "For several years, I was a foster parent to a number of underprivileged boys. Two of my boys have gone on to college."

Jeannie couldn't help picking up on the pride in his voice, but she heard something else, too. "And the others?" she asked.

His eyes turned that deep, gray-green, the stormy sea

color she had come to know well. "Like Eric," he said quietly. "He was eleven when he came to live with me, thirteen when he died."

"He died?"

Denis nodded. "Social Services sent him back to live with his family. Within three months, he had starved to death. I'd told them he was in danger, and I did everything I could to keep him with me, but our system believes in keeping families together. They took a chance, and Eric lost."

"That's horrible!" Jeannie gasped.

Again, he shrugged. "It happens."

"And you could accept that and just keep going?"

"No, I couldn't, but neither could I change what had happened. Eric was gone and I couldn't bring him back. It took me quite a while and several long talks with Alex before I accepted it."

"And that's when you left Washington?"

"Left or ran away. Whatever, I couldn't live there any more."

"It sounds to me like you decided to get on with your life," Jeannie said quietly. "How do you feel about it now? Are you glad you came back to Tulsa?"

With his hand on her shoulder, Denis tipped her back, pinning her down on the bed. His face, just inches from hers, looked deep into her eyes. "What do you think?"

She felt a swirl of desire deep within. "You're glad," she murmured, then watched his face move closer till it blurred. As though in slow motion, her eyelids drifted shut, and his firm lips touched hers. Heat coiled upward and spread to the very tips of her fingers and toes. Wrapping her arms around his neck, she wove her fingers through his thick, springy hair. The kiss went on and on forever, feeling, tasting, hands sliding under her gown, touching her bare skin, filling her with longing.

He eased away, and Jeannie felt his body heave with the

burden of restraint. She opened her eyes. "Wow!"

"Mm-m, you can say that again."

"Wow!'

Smiling, Denis murmured, "One of these days.…"

"But not today."

"Not today," he said, ruefully. "Believe it or not, I have a call to make at the hospital." He glanced at the clock. "At ten o'clock. That's just a little over an hour from now."

Avoiding his eyes, Jeannie stood up and wrapped her robe around her body. She walked over to the closet and yanked on the door. "You'd better get going if you want to make that appointment." As she stared at the rack of clothes in front of her, they all blurred together. So, he changed his mind. No big deal. She blinked rapidly, and the row of colors became a dancing, shimmering rainbow.

He stood right behind her. "Jeannie, I--promise me you'll be careful. Just because Siegel didn't show up last night doesn't mean he won't."

She nodded. *Just go! Please go, before I disgrace myself and embarrass you.*

Two strong arms reached around and locked in front of her. "Jeannie, you are very special to me. I'll call." He kissed her lightly on the cheek, then turned and walked out of the room.

* * *

NICE going, Earley! Real smooth.

Driving along the Expressway, he replayed the past half hour over and over in his mind. She probably thinks--God knows what she thinks, the way he came on to her, then backed off. If he was in her place, he'd have every right to call her a tease. He sure hoped she didn't accuse him of something worse, and all because he wanted her to under-stand him before they rushed into anything.

Groaning aloud, Denis told himself he'd really botched things this time. The woman would be his undoing. She tied him in knots and turned him every way but loose. Stubborn, fanciful, unreasonable, and, God help him, he wanted her more than he'd ever wanted anyone. Since the first moment he'd laid eyes on her--a shy, green-skinned vampire--he'd felt connected. Yes, that was the right word. Even when they argued, and they certainly did a lot of that, it somehow felt right.

With a sigh that turned into another groan, he pulled into his driveway and killed the engine. He had to get Jeannie out of his mind for the next few hours so he could concentrate on the business at hand, an interview with a new patient. Cutting across the front yard, he let himself in through the patio that adjoined the master bedroom suite on the west side of the house. As always when he came home, he felt a surge of welcome from this grand old Victorian house he'd bought. For an eighty-year-old structure, it was in remarkably good condition. Even the yard, an acre-and-a-half on a secluded corner, had been well-kept, its shrubbery and bushes trimmed, the tall oak trees and several elms strong and healthy. He even looked forward to the yard work that lay ahead of him next spring.

Something felt different. He noticed it the moment he stepped into the sitting room that connected with his office.

Someone's been in here. How he knew, he couldn't say, but he was sure someone had walked through this room since he'd left last night. He felt the presence as surely as though he'd seen footprints.

Ridiculous. He sounded like Loren and Barb, talking about their paranormal happenings, or Jeannie, describing her "weird" feelings in their house.

Vivid imaginings, that's all, brought on by heightened awareness and expectations. Still, he tiptoed past the plush, blue and white upholstered chairs and matching ottoman, and past the oversized cherry armoire till he stood in the doorway leading to his office. He scanned the room. At first, nothing appeared out of place, yet the feeling of an intruder persisted.

The first thing he noticed was the Aladdin lamp. It usually sat further back on the desk. Then his chair. He knew for a fact he had not left it back against the wall. And that's when he saw the middle drawer on the right side of the desk, slightly ajar. With a sinking feeling, he knew what he would find even before he pulled it open. Sure enough, the double file box held only one row of cassette tapes, the blank ones. The right side of the box was empty, the ninety-minute tape of Loren's hypnosis session gone. A quick search through his file cabinet confirmed what he'd suspected. Loren's folder had disappeared, too, and with it several pages of confidential interviews and test results.

Denis slumped into his chair. He'd have to report the theft, but it didn't take a genius to figure out who was responsible or why Ron Siegel hadn't showed up at Jeannie's house last night.

* * *

AFTER Denis left, Jeannie showered and dressed in her favorite blue cotton sweater and casual slacks, then, as she made her bed, she tried to decide how to spend the rest of the day. She knew what she'd like to do, but Denis had other ideas. Pounding her pillow back into shape, she allowed herself the pleasure of pretending, for a few seconds, that the feather-stuffed case was a certain good-looking, much too honorable young doctor! Ah well, he did say he would call, and he probably would. With a sigh, she buried her face in the soft down, then set it back on the bed and covered it with a quilted sham.

The small princess phone on her nightstand rang. Sitting on the edge of her bed, she picked it up. "Hello?"

"Jeannie MacLeod, please. This is Mia Andrews."

Immediately, Jeannie remembered her promise, and her failure, to contact the psychiatrist at her Oklahoma City office this past week. "Mia, it's good to hear from you. I'm sorry I didn't call. This week has been pretty hectic."

The woman laughed. "I know what you mean. Sometimes I'm my own worst enemy, getting involved in too many projects. Are you still thinking about writing an article on UFO's?"

"Definitely. In fact, it may turn into a series. The whole phenomenon reminds me of an onion. Peel off one layer and you turn up another."

"It sounds like you've come up with something interesting."

"You don't know the half of it," Jeannie declared. "Do you suppose we can get together sometime soon?"

"Actually, that's why I'm calling. Did I tell you about the support group I've organized for UFO abduction victims?"

"I don't think so."

"We meet once a week at a member's home. Most of the people live in the Oklahoma City area, but today we're meeting in Tulsa, and I realized you aren't that far away. Would you like to come?"

"I'd love to. What time and where?"

Mia gave her the information, then added, "Bring your sister along, if you think she'd be interested. I have to admit I was intrigued when you mentioned that she has a scoop-shaped scar on her leg."

Jeannie felt a tremor ripple through her. Anxiety? Apprehension? "I'm not sure about Barb. She's had a lot on her mind lately, but I'll ask."

As soon as she hung up, Jeannie dialed Barb's number. Her sister surprised her by agreeing to come along, and with very little persuasion. "Loren feels so much better than he did before yesterday's session, he took Buddy to the golf course, and I'm just rattling around alone in this house." Lowering her voice, she said, "He thinks Denis is some kind of miracle worker, although he's still not sure he believes everything he said under hypnosis."

"Neither does Denis," Jeannie replied, then, curious, she

added, "How about you?"

"I'm trying to keep an open mind, although I really don't like the idea of a bunch of--whatever they are--fooling around with my husband."

Or with you either. Frowning, Jeannie realized that's what Barb's scar could mean, and yet she had simply forgotten all about it till Mia mentioned it a few minutes ago. Now she wondered why. Was she afraid of what she might learn?

"Barb to Jeannie. Come in, Sis."

"Mm-m, right here."

"What time will you pick me up?"

"Is one-thirty okay?" As she hung up the phone, she wondered what she was getting herself into this time.

* * *

LATE afternoon shadows spread across the large, comfortable living room at Cheryl Miller's two-story brick home in Tulsa. Eleven people, ranging in age from nineteen to fifty-six, sat on the floor, the couch, two wing-back chairs, and several folding chairs, all their attention riveted on the girl who sat Indian-style on the thick carpet in the middle of the room. Half-filled coffee cups and forgotten glasses of tea cluttered the coffee table. No one moved. The only sound in the room was the clear, though sometimes shaky voice of Diane Merino, a petite, curvaceous teenager with the smooth olive skin and deep brown eyes of her Italian ancestors.

"There's a certain dream," she said slowly. "I've had it all my life, several times a year, and it always seems so real, so different from any other. Sometimes I'm afraid to go to sleep at night. I'm afraid of that dream. I'm afraid they'll come and take me." Her voice faded into a whisper, and she stared down at her hands, which she kept twisting together in her lap. Finally, she looked over at a slender blonde woman across the room "If--I hadn't heard Mary's story, I probably wouldn't have the nerve to tell you this."

Diane squared her shoulders and her voice grew stronger. "My family says I'm imagining things, That it's just a dream and I should forget it. But I can't. Dr. Andrews--Mia--says talking about it will help. So when I was little, maybe three or four, I used to dream they--the little gray men--took me to their home in the sky. It was a big round room filled with purple and gold light. It was pretty, but I didn't like it when they put me on the table and touched me. I always cried. I wanted to go home, but they said they had to do this, that I was helping them.

"When I was thirteen, the dream changed. They started doing other things to me. It was all very clinical, but I felt violated. They never ask permission. They do whatever they want. My feelings aren't important to them." She paused and took a deep breath. "I knew they were using me, using my eggs, experimenting. I hated it. I hate them!

"Then, late last summer, in August I dreamed they--one of those creatures--had sex with me. I had no choice. It was so real, but still I kept telling myself I'd been dreaming. Except, when I woke up the next morning, I was lying at the bottom of my bed, and my pajamas lay in a pile on the floor."

"Oh, my God." Barb's words, barely above a whisper, seemed to express the sentiments of several people, and a buzz of comments echoed through the room.

Jeannie took her sister's hand. It was ice cold, and her mouth had drawn into a tight line in her pale face. "Are you okay, Sis?"

She nodded, but her eyes never left Diane's face.

"I knew something happened that night," the young woman continued, "but I couldn't believe what I had dreamed. I guess I didn't want to believe it, although I couldn't explain why my body ached all over, especially in the pelvic area. So I tried not to think about it or about the dream. Two months later, I couldn't ignore it any more. I had missed my last two periods. I knew I was pregnant."

Her voice had dropped to a whisper and she looked around the room, stopping at each person's face for several seconds. "You all don't know me," she said softly, "so you don't have any reason to believe me, but I swear that what I'm saying is true. I don't sleep around. I've never--I've never had sex, not even with my boyfriend. I've been taught to save myself for my husband, and I plan to do just that. But my body was changing. I could see and feel the differences. I was pregnant. I know I was."

Jeannie believed her. How could she not? No one was that good an actress. A tear rolled down the girl's face, and her voice broke several times as she finished her story. "I didn't know what to do, so I didn't do anything. I guess I was waiting for a miracle--another one.

"Well, I got it. Last month, right before Halloween, I had the dream again. This time I saw myself lying on a hard table with my feet up, like in the doctor's office. *They* were there, those horrible little gray creatures, and I couldn't move or talk or anything. And they took something from me. They reached inside me and took--they took my baby. I know they did. When I woke up the next morning, I felt crampy. There were spots of blood on my sheets and I started my period that day."

Stunned silence, then several people spoke at once. "Unbelievable, but I believe her."

"The same thing happened to me!"

"They're heartless, absolutely no feelings."

"Dr. Andrews, what can we do? Can you help her? Can anyone help us?"

Mia had been sitting beside Diane as she told her story. Now she gave the girl a hug and turned to the rest of the group. "That's a good question, Cheryl, one we've all asked ourselves. I wish I could say I'll make these experiences go away, but I can't do that. Through counseling and some-times hypnosis, I can help you understand and accept what has happened, what continues to happen to you. We can put the abduction experience into perspective, so you understand that you are not crazy, you are not alone, that these things happen to thousands of people all over the world. We can support one another, be there when another 'experiencer' needs us."

"And we can keep hounding the government through our elected officials," Mary Healey spoke up. "We can demand that they let us know about UFO's and abductions, that we refuse to accept any more lies or cover-ups."

"Absolutely," Mia agreed. "Each classified document released through FOIA is another small victory for each one of us." Smiling, she said, "That's one of the reasons I asked Jeannie MacLeod to join us today. As I mentioned when I introduced her earlier, she's a reporter, working on a story that will let people know the truth about UFO's and abductions by UFO entities. What else can you tell us about your work, Jeannie?"

Looking out over the dozen or so faces around her, Jeannie again was struck by the diversity of this group. Just like the UFORA meeting in Tulsa, these people came from all walks of life. Professionals, blue collar workers, housewives and students; rich, poor, young, old, black, white, and an Asian-American, they had come together to solve a puzzle that united them on the most basic level, as human beings. To be part of such a group gave her a sense of purpose she had never felt before, and it felt good.

"I can tell you how much I appreciate being included here today," she said, answering Mia's question. "Hearing your stories has made me realize the importance of my project. I'm more convinced than ever that what is happening to you has profound and far-reaching implications. Someone or something is tampering with the development of the human race and we, all of us, are entitled to know why. We are also entitled to say yes or no to these experiments, if that indeed is what's going on. We are no one's pawns. This is what I will write about, Tulsa area people affected by the UFO phenomenon. And again, let me assure you that anyone I talk to who requests it, will have complete anonymity."

Several people clapped as she sat down. Jeannie felt her face getting warm, but she wasn't embarrassed by what she had said. She meant every word. They broke up into small groups and she spoke with each abductee, ending up with names and phone numbers of eight people who were willing to talk to her about their experiences. Talk about good luck! Her confidence level reached an all-time high, and she began to believe she really might write her big story.

"So, what did you think?" Mia joined her and Barb as they walked toward the door. It was after five and the crowd had started to thin out.

"This was an amazing few hours," Jeannie declared. "I can't imagine anyone denying the existence of UFO's after hearing this testimony."

"You'd be surprised," Mia replied, smiling. "Many people are simply not ready for something so alien to their own perceived sense of reality. What did you think, Barb?"

"I'm not sure what to think. I mean, some of this stuff is too weird, and yet...." She shivered and hugged herself tightly. "I guess it's no worse than what Loren says happened to him."

Frowning, Mia turned to Jeannie.

"Loren is Barb's husband," Jeannie explained. "Denis--Dr. Earley--regressed him under hypnosis yesterday morning, and he related a UFO abduction that supposedly happened just a few weeks ago."

"Just him?" Mia asked. "Or did it involve others in the family?"

"Just Loren," Barb replied quickly. " At least, I hope no one else is involved. I'm not ready for that."

"You do realize, don't you, that very often abductions

include several family members?"

Barb's eyes grew big and round as she stared at Mia. "No, I wasn't aware of that."

Jeannie watched her sister's hand move unconsciously over her stomach. She tried to catch Mia's eyes to warn her, but the woman had focused all her attention on Barb.

Barb blanched. "I think I'd better sit down."

"She's pregnant," Jeannie explained quietly, as they led Barb to the couch. "I didn't want to upset her, so I hadn't mentioned the scar yet."

"What scar? What are you talking about?" Barb demanded.

"That scoop-shaped scar on the back of your leg," Jeannie said reluctantly. "You remember, the one you got when we were kids. I told Mia about it in Tulsa after she showed a similar scar on the leg of an abduction victim."

"I'm so sorry." Mia sat down on the arm of the couch. "I just assumed--are you all right?" she asked Barb.

"I--yes. I just--I'm not usually such a wimp, but all this. Hearing Diane's story." She looked up at Mia. "If what she said is true, could it be? Is it possible?"

"That what happened to Diane could happen to you? How far along are you, Barb?"

"About four months."

"You've had an ultrasound?"

"Yes. The doctor says the baby looks perfect."

"Then he is and you shouldn't worry about it. If something was wrong, believe me, you would know by now. Besides, from all the case studies I've read and heard, what happened to Diane resolves itself by three months."

"You mean, they take the baby within three months?"

"That's right."

Closing her eyes, Barb leaned back against the cushions. "Thank God. I was imagining all sorts of things, and then when you mentioned my scar...." Her eyes flew open. "Do you really think--"

"May I take a look at it?" Mia asked.

Barb reached down and rolled up her right pants leg. "I haven't thought about this in years, but I remember it was right by my knee." She turned her leg. Mia and Jeannie both scooted closer.

"There, I see it." Jeannie ran her finger over the half-inch indentation high on the side of her sister's calf. "It looks just like I remember it."

"I've seen several others just like it," Mia said quietly. "In each case, the person has reported a number of abduction experiences."

"I don't remember anything like that," Barb declared.

"Do you know how you got the scar?"

"We were playing in the front yard."

"It was summer," Jeannie said slowly. "Right before your eighth birthday."

"That's right. I remember the bees buzzing around bothering us. I ran into the woods. A bee was chasing me, buzzing in my ear. I must have fallen and cut myself. We weren't supposed to go into the woods. That's why I didn't want to tell Mom about the cut. I remember it didn't bleed very much."

"Wasn't that the day the new kid came over to play?" Jeannie asked. "I don't remember his name, but he was kind of funny looking."

"I don't remember anyone else." Shrugging, she said, "Anyway, it doesn't matter."

"It might," Mia said softly.

"What do you mean?" asked Barb.

"I find some of the things you've mentioned very interesting."

Jeannie frowned. "What things?"

"The bee buzzing, for instance. Many people report such a sound right before an abduction experience. And the strange little boy you remember, but Barb doesn't. Who was he? Where did he come from? And why did you promise not to tell anyone about the cut on your sister's leg?"

"We weren't supposed to be in the woods--"

"No, there was something else." The answer hovered close, very close. Frustrated, Jeannie shook her head. "I can't remember."

"Then it's probably not important," Barb said.

"I feel like it is," Jeannie insisted.

Mia smiled. "Maybe we've nudged something in your subconscious that's been dormant for a long time."

Jeannie wasn't sure she liked that idea.

"How about you?" Barb said suddenly. "Maybe you have some unexplained scars, too."

She knew she didn't like that idea. "I don't think--"

"Well, why don't you look?"

Jeannie stared at her sister. "You're serious, aren't you?"

"Darned right! I'm not sure if I'll feel better or worse, but I'd like to know if I'm the only one."

"I can't believe I'm doing this!" Bending over, Jeannie pushed up the right leg of her pale gray slacks. "I don't think I can get it up to my knee."

"You don't have to."

"What do you mean?"

"Look here." Mia reached down and ran her forefinger across Jeannie's shinbone. "You do have a scoop mark, and unless I'm very much mistaken, this one isn't twenty years old. I'd say it was made quite recently, within the last few weeks."

13

KENWORTH and the shrill jangle of the telephone greeted Jeannie as she opened the entry door and stepped into her kitchen. The red and white tea kettle clock on the far wall said six-forty.

She set down her purse, scooped up the cat and hurried through the kitchen into the hallway, where the old-fashioned phone sat on a small table. The answering machine was blinking, too. Three blinks, three messages. She sure had become popular lately.

She grabbed the receiver. "Hello?"

"Jeannie?"

A warm feeling shot through her at the sound of Denis' voice. "Don't tell me you expected someone else." Smiling and cuddling Ken in her lap, she settled into the ladderback chair by the phone.

"I guess I expected your machine again. I've been calling all day."

"I just walked through the door. What's up?"

"It's, uh, kind of hard to explain. Will you be home tonight? I could come by."

"I'll be here, but why can't you tell me over the phone?"

"I'd rather not. Trust me on this one, Jeannie."

"I do," she said, softly. "When will I see you?"

"Have you had supper?"

"Not yet. I was about to raid the refrigerator."

"How about pizza? I could stop at Dominic's."

Visions of bubbling cheese and gobs of pepperoni danced in her head, and her stomach rumbled, as though suddenly realizing it hadn't been fed since morning. The sudden noise jolted Kenworth, and he jumped off her lap with a loud protest. "I'd love it, anything but anchovies or pineapple."

"Double pepperoni and extra cheese?"

The man must be psychic! "Just don't take long. I'm starved."

"Forty-five minutes. And don't forget to feed that cat before I get there. I heard what he said when I mentioned pizza, and he doesn't get any."

Laughing, Jeannie hung up the phone. How could one person make her feel so good? She felt like she had known him forever, like they were opposite sides of the same coin.

Uh oh. That line of thinking could get her in trouble.

The man was stubborn and illogical. They didn't agree on anything, except possibly, double pepperoni pizza. Besides, she didn't have time now for a relationship. Just hours ago, her life had been turned into a soap opera filled with UFO's and aliens. She and Barb had talked on the way home from Mia's house, but neither of them was ready to delve too deeply into the possibility that they both may have had a lifetime of abductions. Denis sure wouldn't believe that, and Jeannie just didn't want to think about it now. Sooner or later, she would have to come to grips with what she had learned this afternoon, and it would have to be later. First, she had a story to write, a great story that just possibly could be the start of a whole new career. And second, she had a date in less than an hour with a man who made her want impossible things.

She jumped up and started pacing the hall. It simply wouldn't work, not now, not ever. Somehow, she had to figure out how to stop these irrational feelings that filled her heart whenever she saw Denis. Thank goodness they hadn't made love this morning. Just thinking about his lean body next to hers gave her the jitters. Better think of something else fast, like why he was really coming back tonight.

There. The question she'd been trying to ignore. Why, indeed, if not to finish what they had started this morning.

He wants to talk.

Sure, he does. And what else did he want? After she had practically thrown herself at him this morning, would she resist him now if he wanted what she'd so willingly offered just hours ago?

More important, could she possibly make love with him without losing her heart?

Kenworth brushed against her pants, then wove between her legs. She picked him up again and buried her face in his warm brown fur. "How about Tuna Delight for supper?" she murmured, heading back to the kitchen. "With warm mozzarella for dessert?"

He meowed his complete agreement.

"I just have to be firm," she continued, scooping out the cat food. "If I'm not ready, I'm not ready. It's that simple."

Ken agreed again and attacked his dinner.

"He'll just have to understand that this is a very turbulent time in my life, and I don't need any more complications." *Turbulent.* What an understatement. After learning what she did this afternoon, Jeannie had a feeling her life had changed forever.

But first things first. Right now, ready or not, she had a date to get ready for. Leaving Ken to his meal, she dashed into the bathroom for a quick shower. Twenty minutes later, with her hair brushed and pulled back, and wearing her favorite red and black striped tunic over black stirrup pants, she spread a clean cloth on the kitchen table and then added matching tumblers and plates, silverware, and napkins. Finally, she put on a pot of coffee and sat down to wait for Denis. Two minutes later, she jumped up again, this time to turn on the small radio by the window. Public Radio just happened to broadcast a two-hour segment of romantic classics on Sunday evenings. Coincidence? Of course. Jeannie often listened to NPR.

The problem was, this felt so good. She liked sitting here, sipping fresh coffee, waiting for him to share her supper. Even more, she liked the idea of him sharing her life.

Not that he'd asked. This was one night, not a lifetime. Just because she admitted to certain feelings for the man didn't mean she loved him, or that he felt the same way.

Groaning, she wondered how her life had become so complicated in just a few short weeks.

* * *

"MMM...That was great." With a contented sigh, Jeannie pushed away her plate and settled back in her chair.

"Sure you don't want to share this one?" Denis asked, reaching into the flat cardboard box for the last slice of pizza.

"I want to, but I can't." Out of the corner of her eye, she caught a glimpse of Kenworth sitting between their chairs, following Denis' every move with his big yellow eyes. "Ken will be glad to help you," she said, innocently.

"That cat will burst if he has another bite. And you would blame me." Denis sank his teeth into the thick soft cheese. "I refuse to contribute to your pet's demise."

Ken waited till the last bit disappeared, then with an indignant "meow-rr," he stalked off into the dining room. Grinning, Denis washed down the pizza with the last of his soft drink while Jeannie started clearing the table.

"Don't." His hand reached out and covered hers.

Startled, she looked up and found his eyes boring into hers. "I just--"

"I know what you're doing. Your little chaperone left, and you suddenly realized it's just you and I. And that makes you nervous."

"No." The denial died on her lips. "Yes."

"Good." His hand tightened. "We can be honest with each other."

She sat back down.

"I've been thinking," he began, "about this morning."

"Is that what this is all about?" She looked around at the empty box and dishes.

He shrugged, then grinned sheepishly. "I really did need to talk to you, but I could have done that over the phone, so yes, it's about this morning. I don't like unfinished business."

Jeannie's heartbeat quickened. "That's what you call this morning, unfinished business?"

"Definitely."

Their voices dropped to half-whispers, their eyes spoke of smoldering desires.

"Denis--"

"Jeannie--ah, hell." Even as the muffled oath slipped through, their lips met, and the fire erupted. His hunger matched hers, as though the meal they had just shared had merely whetted their appetites for the love feast they both craved.

Somehow, she was on his lap as his mouth devoured hers, raining kisses on her face, her neck. His hands roamed freely, cupping, cradling, worshipping her body. She answered his assault with her own, matching him kiss for kiss, touch for touch, till finally her breath came in short staccato bursts. "Denis, I--"

He buried his face in the soft knit of her jersey top. "I'm overwhelmed," he whispered. "In over my head." He hesitated, then shifted till he was looking straight at her. "Jeannie?"

"Mm-m?"

"I want you. I need you. I want to make love with you. Right now. Right here."

He sounded a bit unsure of himself, but she couldn't mistake the very real desire in his clear green eyes. Knowing she couldn't deny him, she took his hand in hers. "Right here?" she said, teasing. "My bedroom might be more comfortable."

"Witch," he growled, and nipping her lightly on the ear, he wrapped one arm around her waist and hurried her down the hallway to her room.

Laughing, breathless, they tumbled together onto her big, four-poster bed. From that moment, time stood still for Jeannie. She had lived in this room, with its old-fashioned mahogany furniture and predictable flowered wallpaper, all her life. She and Denis had sat on this bed just this morning and yet now, as she lay in the arms of the man who was about to become her lover, the familiar surroundings edged away, taking on a surrealistic quality instead, bringing the two of them into sharper focus.

"I've dreamed of this for days, weeks." Denis slid his hands under her tunic, letting them roam freely over her warm, smooth skin. "Every time I'm with you, it's been torture keeping my distance, but I knew you weren't ready for this."

Breathless, "I've wanted you, too." She pressed herself closer, reveling in the hardness of his body. "But you're right. I wasn't ready."

"And you are now? You're sure?"

"Yes," she whispered, remembering the feeling she had admitted to herself just a short time before. She had rationalized that they couldn't be together, yet here they were. She might not be ready for love, but she could no longer deny its reality or turn it away. "Oh, yes!" And joyfully, completely, she gave herself to Denis, joining him in the ancient ritual of love, as old as time itself.

* * *

"JEANNIE?"

"Hmmm?"

"We still need to talk."

Unwilling to give up the delicious afterglow of their lovemaking, she burrowed deeper under the quilt they had pulled up.

Denis chuckled and pushed himself back against a pillow, careful to keep his arm wrapped tightly around her. "I'll bet you're fun to wake up in the morning."

"I don't do mornings," she mumbled.

He kissed her lightly on the tip of her nose. "Bet I can change that."

"Bet you can't."

"We'll work on it," he promised. "But since you're awake–"

"I know, I know. We have to talk." With a huge sigh, she scooted back and hitched the quilt up to her chin. Beneath the covers, their naked bodies lay side by side, not an easy thing to ignore, but Denis seemed determined.

"I tried to reach you all day," he began.

Jeannie felt a twinge of guilt that she hadn't told him about the meeting in Tulsa yet. She would, of course. Soon. Very soon.

"I wanted to tell you what happened after I left here this morning. You knew I had an appointment at the clinic."

She nodded.

"I went home to shower and change. As soon as I walked into the house, I knew someone had been there."

Her eyes widened. "Someone broke into your house?"

"Someone came in, yes. Technically, it wasn't a break-in. The police found no sign of forced entry."

Jeannie immediately thought of Ron Siegel's very quiet, very efficient entry into the Sun Building. "A burglary?"

He nodded. "But a strange one. The only thing taken was a single file and a tape from my office."

A sinking sensation settled deep in the pit of her stomach. "Loren's file."

"And the tape of yesterday's hypnosis session."

"What did you tell the police?"

"As little as possible. They'll never get anything on him anyway."

"You think it was Siegel?"

"Who else?"

She nodded. "But we can't prove a thing."

"What I can't figure out is why he's harassing us. Neither the tape nor the records are worth anything to him, so why bother?"

"Maybe," Jeannie said slowly, "he's warning us. He didn't want us in Crossland Park either. Could be we're getting too close."

"To what?"

"The truth."

Denis' eyes narrowed. "About UFO's?"

"Yes. I know it's hard for you to accept, Denis, but you have to admit that Siegel seems to believe in them."

Pulling her tighter against him, he nuzzled his face into her thick hair, which had long since escaped its band and now tumbled loose around her face. "You're right. It's not easy to go against all my instincts."

"Which tell you that UFO's and little gray men can't possibly invade our lives and kidnap people."

"That's right."

"Even though hundreds, even thousands of people claim that's exactly what has happened to them, including your very sensible, down-to-earth friend, Loren Price."

"There has to be another answer."

"And if there isn't?" By this time, their voices had dropped to whispers, and Denis' hands had inched down to lay flat against her belly. His smooth cheek--he must have shaved right before coming here--rubbed against hers, and every few seconds he breathed softly in her ear.

It drove her crazy.

"If there is no other explanation, I'll have to apologize for doubting you," he said, quietly.

"But you don't expect that to happen."

With a deep sigh, he turned her around to face him. "No, I don't. I'm a realist, Jeannie."

A small bubble of anger exploded inside, very close to the surface, and she twisted out of Denis' arms. "I think you're deluding yourself, Dr. Earley. Your view of reality is so narrow, you wouldn't recognize the truth if it slapped you in the face."

"Hey, don't be mad!" Denis pulled her back against him.

"I'm not mad," she sputtered. "I'm--I'm--"

"Mad." Grinning, he bent down and touched his lips to hers.

She swayed against him, powerless to stop the immediate assault on her senses as she slid deeper and deeper into the safe cocoon of shared feelings. Her breath mingled with his. Her eager fingers kneaded the tight muscles of his shoulders and back as she urged him closer, ever closer. They shuddered, then sighed deeply in unison, as the tension eased and they spiraled together back to earth.

"Wow."

She couldn't say a word, but held him tightly till her world stopped spinning.

"You are something else, woman. What am I going to do with you?"

Love me, love me, love me.

But he didn't, and reluctantly, Jeannie moved to the edge of the bed.

She felt like she'd been cut loose from her lifeline.

"You could help me figure out what to do about Siegel," she said, avoiding Denis' eyes. "Isn't that why you came here? And insisted that we talk about him? Right now. Tonight."

For just a second, she thought, hoped he might not

accept her decision, but finally, he nodded. "That's why I came. But not why I stayed. Or why I'll be back. What we shared tonight was very special, Jeannie."

Special. Oh, yes. Loving Denis Earley was definitely special, almost as special as being loved by him. But she would never beg him to say the words. It took all her will power to stay quiet and watch him ease his lean body into his jeans. Just a word or two and he would hustle her right back into bed, and now she knew the experience would be breathtaking, beautiful, incomparable. Was she making a mistake?

No. Much as she wanted to, she couldn't make Denis love her. Maybe someday....

And maybe not.

She pushed that painful thought to a faraway corner of her mind and concentrated on Siegel. He was something they could deal with right now, before he really hurt somebody. He'd already come too close. "I wish Siegel would go away and leave us alone."

"Not likely," Denis said, frowning at her abrupt change of subject. "Unless he finishes his job here or gets called back to Washington."

"Called back? You mean, if they put him on a different project?"

"That, or maybe if he goofed up big time, although I can't see that happening. The guy is a royal pain, but he's a pro. He hasn't made any mistakes."

"So far." The germ of an idea began to skip around in Jeannie's mind.

"I'm almost afraid to ask what's going on in that fertile little brain of yours."

She ignored him. "I wonder what would happen if Siegel got mixed up with the local police."

"Not much," Denis replied. "One call to whatever agency in Washington, and he'd be free and clear."

"Even if he's charged with a crime like armed robbery?"

"That might take two phone calls."

"Be serious!" With the twisted sheet pulled up to her chin, she grabbed the clothes she had left lying on the floor and quickly slipped them on. "It might just get him out of our hair."

"How? We may suspect him, but we don't have a shred of proof that he got into my house."

"That was last time."

"Last?" Denis quickly pulled his knit shirt over his head. "Why do I have the feeling I'm not going to like what you're thinking?"

"I can't imagine." Jeannie stood at the dresser, trying to tame her flyaway hair. "I rather like it myself." In fact, the more she thought about it, the better her idea sounded. Not only could they get rid of Siegel, she might also get the answers to some very puzzling questions, answers that could help her with the UFO story she was more determined than ever to write.

"Okay." A deep sigh. "Let's have it."

The words tumbled out quickly as ideas formed in her mind. "Suppose we catch Siegel breaking into your office? We know he carries a gun. Voila! Armed robbery! Even if he weasels out of charges, he'll be in enough hot water that they'll call him back to Washington. And we'll be rid of him."

Halfway through her spiel, Denis started shaking his head. "It won't work. The man's not a fool. Why would he come back? I don't have another thing he could possibly want."

She played her trump. "But you will. Another tape, after my hypnosis session."

For once, she had the satisfaction of seeing Denis absolutely speechless for about five seconds.

"That's crazy," he sputtered. "Why would I hypnotize you?"

"Because another abduction victim is the one thing that

will flush Siegel out," she replied calmly.

Shock, then disbelief registered on Denis' face. "Come off it, Jeannie. You don't believe that any more than I do."

Not knowing what to believe at this point, she said simply, "It's what Siegel believes that counts. More than one victim in a family is completely plausible. I've read about it any number of times. I'm telling you, this will get him off our backs for good."

"Even if I agreed with you, which I don't, it's not necessary to hypnotize you. What difference does it make if Siegel comes after a blank tape or a real one?"

"I'd agree, except this guy always seems to know exactly what's going on. I don't know how he does it, but he does, so I figure we ought to make it as legitimate as possible. Besides, if I'm going to write about hypnosis, then I should experience it. It will make my story more believable."

"Ah yes, your story." As he strode the length of the room and back again, Denis rubbed the muscles in the back of his neck.

Back to that again. With a sigh, Jeannie said, "It still bothers you that I want to write about UFO's, doesn't it?"

"Yeah, I guess it does."

"Even though I've told you I'll protect the identity of anyone whose experience I use. Don't you trust me, Denis?"

"Of course I do." Leaning over, he cupped her face in his hands and kissed her gently. "I know you would never deliberately hurt anyone."

"Then what?"

"This whole business is so--" He threw up his hands. "I don't understand it. And I don't know why you're so fascinated by it."

"Neither do I."

"It's almost as if--" Halting, he turned around slowly. "What did you say?"

Looking down at her hands, she said softly, "I don't

understand either. I just know this is important."

"How do you know?"

She shrugged. "I just do."

Denis rolled his eyes. "I don't believe we're having this conversation."

"Not real scientific, huh?"

In spite of himself, he grinned. "Let's just say I won't be writing it up for any of the psych journals."

"Want to bet on that?"

He stared at her. "You're serious."

"Absolutely." And she meant it. At that moment, she knew for certain she would write her story, maybe more than one. They would be important stories, and Denis would agree with her. How she knew this she couldn't say, but she was as sure as if it had already happened.

"Shall we seal our bet with a kiss?" And he bent down to do just that.

Breathless already, she forced herself back to the issue at hand. "Does this mean you'll do it?"

"Do what?" Completely distracted, Denis nibbled his way down her neck.

Tiny ripples of pleasure surged through her. "Hypnotize me?" she gasped. Much more of this and she would be under his control without hypnotism.

Backing off, he muttered, "You are one persistent woman."

Jeannie took several quick, deep breaths and pursued her advantage. "What should I do? Sit down? Lie down? Why don't we go into the living room? It's more comfortable there." *And lots safer.*

"You want me to hypnotize you now?"

"Sure. The sooner we have that tape, the sooner Siegel will leave Tulsa and leave us alone." She headed toward the living room. "Why don't I sit on the couch? You can pull up a chair."

Reluctantly, Denis dragged a straight-backed chair

across the room and set it next to the couch. "Are you sure you didn't have this all planned? I feel like I've been set up."

"I swear, I didn't even think of this till just a few minutes ago, but I'm glad I did." She kicked off her loafers and stretched her legs out on the coffee table. "Another tape is the perfect bait for that guy."

Denis turned the chair so the back faced him, then swung his right leg over, straddling the seat. "You know, I've been thinking about Siegel knowing what we're up to and when. Don't you find that a little strange? I mean, why did he come to my house last night, not the night before? How did he know when you'd be working late at your office?"

"What are you trying to say?"

"I'm wondering out loud, that's all."

"Do you think my house is bugged? Is that what you mean?"

Denis shrugged. "It was a thought, that's all. When you say it out loud, it does sound pretty far-fetched. I'm probably way off base."

"I wish you hadn't said anything," Jeannie declared. "Now I'm going to be looking over my shoulder every time I say something."

"If the house is bugged, he can only hear you, not see you."

"Great. That makes me feel a lot better."

"Jeannie, just forget I mentioned it, okay? It was a crazy idea. The chance that the guy has gotten into both our houses, well, I just don't think you have to worry about it. Besides, if you don't relax, I can't hypnotize you."

"Okay, you're right." With a sigh, she settled back against the cushions. She would put his idea out of her mind for now, but later, after he left, she would do a little checking. Just in case.

She looked at Denis. "I'm ready any time you are."

"I still can't believe I'm doing this," he said, shaking his head.

Jeannie smiled but didn't say a word. She had already decided she wanted this experience. Denis was the one having a problem with it.

His eyes focused on hers. "First, let's be sure you understand what's about to happen here. Hypnosis is a normal state of mind, actually the second of the four natural levels of mental activity. The first level, called *beta,* is that of complete consciousness. We function at this level approximately sixteen hours a day. The second stage, which we deal with in hypnosis, is called *alpha,* and it corresponds to the subconscious mind. *Theta* corresponds to light sleep, that is, the unconscious mind is unawake and unaware. *Delta* refers to deep sleep."

Jeannie nodded. So far, so good.

"When you're hypnotized," Denis continued, "you are in the alpha state. You are not asleep. You're fully aware at all times. Hypnosis simply sets aside the conscious mind so we can deal directly with the subconscious. Your concentration becomes more focused, and you become completely relaxed, so much so, you don't even want to move. You *can* move at any time, but under hypnosis you don't want to. Understand so far?"

"I think so. What you're saying is I won't go to sleep, and I won't become a zombie. I'll know what's going on, but my concentration will be so focused, I won't care about anything else."

"That's about it. Oh, one other thing. You will need something to focus on. Is there any habit you'd like to eliminate, any minor medical problem, any childhood incident you want to clarify?"

Jeannie had anticipated this question. "I'd like to go back to the day Barb got her scar on her leg," she replied promptly.

Denis scowled. Clearly, he didn't like her choice, but he

didn't challenge it either. "Okay. First, you need to relax. Close your eyes."

Following his deep soothing voice, Jeannie became conscious of her breathing. In and out, in and out. Relax... relax...relax....

She felt good, very good. Her face, her neck, her shoulders, her back. Light and loose. Her legs, her feet....

A bright white light sifted down into her body, through every pore, every cell. It filled her, surrounded her. Down and down....

She sighed deeply.

"Jeannie...." His voice sounded close, yet strangely detached. "I'm going to count backward from ten, very slowly. You will hear only my voice. With each number, you will sink deeper and deeper. By the count of one, you will be in a deep state of relaxation. Ten. Nine. Eight."

Like sinking into a cloud.

"Two. One. How do you feel, Jeannie?"

"Good. Relaxed."

"That's fine. What I'd like you to do now is talk to your subconscious. Why don't you silently ask your subconscious if it is willing to communicate with you? Ask if it will talk to you about the day Barb got the scar on her leg."

Sure. Why not? *Subconscious, are you willing to talk to me about Barb's scar?*

Nothing. Then, finally, an answer. *Yes, I'm willing.*

She felt her head nodding. "It says it will talk to me."

Denis' voice replied, "Fine. Go ahead. Anytime."

Wrapped in her cocoon of dark silence, Jeannie felt tuned in and secure, calm, yet expectant. A different feeling.

The picture in her mind started as a point of light and grew bigger, clearer, till it completely enveloped her. A bright summer sun, high in the clear blue sky, warmed her bare legs--her *small* arms and legs--as four-year-old Jeannie sat on a faded patchwork quilt in the back yard. Her

big sister, Barb, sat cross-legged next to her, and their dolls
had been propped in a semi-circle in front of them.

"We're having a tea party," Jeannie explained, delighted
with the scene her mind had conjured. "It's one of our
favorite games. Mama lets us have soda and cookies." She
giggled. "Barb and I eat all the cookies. The dolls don't
mind."

A third person joined the party, and Jeannie felt her body
stiffen. "Oh no! It's him! Go away. We don't want you
here."

"Who is it, Jeannie?"

"It's that funny-looking little boy. I've seen him before,
and I don't like him. Go away!" Frozen, she watched the
boy walk toward them from the stand of tall pine trees near
the fence. "He dresses funny, and his head's too big. No!
Don't go with him, Barb! Mama said to stay here. She's
gonna be mad!"

The scene shifted, and Jeannie watched herself and Barb
walking behind the little boy past the pine trees. "I wonder
where he's going. We're walking toward the fence. Stop! I
can't climb that fence. Oh! That's neat. We went through
the fence, right into Mrs. Rampolla's garden."

"You went *through* the fence?" Denis' voice cut in.

"Uh huh. Right through. Oh, there's a little house. I don't
remember a house here. What a funny-looking family.
They all look like the little boy. He takes us into his play
room."

A chill washed over her and she shivered. "It's cold in
here. I don't like this house."

Again, the scene shifted. Little Jeannie lay flat on her
back on a hard cold table. So cold. She thought she'd been
frozen into a block of ice. The little boy stood beside her,
his big black eyes staring, his long thin arm stretched
toward her.

She panicked. "Get away from me! Leave me alone!"

Something cold touched her leg, her stomach. "Don't do

that! No!"

"Jeannie! Listen to me."

That voice. Something familiar about that voice.

"Jeannie, you're okay. This is all in the past. You're fine. Very relaxed. Breathe deeply, in and out, in and out."

The deep soothing voice held her now, and she felt her body go limp. Sighing, she watched the image in her mind change once again.

"What do you see now, Jeannie?"

"I'm running. Hard. Fast. Up the stairs, through the sewing room, out to the eaves." She breathed faster. Her right hand gripped the sofa arm hard. "It's dark in here, real dark. I'm so glad Mama's here, and Barb. We're holding hands, waiting."

She leaned forward. "Someone's coming. We knew we couldn't hide. They always find us, no matter where we are. We all stand up. Mama goes first, then Barb, then me, right through the door. They're waiting for us."

"Who? Who is waiting, Jeannie?"

Her voice dropped to a whisper. "Someone." Frowning, she watched the image in her mind slowly fade away. "It's gone."

"Don't worry about it," Denis said softly. "Why don't you ask your subconscious if it is still willing to communicate with you?"

Again, she felt her head nodding and heard the words in her mind, *Subconscious, are you still willing to talk to me?*

Nothing. She waited. Still nothing. Then, very clearly, *No more today.*

She sighed. "It says not today."

"Okay. That's fine. Jeannie, I'm going to count to ten very slowly. When I reach ten, you will open your eyes. You will be wide awake and feeling fine. You will remember everything we have talked about. One. Two."

It felt like climbing a long flight of stairs, and with each number the air around her became a little lighter.

"Nine. Ten."

Her eyelids fluttered and then slowly opened. Blinking to readjust her contacts, she gradually brought the room and the man in front of her into focus. "Hi."

"How do you feel?"

"Fine. Great." She stood up, stretched, and then it hit her. "Oh, God!" She sat back down. From the corner of her eye, she caught a glimpse of Denis with a perplexed scowl on his face.

"You remember everything?"

"Yeah, I--"

"You knew," he said tightly. "You knew exactly what would happen if we went back to that incident."

"No. That's not true." She saw the disbelief in his eyes. "I wondered," she said quickly. "I didn't know for sure. I couldn't."

He didn't answer. He didn't have to. She watched his eyes turn from a soft pale green to dark, smoky gray. Stormy eyes. She shivered and waited for the storm to break.

It didn't take long.

"You used me, Jeannie."

The words pierced her like a knife in the gut, taking her breath away.

"You had this all planned, didn't you? What better way to 'prove' your UFO theory and get material for your story?"

"No! That's not true."

He loomed over her, his face no more than six inches from hers. "Isn't it, Jeannie?" Soft and calm, his voice was as cold as the emotions he had frozen away inside him. "Can you deny that this is the 'proof' you've hoped for all along? Your very own abduction. How wonderfully convenient, especially since your whole family is involved. You certainly have enough material for your story now, for two or three stories. Hell, now you can write a book.

"And what about that little bedroom scene? A little sex with the big, bad, doubting doctor thrown in for good measure. That ought to make great copy."

She wanted to defend herself, to tell him he had this all wrong, but he didn't give her a chance. Turning abruptly, he strode out of the living room and into the kitchen. He grabbed his jacket from the back of a chair and headed for the door.

"Denis, don't do this." She ran after him, reaching for his arm, but he shook her off. "No!" She wrapped her arms across her chest and backed away. "You're wrong," she whispered. "All wrong."

"I don't think so, although I admit you had me fooled. I really believed in all that shy innocence. I was even happy for you when you started digging into this story. 'Sure, Jeannie, go to Washington. Spread your wings a little.' Boy, did you ever! You didn't need my encouragement, that's for sure. You knew exactly where you were going and how to get there."

When the door slammed shut behind him, she was still shaking her head in silent denial.

14

SWIRLING pockets of dense fog had moved into the area, covering the familiar landmarks of Benton's Valley Road with a gray shroud.

Cursing the weather, the night, and life in general, Denis downshifted the car to second and hoped there weren't too many other fools heading toward Tulsa tonight. His low beams couldn't penetrate the thick mist and high beams blinded him.

Don't think. Just drive. Concentrate on getting the car safely from Point A to Point B. Not an easy task when the rage and hurt inside him had become an actual physical pain.

Two hazy pinpoints of light appeared somewhere up ahead. He slowed again, shifted to first, and crawled along the winding, two-lane road. The lights grew bigger, then passed him. He never did see the car.

Without warning, the country road dead-ended, and the highway appeared ahead of him. Denis hit his brakes hard to keep the front end of his car out of the path of northbound traffic. Very carefully, he turned right and visibility improved, thanks to streetlights and a slightly higher elevation. He had just started to breathe easier when the first tiny pellets of freezing rain struck his car. Within minutes, his wipers were laboring to keep the windshield ice-free.

"Great," he muttered, gripping the wheel harder. "Just what I needed."

He didn't remember making a conscious decision to turn onto Bentonville Road, but somehow it happened, and here he was urging his car up the long steep hill that was already covered with a thin layer of ice. "Come on, baby. Don't stop now."

When his headlights finally caught the amber reflector at the bottom of Loren's driveway, Denis knew how fog-bound sailors must have felt when they finally saw the saving yellow beam from a lighthouse. He didn't slow down at the foot of the hill, just swung wide and gunned the engine. By the time he reached the top, the little car had just enough left to ease over the edge onto the flat. "Nice little car," he breathed, turning off the key.

Okay, Earley, it's nine-thirty at night. You're sitting unannounced in your friend's driveway, in the middle of a damned ice storm. What the hell are you doing here?

The house was dark. They'd probably already gone to bed.

He couldn't do it. No matter how badly he needed someone to talk to, he couldn't barge in there.

The outside lights suddenly flooded the yard and driveway. The front door opened halfway, and he saw Barb huddled in the doorway, looking toward his car.

Now he couldn't *not* go in. Turning off his lights, he pushed on his door and made the long dash through the freezing rain, into the house.

Barb just shook her head. "And here I thought you were the sane and sensible one." She sighed. "Go out to the kitchen, Denis. I'll get you a towel."

"I'll drip on the floor," he protested, looking down at his wet jeans and jacket plastered against his body.

"It won't be the first time. Now, get going. Loren's on

the phone, and the coffeepot's full." Still shaking her head, she walked off toward the bathroom.

"Look, Gates, it's not something I want to talk about. Understand?" Loren's normally calm, even voice boomed through the kitchen as Denis walked into the room.

"Yes, I do mind, and besides, he's an old friend. He won't talk to you and neither will I." Loren slammed down the phone, then looked up and saw he wasn't alone. "Hi, Denis." Then he muttered, "Damned nosy reporters."

Reporter? No, of course not, but who?

Loren started rubbing his temples with the thumb and forefinger of his right hand. He didn't seem to find anything unusual about his friend's sudden appearance in his kitchen on a stormy Sunday night, and Denis found that comforting. He'd made the right decision coming here tonight.

"Here's a towel to dry your hair," Barb said, coming up behind him. "And a hot drink so you won't catch pneumonia. I'll take your jacket and hang it up, then you can tell us what you're doing out in this weather. Who was that on the phone, Loren?"

"Some reporter for the *Tulsa Star*." He reached into the cookie jar and pulled out a handful of chocolate cookies, then pushed the jar toward Denis.

"What did she want?" asked Barb.

"He, not she, and he's looking for information about strange lights people have seen in Crossland Park. The Tulsa Lights, he called them."

Barb stopped in the doorway. "What did you tell him?"

"Nothing. I said I don't want to talk about it, and neither will you or Denis."

"How did he know about Denis?"

Loren shrugged. "Beats me, but he did. He even knew I had consulted Denis."

"I wonder what else he knows. He's not going to write a story, is he?"

"He'd better not. I told him I would deny everything, and

then I'd sue him and the paper both!"

Barb looked relieved. "Then I guess he won't."

"I wouldn't bet on that," Denis said slowly.

Loren and Barb stared at him. "Why not? What do you mean?"

Very carefully, he spread the damp towel over the back of a chair, then pulled out another chair and straddled it. "I'd say it depends on how good this guy's source is. If he considers it reliable, he'll probably run the story."

"But we're the only ones who know what's been going on," Barb protested.

"Jeannie knows," Denis said quietly. "And one other person." Even as he said the words, however, he found them hard to believe. But damn. She'd betrayed him once. Why not twice? Or three times?

"Not Jeannie," Barb declared emphatically. "So, who is this other person?"

Denis hated to tell them about Siegel. God knows they had enough to contend with right now, but they also had a right to know what was going on. He took a deep breath and started talking. One thing led to another, and pretty soon he had told everything, including a censored version of what happened tonight. Since Loren and Barb knew all about his disastrous marriage to Suzanne, they understood all too well why he would consider Jeannie's actions the worst kind of betrayal.

Except Barb didn't see it that way. Loren sat and listened, offering little comment, but by the time he described leaving Jeannie's house and unconsciously heading toward their place, Barb looked like a small volcano about to erupt.

"Men!" She plopped herself into the chair next to Denis. "How do you do it? I mean, for fairly intelligent creatures, why do you do such dumb things?"

Denis didn't need this. "Now, wait a minute Barb."

"No, you wait. I know there's some good thinking matter

up there." She leaned over and tapped his forehead. "Besides what Loren has told me, I've seen you in action myself, so I know you're plenty smart." Before he could reply, she demanded, "Do you love my sister?"

"Barb, I don't think--"

"Hush, Loren. Denis knew he'd face the third degree if he came here tonight. Right, Denis?"

"No. I--"

"And he knows we want to help him, and Jeannie, too. Of course," she added sweetly, "you don't have to answer if you don't want to."

Denis couldn't help smiling, just a little, at Barb's tactics. "You're incorrigible," he told her, "but I suppose you're right. Deep down, I knew what I'd be up against if I came here, and I came anyway. So, go ahead. I'm listening."

She reached into the glass jar sitting on the table and pulled out a homemade chocolate chip cookie. "Okay. First of all, you didn't answer my question. Do you love my sister?"

A dozen different emotions churned through him as Barb's words echoed through his head. He knew that Jeannie delighted him and confused him. She made him happier than he'd been for years, but she had hurt him deeply. She was sweet and shy, yet she had loved him tonight with total abandon.

"It's not that simple," he mumbled, running restless fingers through his damp hair.

"Of course, it is." Barb took both his hands in hers and looked him straight in the eye. "Can you imagine the rest of your life without Jeannie?" she asked, softly.

Oh, yes. Yes, he could, year after cold, empty year. His heart thumped so hard it almost hurt. "I guess I love her," he admitted.

Barb looked pleased. "Good, because she loves you, too."

"You couldn't prove it by me. And I sure haven't heard

her say so."

"Have you told her how you feel?"

"Well, no, but--"

Barb threw up her hands. "That's what I mean. Not just one, but two stubborn idiots. She loves you, believe me."

Looking down at the table, Denis said quietly, "I'd like to, Barb, but it's pretty hard when I remember how she set me up to prove her UFO theory. Not that I'm convinced, but she is. She admitted that she suspected what would come out during hypnosis. How do you think that makes me feel?"

"How do you think she feels?" Barb countered.

"What do you mean?"

"Exactly what I said. Think about it, Denis. You say Jeannie used the hypnosis to prove her UFO theory. I say she wanted to prove it *isn't* true."

He shook his head. "I can't buy that. She has talked UFO's since the first time I met her. She's convinced herself they're real. They've become an obsession with her."

"Why do you suppose that is?"

He stared at the slim, dark-haired woman sitting next to him and realized for the first time how very much Barb resembled her sister. The hurt hit him again, harder than ever. "Why?" he repeated.

"Yes. Why this big fascination with something most people consider pretty far-out?"

"I asked her that. She doesn't know herself."

"Oh, I think she does, but she's afraid to admit it, even to herself. No, hear me out," Barb said, when Denis would have protested. "I've thought about this constantly for two days, and I believe I'm right.

"If what came out in both hypnosis sessions is true, then our family has been intimately involved with this phenomenon for years. Quite possibly for generations. If UFO's and the entities are real, then Jeannie has been responding to something she recognizes on a subconscious level. She wants it to remain subconscious, but the fascination is there, so she investigates sightings. That's safe, as long as she herself isn't involved.

"When she asked you to hypnotize her tonight, I think she was trying to prove that what she fears--our family's involvement--wasn't true. Instead, she revealed an encounter we were both involved in years ago. Can't you imagine how she must have felt?"

Denis figured he knew exactly how Jeannie felt, thrilled and excited, but he couldn't very well tell Barb he didn't buy a word of the fairy tale she had spun for her sister's benefit. Fortunately, Barb didn't give him a chance to reply.

"Scared to death. That's how she felt, how she still feels."

And you sure didn't help. He could almost hear the words in her head, accusing him of abandoning Jeannie in her hour of need. The worst part of it was, for a few seconds he actually felt guilty! Then common sense took over. "That may be, Barb, but right now I don't see it that way. I only know how *I* interpreted her actions and how *I* feel."

"And that's all you will know until you talk to her and listen to what she says."

Denis shrugged. As far as he was concerned, the subject was closed.

Barb stood up and stalked across the room, stopping in the doorway for one, last parting shot. "Well, I, for one, happen to care about Jeannie, and I think she might need someone to talk to--right now."

He watched the louvered kitchen doors swing back and forth half a dozen times after Barb disappeared into the family room.

"She doesn't often get worked up like that," Loren commented. He settled back in his chair, cradling his cup thoughtfully. "Must be the pregnancy. It does funny things to a woman.

"About this Siegel," he said, changing the subject abruptly. "You really think he's the one who tipped off the Tulsa paper?"

"Probably," Denis replied. "It's the kind of thing he would do. I think. I haven't figured out what he's up to, but whenever there's trouble, he seems to be around."

Nodding, Loren wandered over to the window and peered into the darkness.

"Still sleeting out there?"

"It's coming down hard. Weather forecast says it's supposed to keep up all night. You'd better figure on staying over."

Denis looked over Loren's shoulder. Everything, as far as he could see, was covered in a glistening layer of ice. "It doesn't look good out there," he admitted.

"Don't look so glum." Loren clamped one hand on his shoulder. "It could be worse. You could have been stranded at Jeannie's house."

If Loren hoped for a reaction, he was disappointed. Denis gave one great sigh, asked which room he should take, and made his way slowly toward the stairs.

* * *

JEANNIE'S room. By some crazy quirk of fate, he'd managed to end up in her bed tonight. Alone, but still in the bed she slept in when she stayed at this house.

Lying there in the dark stillness, Denis tried not to think about her soft body with its gentle curves settling into this very spot in the mattress, tried not to remember how well his body had meshed with hers in another bed just a short time ago.

His eyes popped open, and he rolled onto his back. What had Barb said to her sister? Had she explained how Denis felt, how much Jeannie had hurt him? Although what difference did that make, unless Barb was right and Jeannie had simply meant to prove to herself that nothing had happened to her or her sister.

Damn. He'd never get to sleep this way.

Turn it off, he told himself. *Empty your mind. You can deal with it tomorrow. Relax.*

Surprisingly, he did just that, and several minutes later he dropped off into a deep, dreamless sleep.

He came awake suddenly. One second, he was sleeping soundly, the next, he was aware of his body lying tense and motionless in the center of the bed. What had awakened him? Listening intently, he heard nothing, yet something didn't feel right. Slowly, he opened his eyes.

Total blackness, total stillness, except for the rapid thumping of his heart, which made no sense, unless he'd been dreaming and didn't remember.

By this time, he could distinguish vague shapes and shadows. Dresser, desk, the dim outline of the east window. And something else--something moving in front of his bed. No, it had to be his imagination. Keeping his body perfectly still, he blinked his eyes. What looked like the silhouette of a child glided from the window on his right to the foot of the bed, and on through the door.

Through the door?

He blinked again. The door *was* closed, and the figure *had* disappeared.

Another movement to his right. Another figure appeared from the direction of the window, which seemed brighter now, as though a full moon had risen, lighting the whole area outside. Fascinated, Denis watched the second figure, an exact duplicate of the first, glide across the room and through the door.

He must be dreaming. His body felt lethargic, as it would in a dream. He thought about moving, following the figures, but he didn't do it. Maybe he *couldn't* do it.

His eyelids felt heavy. Fighting to keep them open, he seemed to have no control. He thought he saw one more figure glide along the same path the others had taken.

Where are they going? he wondered, just as his eyes slid shut.

* * *

MONDAY mornings had never been Jeannie's favorite time of the week, and this particular day promised to be worse than usual. Even after talking to Barb last night, she still couldn't believe Denis had misunderstood her so badly. Her sister had assured her that he loved her, but remembering his anger, she found that hard to believe. She was worried, too, that Siegel would break into her house. All said, she hadn't slept much the night before, no more than an hour or two, which meant she'd turned off the alarm and dozed again, putting her forty-five minutes behind schedule. Which meant she didn't leave her house till nine-thirty.

The sun was shining and the roads, frozen from last night's ice storm, had already turned to slush. Traffic was slow, so she didn't bother stopping for gas, and that meant her car ran out six blocks from the office. She finally burst into the Sun Building at ten-ten instead of nine o'clock.

Billy Whitecotton had perched himself and his coffee mug on the corner of the front desk, so he could talk to both of the pretty little receptionist/copy editors who worked for the paper.

"'Morning, Gang!" Jeannie gave the three young people her normal breezy greeting and kept on going. She had almost crossed the huge square room when she noticed the sudden silence behind her. She stopped and turned around slowly, her eyes skipping from one to another. "Something wrong?"

As soon as she spoke, Beverly and Ginger found urgent business at their keyboards, while Billy continued to stare at her as though she had grown a second head. Maybe she'd better check this out. "What's up, Billy?" she asked, walking back to the desk.

He didn't meet her eyes but looked over Ginger's shoulder, focusing all his attention on her computer monitor.

Jeannie reached over and tapped his shoulder. "Billy? Talk to me."

Reluctantly, he looked up, his dark brows furrowed into a deep frown. Glancing toward the offices down the hallway, he said softly, "Eddie'll probably fire me if he sees me talking to you, but I hate for him to catch you unaware."

"Unaware of what?"

He studied her face. "You really don't know?"

Jeannie felt her patience stretching very thin. "No, I don't, and if you don't tell me in the next five seconds, I'll probably scream. Very loud."

"No. Don't do that. It's--well, it's that article in this morning's *Tulsa Star*. Eddie says you sold us out. I've never seen him that mad."

"What article? What's this all about, Billy?"

"How could you not know? You're on the front page of the *Star's* 'Statewide' section."

She shook her head. "You're kidding, right? This is a big joke."

Billy didn't even crack a smile. "No joke, Jeannie. Neil Gates did a column about you and your family being abducted by aliens."

His words slammed into her with all the force of a speeding train, and she felt herself swaying. Gates. Barb had told her that was the name of the reporter who had called Loren last night. But her brother-in-law had refused the interview, so how…?

"Well, well, if it isn't Ms. MacLeod, ace reporter." With his hands jammed into the pockets of his wrinkled pants and his oxford shirt sleeves rolled up to his elbows, Eddie Barnes strolled into the lobby. He held up his left arm and pretended to study his watch. "Nice of you to join us today."

Still reeling from Billy's announcement, Jeannie had no patience with her boss' attempt at humor. "Come off it, Eddie. You get more than any forty hours a week from me, and you know it."

Eddie's face turned red. "The only thing I want right now is answers. I'll see you in my office, MacLeod." He spun around and stomped off.

Watching his retreating back, Jeannie scowled. "You were right, Billy. He's hacked off, but not half as bad as I am. Somebody has some fancy explaining to do."

Billy's hand on her shoulder stopped her as she started off after Eddie. "Uh, Jeannie, there's one more thing you should know, just in case Eddie 'forgets' to mention it. He's been into your computer. I don't know what you have in there, but whatever it is, he was spitting nails when he pulled it up a while ago."

Oh God! Her "Lights" file, with the UFORA data, John Gregory's letter, her report on Loren's hypnosis session, and a bunch of other material. The only thing not in it was her own hypnosis session, which she had planned to enter today.

Dismay quickly turned to anger. Eddie had no right to snoop in her computer, no right at all. Taking several deep breaths, she managed to calm down a notch or two. A shouting match wouldn't prove anything. "Thanks, Billy," she mumbled, and even managed a half-smile. "I appreciate the information."

"Yeah, well, I hope you can calm him down." He punched her lightly on the shoulder. "Give 'em hell, Jeannie."

Nodding, she walked away, but her mind had already jumped ahead to what would surely be an unpleasant scene. And with good reason. Eddie was out of line, messing with her computer. If he'd had questions, he should have called her.

His door was open, and he sat at his desk, his swivel

chair tipped back, one knee propped up on the other. As she stepped through the doorway, his eyes narrowed and his mouth opened.

Jeannie didn't give him a chance. Seeing the *Star* lying on his desk, she reached over and picked it up. "Is this the one?"

"Hell, you should know. You're plastered all over page one."

"Well, I don't--oh, no!"

"Don't tell me you're disappointed. The only thing missing is your picture."

"Area Residents Snatched by Little Green Men," she read. "Two prominent Benton citizens, who wish to remain anonymous, have reportedly become victims of a local phenomenon appropriately named The Tulsa Lights."

Neil Gates' tongue-in-cheek expose went on, dropping hints, but never naming names, subtly suggesting, yet with no outright accusations:

"A Northwest College professor hoping to make *history;* his lovely young relative, *reportedly* a childhood abduction victim."

Continuing, the column speculated on the aliens' motive for abducting people. It concluded that the little gray "space brothers" had nothing but altruistic motives. They knew how profitable it was these days to report an encounter. What with talk shows and books and movies, the possibilities for profit were almost endless.

Gates did leave one question unanswered. He wondered why the aliens found this particular professor and his relative worthy of abduction, when they usually concentrated on taking rednecks in pickups from the backwoods of Georgia or Tennessee. Perhaps their taste in victims was improving?

"How could he!" Jeannie sank into the small sofa against the wall.

"You mean, how could you!" Eddie jerked the paper out

of her hands. "You let a second-rate columnist scoop you, MacLeod, and in the process, he trashed a perfectly good story. What's the matter with you?"

"With me?" Jeannie couldn't believe she was hearing this. She stood up and planted herself directly in front of Eddie. "You're blaming me, when I'm the one who will be the laughingstock of the whole area, me and my family? Don't you even wonder how Gates got his information? I sure didn't give it to him...." Her voice trailed off, and she answered her own question. "Damn," she whispered.

The puzzle pieces suddenly slipped into place.

It had to be Siegel.

She shouldn't have worried about him breaking into her house. He already had what he wanted, and last night he was very busy giving it to someone else: Neil Gates, who knew exactly how to use it. From the information in the column, he must have known about her hypnosis session, as well.

That meant Denis' suspicions were right. Siegel had bugged her house.

Squeezing her eyes shut, she slammed the paper onto the desk. "Damn, damn, damn!"

"I don't care how Gates got his information," Eddie declared, ignoring her outburst. "He doesn't use anything he can't prove. What I do care about is you letting a great story just sit in your computer. This UFO stuff is hot right now. The *Star* has already run a couple of news stories on these Tulsa Lights. What you've got could have been bigger than both of them. And you didn't do a thing about it."

Pacing the floor, he picked up the folded paper and waved it in front of his face like a fan. "Maybe it's not too late. If we get our stuff together, set up a couple of interviews with your brother-in-law and that doctor, the psychologist. What's his name?"

Jeannie shook her head. "No way. We're not doing it."

"Earley, that's it. Denis Earley. He'll confirm what Price

says and--"

"Stop it, Eddie!" She leaned over and pounded her fists on his desk.

He turned around and stared at her. "What are you talking about?"

"I'm talking about this--this story." She pointed at the paper in his hand. "We're not going to do anything with it. There won't be any interviews."

"Are you crazy? Of course, we'll do interviews. You've already got a bunch of info in your computer and--"

"Hold it right there." This time her voice was very low and very calm. Eddie stopped in mid-sentence. "What's in my computer is privileged information, Mr. Barnes. I thought it was safe there, but I was wrong. I won't make that mistake again. I'll take it out today, so you won't be tempted to snoop again. And I would appreciate it very much if you would forget anything you saw in there on the subject of UFO's."

"Wait a minute, MacLeod. I'm the one directing the show around her, and I say we're doing this story. If you won't write it, I will."

Jeannie's heart was pumping so hard and so fast she was afraid it might explode, but she was on a roll now. "I'm only going to say this one more time, Eddie, so listen good. What's in my computer is privileged and personal. It belongs to me, and when I walk out of this room I'm going to my office and I'm going to delete everything I consider confidential."

Jeannie might be concerned about her heart, but Eddie looked positively apoplectic. His round face had turned bright red, and his hands, squeezed into tight fists, were shaking. "If you take one single thing out of that computer, MacLeod, you're fired."

"Uh-uh, that won't work, Eddie." Jeannie realized she was smiling. "I *am* taking my files, and you can't fire me because I quit."

As she spun around, she heard a chorus of gasps from the doorway. Ginger, Beverly and Billy moved aside as Jeannie swept past them all, still smiling, on her way to clean out her office.

15

"YOU did what? Oh, Jeannie!"

Standing in her sister's big warm kitchen, Jeannie felt her eyes burn as Barb hugged her tightly. "I'm okay, Sis. It's been a long time coming, and today just happened to be the day. I'm glad to be out of there. Honest." Reaching for the coffeepot, she poured two cups and carried them to the table.

"We saw what Gates wrote," Barb said, taking a coffeecake out of the freezer and setting it in the microwave. "Loren said he'd sue him, but the guy's not worth it. Did he have anything to do with your trouble at the paper?"

"You might say that. What did you think about the column?"

"I think the man's an idiot, and so will everyone else with a lick of common sense."

Jeannie laughed. "That's what I like about you, you're completely impartial. Mmmm, that cake smells wonderful."

"I haven't decided if this is a party or a funeral," Barb declared. "Either way, I figure we need calories."

Minutes later, they were digging into thick chunks of cinnamon pecan cake.

"I'm glad to see that your appetite has finally picked up," Jeannie said, watching her sister enjoy the sweet treat. "I was beginning to think you might set a record for no weight gain during pregnancy."

"No chance of that." Barb patted the slight swell of her stomach under her sweatshirt. "We're both doing just fine, thank you. Actually, I can't believe I feel better since Loren's session with Denis, but it's true. We both do. I still worry about him and the baby, but after talking to your friend, Mia, I don't think I'll go off the deep end like I did when I was expecting Buddy. At least now I know why I'm worried.

"I know Denis doesn't take Loren's explanation literally, but we both think it makes sense." She shivered. "It's horrible to think that someone or something we don't understand has this control over our lives, but it explains so many things. And so many people have the same experiences. They can't all be crazy. Besides, you believe it, too."

She reached over to touch Jeannie's arm. "Now, tell me what happened this morning. When my very practical sister walks out on the job she's held for six years, something is very wrong."

"I should have done it ages ago," Jeannie muttered, and quickly explained what had happened at the newspaper office.

"You're right. That guy is a real jerk," Barb said, referring to Eddie. "Did you get all your files copied and deleted?"

"I took all my personal data and left everything I was working on for the paper. Maybe somebody else can use it."

"What are you going to do, Sis? Can you manage without a job?"

"For a while. I have some savings."

"I just can't believe all this happening at once." Barb pushed away her empty plate and reached for her cup. "First, the hypnosis session with you remembering both of us being abducted years ago. Then Denis thinking you used him to prove your UFO theory. And now, no job. It's all so bizarre."

"Don't tell me!" Cradling her cup, Jeannie stared into the steaming liquid. "I can't even begin to tell you how I felt when I remembered what really happened that day when we were kids. It felt like it was going on right then, like I was living that day all over again. I was so scared, and I know you were, too. Maybe it's a good thing they make us forget. I don't think most people could handle it, knowing they'd been used like that."

"That's what Loren says." Barb looked at her sister thoughtfully. "What happens now? Where do we go from here? What are you going to do?"

Jeannie had been expecting and dreading that question. She knew the answer, knew she had no real choice. She just didn't know if Barb and Loren would accept her decision. "I have to see this through," she said finally.

"You mean, your investigation?"

"Yes. I'm absolutely convinced that UFO's do exist somewhere. I know they interact with us somehow and have for years, even centuries. They leave behind physical evidence, burned grass, scars that we can see and touch and feel. And they leave people changed forever. I think, when we finally solve the mystery, we'll find our ideas of reality changed, too. It seems to me that's reason enough to continue until we have the answers."

"Do you think we ever will have all the answers?"

"Oh yes. Every little question answered adds another piece to the big puzzle. One of these days, we'll see the whole picture, even though Siegel and others like him keep trying to confuse us and take away the pieces."

"And you think Siegel equals government?"

"Some part of our government, yes."

Barb shivered. "It's scary to think our government might be responsible for breaking and entering and robbery."

"And worse," Jeannie added, thinking about the night she was attacked in Crossland Park.

Barb refilled their cups. "Well, whatever you do, Loren and I are with you all the way."

Again, Jeannie's eyes burned. "Thanks, Barb. That means a lot to me. I just wish--" She paused and blinked rapidly. No use wishing for the impossible.

"He'll come around, you know," Barb said softly, reading her thoughts. "He does love you."

"Maybe once he thought he did," she murmured. "You know, the irony of it is, as strongly as I believe in UFO's, I just didn't think my hypnosis would reveal anything. I guess it's the old story, everybody else but not me. Nothing will happen to me." She gave a quick laugh and her voice caught. "Boy, was I wrong."

"One of these days, Denis will figure out he's wrong, too," Barb declared. "Wait and see."

Jeannie nodded, but she felt pretty sure he wouldn't change his mind. Barb hadn't seen his face or heard his voice when he talked about his wife's betrayal. A man wouldn't take a chance on that kind of hurt again. No, she'd had her chance with Denis Earley and she blew it. Inadvertently, but it still happened. He wouldn't let her close again.

They talked well into the afternoon, everything from job possibilities to how Jeannie would continue her investigation of the Tulsa Lights, and they agreed they should both explore the possibility of more UFO experiences over the past years.

"But I don't think Denis will help us," Barb said. "He'll work with Loren because he believes something else is causing his problems, but I can't see Dr. Earley agreeing to uncover a series of UFO abductions that have affected our whole family for several generations. Although," she added, "he did have a lot of questions this morning."

"What kind of questions?" Jeannie asked quickly.

"Oh, he talked about the noises we hear at night, the lights going on and off, that kind of thing."

"Like that last night I stayed here."

"Right. I thought he might have heard something, but he never admitted he did."

"I'm not surprised. If something did happen, he's probably trying to convince himself it didn't. But even if he won't work with us, I'll bet Mia will." Jeannie's mind was already racing with possibilities. "And Allen will use UFORA personnel and resources to help with the investigation. I've already given him the grass sample from the woods here, and Virgil Owens gave him permission to have his film analyzed. I know Allen wants to be involved. I'll concentrate on compiling the material into a book."

"It's probably not too early to get a proposal together and start contacting publishers," Barb added.

Jeannie agreed. "And while I'm at it, I may as well talk to a couple of people at the *Tulsa Star*."

"Even though Neil Gates works for them, too?"

"Yeah, even though. Let's face it. This could be a lengthy project, and I'm going to need a job. In spite of Gates, it's a good paper and I've always wanted to work for them." She shrugged. "The worst they can do is say no."

Smiling, Barb squeezed her hand. "I'm so glad to hear you say that. You've always been the strong one in the family, doing what's best for everyone but yourself."

"That's not true," Jeannie protested.

"Yes, it is. Mom worried about you all the time. She hated asking you to leave college to take care of her when her MS got so bad, but she didn't know what else to do."

"She didn't ask. I told her I was coming home and I just showed up. I did what I wanted to do."

"Maybe. Anyway, she would be glad you're trying something new, spreading your wings a bit."

Denis' words. He'd been happy for her, too. Once.

Pushing the painful memory aside, Jeannie tried to

concentrate on her sister's ideas for possible publishers, but it wasn't easy. And this was just the beginning. In the few short weeks she'd known him, Denis had become a vital part of her life. She'd dreamed about their future together. And yet, he'd rejected her.

That hurt, a deep raw hurt that would take a long, long time to heal.

Maybe forever.

* * *

HE'D probably had worse days, but Denis couldn't remember when. After spending a restless night, more often awake than asleep, he'd left Loren's house around nine the next morning. The sun was already shining and traffic was heavy, leaving the roads messy but drive-able. Thank goodness he had only one appointment later that afternoon. Right now, he wasn't at all certain he could even talk coherently, much less analyze a patient's problems.

Moving along the crowded expressway, he tried to keep his mind on driving, but he found himself thinking about the night before, or worse, not thinking at all but simply *spacing out* for half a mile, even a mile at a time. Highway Hypnosis. Normally not a dangerous situation, but today, considering the amount of sleep he'd had, it could be.

Think, he told himself, and an image of Jeannie appeared in his mind.

No, not that! He'd already replayed their last minutes together over and over, and he'd thought about what Barb had said. Obviously, one of them had misjudged Jeannie, but for the life of him he couldn't figure out which one.

Then there were the hours he'd spent in Loren's house last night. Had he been dreaming when he imagined those childlike shadows flitting by his bed? It hadn't seemed like a dream but they couldn't be real. Yet, according to Loren and Barb, other strange things happened there at night, noises they couldn't explain, lights flickering, and Loren's dreams that scared him to death.

Denis shook his head hard and gripped the wheel tighter. Just a few more blocks and he'd be home. And he would make that call to Alex MacGregor in Virginia he'd promised himself as he lay alone in the long silent hours before daylight.

* * *

"DENIS? Man, it's been a long time. How are you doing?"

Sitting at the desk in his office, Denis nursed the mug of instant coffee he'd fixed on his way through the kitchen. "Not bad, Alex. Not bad."

There was a slight pause at the other end of the line. "But not good either?"

"Well, now that you mention it...."

"Okay. Let's have it. I'm off for a few days, and I've got nothing but time this morning. Maryann took the girls to the mall. I don't have a thing to worry about till I get the bills."

Usually, Denis would have appreciated his friend's quiet humor. It had helped him through some bad times after the divorce. But not today. "I met a woman," he said.

"Hey, it's about time. Congratulations."

"Not yet. Probably never."

"Uh oh. Sounds serious."

Leaning on his elbows, Denis rubbed a nagging ache at the base of his neck. "You don't know the half of it. Do you remember me talking about Loren Price, my old roommate from OU?" Once he got going, the story rolled out easily, though it really hurt to talk about Jeannie.

"Let me get this straight," Alex said finally. "Loren, his wife, and his sister-in-law all believe they have been abducted?"

"I know it sounds crazy, but they're not--crazy, that is. I've just never encountered anything like this before. Frankly, I don't know what to make of it."

"What about the boy, Loren's son? Has he been involved, too?"

"I don't know. No one ever mentioned--"

"Haven't you asked?"

"I didn't think--"

"Good grief, man. Don't you realize what you have there? Probably the story of the century, maybe the millennium! No wonder your reporter friend wants to write it up. Leave it to you, Doubting Thomas, to have something like this dropped in his lap."

Denis couldn't believe what he was hearing. "Are you saying you believe this stuff?"

"If you could hear some of the sessions--hypnosis and simple consultations--I have on tape, you wouldn't even ask," Alex replied. "Several of my patients have been involved in encounters that make Loren's, well, I won't say insignificant, but at least a lot more believable. But I've never come across several members of one family spanning several generations, although I've heard of it."

For the next few minutes, Denis listened to his good friend, his conservative, professional friend, explain to him why the scientific community should take the claims of UFO abductees, *experiencers* he called them, seriously.

"You're not putting me on?" Denis asked, when he could finally get a word in.

"Absolutely not. I believe what I'm saying, and you will, too, if you just open your mind a little. Remember what the Bard told us? 'There are more things in heaven and earth--'"

"Spare me," Denis groaned. "Not Shakespeare this early in the morning."

"Never too early," Alex replied cheerfully. "Will always has something to tell us, if we just listen." Abruptly, he shifted gears. "Got a pen handy?"

"Sure. What do you have?"

"Books and authors. Take down these titles and read them. You need to have your viewpoint expanded."

Denis wrote for the next five minutes. "It'll take me a month to get through all these. That's six books!"

"You'll be surprised. It's fascinating reading. When you finish, call me again. Better yet, why don't you come this way and spend Thanksgiving with us? We can do some serious talking, and you can hear some of the tapes I have. I guarantee you'll go away convinced that something really strange is happening in our world. What do you say?"

Denis hesitated. He wasn't at all sure he wanted to be convinced that UFO's were real. How could he live with such a radical idea? It would change his concept of reality.

"Will you come?"

"I'm not sure, Alex."

"Hey, I know it's a scary idea, but I've never known you to back away from the truth."

The truth. Suppose, just for a minute, that Alex and Jeannie were right? Faster-than-light spaceships? Alien abductions? Genetic tampering with the human race? Common sense told Denis these things were the stuff of science fiction, yet some other part of him, a part he didn't even begin to understand, whispered, "It might be true."

He owed it to himself--and Jeannie and Loren--to decide one way or the other. To find the truth.

He heard himself saying, "Okay. I'll come."

"Great. Maryann will be thrilled. She loves a crowd for the holidays. I'm proud of you, man," Alex added. "You've just taken a giant step forward."

A few minutes later, Denis set the receiver in its cradle and pushed back his chair. "*The UFO Enigma*," he read, scowling at the list on his desk. "*The Abductee Experience.* Hell, why not?" He shoved the list in his pants pocket. "All I've got is time."

16

ON a bitter cold night in mid-December, Jeannie opened the Bainbridge East Library's front door, her immediate objective to get warm.

A blustery wind blew from the north, forcing her to use every ounce of her strength to hold the heavy glass door while she slipped inside. She tried not to think about last month, same time, same place, when Denis had held this same door. Tonight she had no idea where he was. She hadn't seen or talked to him in almost a month.

The longest month of her life.

She had survived by staying so busy she had no time or energy to think about him. It didn't always work, but usually she managed to push the worst hurt into a deep enough pocket of her heart. That way she felt only a constant dull ache, uncomfortable but bearable. Like now, when her memories of another night in this building threatened to bubble up to the surface and spill over. A deep steadying breath, a smile on her face, and she walked quickly through the lobby to the room where the UFORA group met.

"Jeannie?" A familiar voice called out from across the room. She waved to Allen and watched him make his way toward her.

He shook her hand warmly. "I'm so glad you could make it tonight."

"So am I." She patted her bulging shoulder bag. "I have some things to show you, material Mia and I have been working on."

"Excellent. The business meeting shouldn't take long tonight. We'll have plenty of time to visit." Looking around the room with its red and green streamers, holly and mistletoe, he added, "Looks like they've planned on partying anyway."

Which was the last thing Jeannie wanted to do. So far, she had simply avoided the idea of holidays this year, even refusing to go shopping with Barb. She knew her sister expected her to spend Christmas and New Year's with them as she did every year, but she knew they would invite Denis, too, and she didn't think she could handle that. Not yet. Loren had asked him to Thanksgiving dinner, but he'd decided to make a last-minute trip and spend the weekend with friends in Virginia. Only then did Jeannie breathe a sigh of relief and settle down to eat her fair share of turkey and trimmings. She knew she couldn't avoid him forever, but it would hurt too much to spend Christmas with him, knowing how close they had come to something very special between them, knowing how much she still loved him.

"Jeannie?"

She jumped at the sound of Allen's voice next to her ear. "Sorry. I guess I took off for a minute there."

Allen chuckled. "No problem. My wife does the same thing. Oh, there's Mia now." He waved at the petite blonde woman standing in the doorway.

Smiling, she walked quickly across the room. "Jeannie. Allen. Good to see you. Looks like we have a pretty good turnout tonight."

"Even UFO researchers like to party," Allen said, grinning.

Mia turned to Jeannie. "I thought Barb and Loren might come with you tonight."

"They had a faculty party at the College. It sounded like a command performance. I think they'd both rather have come here. How did you get out of it, Allen?"

He shrugged. "Told the Dean I had a prior engagement. Which was true. He usually doesn't press. Thinks I'm weird anyway."

"Because of this?" Jeannie indicated the group around them. "He knows about your interest in UFO's?"

"Oh, yes, but he chooses to ignore it. As long as I don't do anything to implicate or embarrass the College, he pretty much leaves me alone."

"Loren is still feeling his way through the situation. He's had two more hypnosis sessions, and he still can't quite believe what's coming out."

"Is he feeling better?" Allen asked.

"Much better," Mia replied. "He now has a reason for his fears and anxieties, and therefore, something to talk about. Denis says this last session was particularly helpful."

"Denis?" Jeannie said, startled. "You've talked to him?"

"Some," Mia admitted.

She shouldn't care. And yet, irrationally, Jeannie felt slighted. Mia had talked to Denis and she hadn't

"Looks like they're getting ready to start," Allen said, as the crowd began to file into the rows of chairs. Jeannie followed him to a spot in the middle of the room and sat down.

The business portion of the meeting moved along quickly, yet Jeannie found it difficult to keep her mind on the reports being read. She had come here tonight to meet with Allen and Mia and to discuss UFORA's ongoing investigation of the MacLeod family's abductions. Allen had taken charge of the overall investigation, while Mia conducted Jeannie and Barb's hypnosis sessions. It was Jeannie's job to assimilate all the information into a book proposal. She had found only one drawback to an otherwise smoothly run operation, the fact that Denis, not Mia, was working with Loren. Jeannie couldn't imagine Denis ever agreeing that Loren's case study should be included in her book, even though Loren didn't mind, as long as he remained anonymous.

She heard a shuffling of chairs in the row behind them, as a latecomer made his way to an empty seat. She forced her attention back to the speaker at the front of the room. Later, she would ask Mia if there was any chance Denis might eventually cooperate in their project. Maybe her friend could talk some sense into the bull-headed man she'd had the misfortune to fall in love with.

Two or three minutes passed. Jeannie shifted around in her chair. Another minute. She shifted again. Something was bothering her, but she couldn't pinpoint exactly what.

She became aware of a slight prickling at the back of her neck and suddenly she recognized the feeling. Someone was staring at her. She glanced around, but everyone she could see appeared focused on the speaker.

The feeling got stronger. It must be someone behind her. Who? And why?

On an impulse, she grabbed her purse and stood up. "Excuse me," she murmured, stepping over Allen's feet. "Excuse me." Reaching the aisle, she looked into the row of seats directly behind them and into a pair of familiar but wary gray-green eyes.

She gasped and stood rooted to the floor.

Never taking his eyes from hers, Denis got to his feet, and with two long strides he stood beside her. "Shall we?" His voice was low enough that only she could hear. He looped his arm through hers, gently encouraging her to obey his words.

She did. Quickly, quietly, they walked to the back of the room and out the door. It swung shut, leaving them alone in the silent, empty lobby.

Denis still held her arm. She didn't move, didn't want to move. Looking up into his rugged face, she felt like she'd come home at last.

"Jeannie, I'm sorry. I was a hot-headed fool to leave you the way I did." He sighed. "I've been waiting days, weeks to get that off my chest."

Stunned, thrilled, Jeannie unconsciously moved closer to him. "What are you doing here?" she asked, hoping for the answer she wanted desperately to hear.

"I came to see you."

"All this way? Benton is a lot closer than Oklahoma City."

"Okay. There is another reason. Mia said she and Allen have been working with you on your book. I want to help, Jeannie."

Closing her eyes, she leaned in to his hard body. "I'm so glad," she whispered.

His arm tightened around her. "Just like that? No questions?"

She smiled. "Well, maybe a few. Like, what made you change your mind?"

"I guess you could say I didn't change my mind as much as open it, thanks to Mia and Alex MacGregor."

"Your psychologist friend in Virginia?"

"That's right. You probably knew I spent Thanksgiving with him and his family."

Jeannie nodded.

"Well, Alex made it pretty plain he thought I was a *narrow-minded fool*." Denis grinned sheepishly. "I believe that's an exact quote. Anyway, he made me read a bunch of books and we talked, really talked, about UFO's and paranormal phenomena in general. I began to understand that I *have* been narrow-minded and opinionated and a few other things I'm not proud of."

"He *made* you read some books? I have to meet this man. I didn't think anyone could make you do anything!"

Denis gently tipped up her chin till she looked directly into his eyes and saw his love reflected there. "You made me love you," he said softly. "I didn't think I would ever love again, but I do. Marry me, Jeannie. Share my life. I promise to share yours. You've taken on a big job with this UFO research project. Let me help you."

"Yes," she murmured, as his lips moved closer to hers. "Oh, yes!"

Epilogue

ONE year later--

Shortly after sunset on a cold cloudy Saturday in December, a dark red sedan, successor to a smaller sporty model, cruised westward on the Broken Arrow Expressway. Inside the car, two passengers talked softly, while the third one slept.

"I can't believe I've used up my maternity leave, and I'll be back at work in a couple of weeks." Jeannie Earley turned to watch the small, tawny-haired baby napping in his car seat. "I've loved staying at home with Eric these last couple of months." As she spoke, she felt again the wonder of this living miracle they had named after Denis' foster child in Virginia.

"You don't have to go back," Denis reminded her. "My practice is more than enough to take care of us."

"I know, but I love working for the *Star*. It's a great job."

"Better than the *News and Sun*?" Denis teased.

She wrinkled her nose. "I still can't believe Eddie tried to claim copyright infringement when I wrote that series of articles on the Tulsa Lights last summer."

"He did back down eventually."

"Right. When my editor threatened to sue him for harassment."

"At least he hasn't bothered you lately. Speaking of

harassment, has Allen ever gotten a line on Ron Siegel? I always figured he was the one who tipped Eddie off about what was in your computer."

"Allen says the UFORA office in Washington has an open file on him. He hasn't surfaced recently, but I'm sure he'll show up again, making trouble for some UFO investigator who's trying to uncover the truth. Maybe us. I expect that some of the 'Powers That Be' won't appreciate our book when it comes out next fall."

Denis nodded. "You're probably right, although I can't imagine what Siegel or anyone else can do about it. We can substantiate everything we've put in that book, and we haven't betrayed any confidences. I think we've pretty well protected ourselves."

"Maybe, but if he or anyone else really wants to make trouble for us, it won't be hard. Remember how he bugged my house? I had no idea until it was too late. Who's to say he won't do the same thing again, or get to one of the other people we've written about? If he wants to know who we've talked to, he can find out pretty easily. I imagine Siegel and whoever he's working for know as much about that book as we do."

"I hate to admit it, but you're probably right." Scowling, Denis added, "I sure don't want anything to happen now to set Loren back. His symptoms have just about disappeared since I figured out what his problem was."

"Who figured it out?"

"Okay, okay. Since I recognized that your diagnosis of Post-Traumatic Stress was completely accurate." Grinning, he added, "You'll never let me forget how wrong I was, will you?"

"Never," she replied, cheerfully. "I like having something to hold over your head."

"Witch." Lifting her hand to his lips, he ran his teeth across her knuckles.

Jeannie shivered with pleasure. It never ceased to amaze

her that the simplest touch from this man could set her on fire.

He must have been thinking the same thing. His voice husky, he murmured, "If we hadn't promised Barb and Loren that we'd be there by seven, I'd turn this car around and head home right now."

"We don't have to stay long," Jeannie replied. "They'll understand."

"They'll probably be grateful. Since little Grace started walking, neither of them gets much rest. Loren told me that when nine o'clock comes, he's ready for bed."

"Barb says the same thing. Wait till she starts babysitting Eric, too. I tried to talk her out of it, but she insists no one but family can take care of her nephew properly."

"That's fine with me. I won't worry about him when he's with her. Of course," he added, "we're talking about a rather strange family here. UFO abductions. Paranormal phenomena."

"Don't forget, it's your family, too," Jeannie replied, quite used to his teasing by now. "If we're strange, so are you." She smiled.

"But those things don't happen to me. It's only--uh oh! Hang on!" He braked, glanced over his shoulder and headed into the right lane, then down the exit ramp. At the bottom of the slight hill, he turned left onto Shannon Boulevard and then settled back in his seat. "Sorry. I almost missed the exit."

Jeannie shook her head. Maybe she'd better keep quiet and let her husband concentrate on his driving, although she noticed that the traffic had thinned considerably here. In fact, looking out the window into the early evening darkness, she didn't see another car. Strange, since this was a popular residential neighborhood.

An eerie silence filled the car. Did Denis feel it, too? She wanted to ask him, but instead she simply stared out the window. She had felt this stillness before. Where? When?

The question faded away.

Crossland Park appeared on her right. There was something about this park she should remember, but again the thought slipped away.

The sky brightened now, as the moon appeared from behind the trees. No, that was wrong. No moon tonight. Then what?

Without warning, Denis put on the brakes, turned and followed the two-lane road that led into the park.

Why? She tried to think, but her head felt heavy, her body listless.

The moon. Something about the moon. It was getting bigger, brighter.

Denis stopped the car, but he didn't move. Nor did Jeannie or Eric. They simply sat and stared at the glowing white light that filled the car.

They sat and waited.

* * *

About the Author

PAULA BLAIS GORGAS, a native Rhode Islander, lives in the Green County of eastern Oklahoma with her husband, a retired Navy officer turned pro-golfer. While traveling around the United States and raising four sons, Paula worked as an NSA intelligence analyst and as a children's librarian before returning to her first love, books. Always an avid reader, she has sold many short stories, both romance and fantasy. Her young adult novel, Court of Honor, won the Romance Writers of America's Golden Heart Award. Her young adult fantasy novel, Earth Magic, won the Oklahoma Writers Federation Inc.'s trophy award for the "Best Juvenile Book of 2002." Because she loves to explore mysterious and unexplained phenomena, Paula has turned to science fiction and fantasy for her latest writing projects.

* * *

www.ingramcontent.com/pod-product-compliance
Lightning Source LLC
Chambersburg PA
CBHW050024180626
46810CB00002B/569